Ra...

MAZEY E...

'Mazey Eddings's writing is authentic, emotional, and intensely romantic! To me, it's like a Taylor Swift song in book form'
Ali Hazelwood, *New York Times* bestselling author

'So freaking cute. *Tilly in Technicolor* will have you aching with love for these characters while swooning at their awkward adorableness together. I want to hug this book to my chest'
Chloe Gong, *New York Times* bestselling author

'*Tilly in Technicolor* captures the giddy thrill of finding the person who sees you, who gets you, and who, ultimately, adores you exactly as you are . . . This is an affirming and joyful novel about rediscovering yourself outside of boxes, expectations, and comfort zones'
Lillie Vale

'I don't know how she does it, but somehow every book Mazey Eddings writes becomes my new favorite. *The Plus One* is deliciously tropey, but also raw, honest, psychologically rich – and scorchingly hot'
Ava Wilder

'Prepare to smile, laugh, and cry your way through this witty, fast-paced rom-com debut starring a passionate heroine and a delicious cinnamon roll hero who knows how to love her just right'
Evie Dunmore, *USA Today* bestselling author

'*A Brush with Love* reads the way young love feels. Mazey Eddings stole my heart with this laugh-out-loud funny, almost unbearably cute debut (and she made me care about dentistry)'
Rosie Danan

'An adorable love story. *A Brush with Love* blends sweetness, breathless romance, and moments of striking vulnerability'
Helen Hoang, *New York Times* bestselling author

'With a shimmering voice and razor-sharp wit, Mazey Eddings has crafted a contemporary romance masterpiece that made me want to hug my dentist . . . The most intoxicating slow burn I've read in ages'
Rachel Lynn Solomon

'Tenderly written and oh-so-sexy, *A Brush with Love* brims with emotional depth, whip-smart banter, and sizzling chemistry. This romantic comedy completely stole my heart'
Chloe Liese

Mazey Eddings is a neurodiverse author, dentist, and (most importantly) stage mom to her cats, Yaya and Zadie. She can most often be found reading romance novels under her weighted blanket and asking her boyfriend to bring her snacks. She's made it her personal mission in life to destigmatize mental health issues and write love stories for every brain. With roots in Ohio and Philadelphia, she now calls Asheville, North Carolina home. She is the author of *A Brush With Love, Lizzie Blake's Best Mistake* and *The Plus One*.

To learn more, visit: **www.mazeyeddings.com**
or follow Mazey on Instagram: **@mazeyeddings**.

By Mazey Eddings

A Brush With Love
Lizzie Blake's Best Mistake
The Plus One
Tilly in Technicolor

Tilly in Technicolor

MAZEY EDDINGS

HEADLINE
ETERNAL

Published by arrangement with St. Martin's Griffin,
an imprint of St. Martin's Publishing Group.

First published in Great Britain in 2023
by HEADLINE ETERNAL
An imprint of HEADLINE PUBLISHING GROUP

1

Cataloguing in Publication Data is available from the British Library

ISBN 978 1 0354 0398 1

Offset in 11.12/14.21pt Adobe Caslon Pro by Jouve (UK), Milton Keynes

Printed and bound in Great Britain by Clays Ltd, Elcograf S.p.A.

MIX
Paper | Supporting
responsible forestry
FSC® C104740

Headline's policy is to use papers that are natural, renewable and recyclable
products and made from wood grown in well-managed forests and other
controlled sources. The logging and manufacturing processes are expected to
conform to the environmental regulations of the country of origin.

HEADLINE PUBLISHING GROUP
An Hachette UK Company
Carmelite House
50 Victoria Embankment
London EC4Y 0DZ

www.headlineeternal.com
www.headline.co.uk
www.hachette.co.uk

To my fellow neurodivine individuals
navigating a world not built for them.
Your brain is beautiful, and
I'm so glad you're here.

Tilly in Technicolor

Chapter 1

Panties in a Twist

Tilly, are you sure you have enough underwear?"

I stare at the massive lump of underwear shoved into my suitcase. Are thirty-nine pairs enough? What if I pee and/or crap my pants multiple times a day for the next three months? What if I absolutely demolish my underwear, turning pair after pair from sturdy to crotchless, and Europe suddenly experiences a massive underwear shortage?

"Can never be too prepared," I say, nodding at my mom and fishing out the last handful of underwear I have in my drawer. I try to wrestle them into the pocket of my suitcase, but they won't fit without busting the seams, so I stack them on top of the six boxes of tampons I've packed. Size super because I don't do anything by half measure.

"Good girl," Mom says, smiling at me like I just came up with a cure for global hunger. "There's hope for you yet."

That look and her words send a sharp mix of shame and annoyance dancing across my skin, making it prickle. I turn away, crawling into my closet and pretending to search for a pair of tennis shoes while I gulp down a frustrated scream trying to claw its way out of my throat.

It's moments like this that confirm how badly I need my life to change. I need to leave this house. Get out from under my mom's thumb. Get the hell out of Cleveland.

Which is exactly what I'm packing for: my great escape.

Or, as much of an escape as a trip around Europe financed by my parents while acting as my sister's lowly intern can be. I'd rather not get lost in the semantics of it all.

"Have you programmed our calls into your calendar?" Mom asks, in that perfectly practiced casual tone that means she expects me to have forgotten and is going to be let down but not surprised when I prove her right.

"Of course," I lie. It's hard to force myself to do things I really, *really* don't want to deal with, and my scheduled calls home to my parents while I'm away are pretty high on my list.

This trip is a combination of a birthday and a graduation present with just enough built-in structure that my parents agreed to it. They're paying my way to Europe, and, in exchange, I'll be traveling around the continent for the next three months with my sister, Mona, as she tries to grow her start-up. Mom plans on meeting me in London when it's over to spend a few days there before taking me home . . . likely kicking and screaming.

The trip doesn't come without a few catches, one being weekly check-in calls with my parents, where I tell them how much I'm growing as a person and learning so much, la la la.

The second is that I'll technically be Mona's intern, but I think that label is more for my dad's sake and his big dream (read: capitalist-inspired nightmare) to see his two daughters become some sort of heavy-hitter business moguls.

"I told Mona to set an alarm on her phone to remind you to take your medicine. I'll text you, too, so you don't forget," Mom says, her words pinching at a soft spot between my ribs.

"I'll remember, Mom," I mumble, my cheeks burning. The problem is, I do have a tendency to forget to take the tiny little pills that help me with basic tasks like remembering, one of ADHD's fabulous ironies. But I also don't need my mom recruiting my perfect older sister in this endless plight to make me feel as helpless as a two-year-old.

"And Tilly, please make sure you listen to Mona while you're gone. I know you tend to wander off and do your own thing or get lost playing on that laptop of yours, but she'll know how to navigate better than you will and the whole point of the trip is for you to gain some life experience. You wouldn't want to cause a scene while you're away."

This is the point where I shut down.

Back still turned to her, I squeeze my eyes shut, gripping my hands into tight fists and biting my lip to tamp down the swell of feelings. I'll be out of here soon.

No more gentle, disappointing sighs when I forget to do something. No more glances of weary defeat—an acknowledgment of a shared burden—between Mom and Dad when I get worked up and emotions pour out of me with the force of a waterfall but none of the beauty. No more comparing my consistent failures and shortcomings to perfect Mona's endless successes.

Mona is five years older than me, and we used to be super close. Best friends. But then she went off to Yale for college and was never quite the same. She traded her silly personality and long flowing dresses for a crap ton of power suits and more sweaters with elbow pads than one person has a right to own. Every visit home on breaks and holidays, she was a little different. Less fun. Way more serious.

Instead of fangirling with me over *Supernatural* or *Doctor Who*, she started discussing market trends with Dad. Neighborhood gossip with Mom.

Mom says she became a true New Englander. I think she became a stuffy dud.

As if attending an Ivy League university (completing an accelerated MBA program, no less . . . gag me) wasn't enough, she started her own company during school, partnering with some genius engineering-business double major named Amina. The duo developed a bougie, eco-friendly, organic, nontoxic, insert buzzword here nail polish brand—excuse me, I mean luxury nail *lacquer* . . . because, apparently, the word *polish* isn't classy enough.

After graduating last year and winning seed money in some *highly competitive* women in business competition (which Dad went ahead and made his only talking point and entire personality), Mona moved to London, where Amina's originally from, and the pair have been growing the business there ever since.

They named the company Ruhe, which is a German word that "doesn't translate exactly to English" meaning nothing around you bothers you. I'm pretty sure she found it on some *BuzzFeed* article about fancy foreign words without an exact translation. I am once again requesting that you gag me.

Mom and Dad might as well have set up a Mona altar in our living room for how much they worship her accomplishments.

"Oh Tilly, don't get upset. I'm not criticizing you," Mom says, walking over to where I'm scrunched up in the closet, back rounded like a turtle shell. She rubs lightly between my shoulder blades and my muscles lock. "You know that your ADHD causes these issues, not you."

My mom talks about my diagnosis like it's a separate entity from me, some awful parasite hijacking my system and changing who I actually am.

"Dr. Alverez told us it can cause impulsivity. Recklessness.

I just want you to be aware of those things so you can over-come them," she continues, rubbing soft circles on my back that make my skin crawl and my body shudder. I don't like soft touches.

I want to scream. I want to blow up. I want to say *Stop, Mom. Just stop. Stop laying out all the things you'd change about me and blaming them on a diagnosis.*

ADHD hasn't "changed" me, which is how my mom views it. It *is* me. It's an undeniable and simple fact of who I am. Like my black hair or my gray eyes or the bump on the bridge of my nose. It exists in my DNA, probably right between my hopeless romantic gene and the raunchy sense of humor allele. It's woven into who I am. It's not some disease that needs to be cured.

I duck and roll away from her touch, standing up and doing a bizarre spin and leg kick like I'm a modern dancer. I sashay toward the door.

"What are you doing?" Mom asks, sitting on the floor, her eyebrows drawn and frown fixed as she looks at me in confusion.

"Dancing for joy," I lie. "I'm just so excited for the trip," I add, traipsing into the hall. "And I need a snack."

I continue my impromptu dance down the stairs, leaving my mom to probably jot a note about my erratic behavior. She doesn't know I know about her notepad of instances she takes to Dr. Alverez, documenting moments to bring up during the part of appointments I'm not in.

I hate that notebook.

But I do have a tendency to do odd things like this, some-times. When feelings build and overwhelm me, pushing at my joints until I feel like I'll fracture from them, I do something explosive with my body. It just feels . . . *good* to move. To get it out.

I know my mom thinks it's bizarre and some sort of defect in my programming, but I've given up trying to hide it.

Maybe if I'm fully myself for long enough, she'll finally give up on me. And I can just be.

Chapter 2

Future?
I Hardly Know Her.

W hile we're aware you are looking at this trip as a vacation, don't forget you're going to help Mona and learn about business. I also encourage you to utilize any free time for educational and enlightening pursuits," Dad says, carefully changing lanes on the highway as we head to the airport. "Try to learn all you can about the history of the places you visit. Become more cultured."

History. Right. Because the last twelve years of my public school education didn't focus enough on Eurocentric history. How tragically I've been deprived.

"Write down all your experiences!" Mom says, turning around in her seat to smile at me. "You won't want to forget a thing."

I smile. A real, genuine smile. Because that's the first time in a long time she's brought up my writing in a positive light. I love to play with words, swirl and shape letters until I've translated a feeling into an expression.

I've filled hundreds of notebooks with thoughts, getting lost in the creamy lined pages. Much to the dismay of Mom, who flips out anytime she finds me (more frequently than I'd like to admit) at two a.m., eyes crusty from not blinking and hand smudged with ink and a journal stained with my heart on its pages, while none of my homework for the next day is done.

"This will all be perfect for a college application essay," Mom continues, reaching back to give my knee a squeeze.

I pull away. Not this again.

"Yeah, it would," I say, picking at my nails. "For someone actually applying to colleges."

Mom frowns at me for a moment before turning around in her seat.

"It's not too late to change your mind about college," Mom says with forced lightness. "You can enroll in community college classes for the fall, or even try to get into a four-year university for the spring semester. You have options, Tilly. I'd hate to see you waste your potential."

"A college degree doesn't even cut it anymore," Dad adds, looking at me through the rearview mirror. "You're setting yourself up for a lifetime of struggle if you don't get an advanced education."

"Right. Never mind the crushing student debt and the mental gymnastics I'd have to force myself through to do it," I whisper to myself.

"What was that?"

"I said I get it, Mom." I press my forehead against the window. This is the passive-aggressive argument we've had more times over the past year than I can count.

College is not for me. End of story.

My grades in high school were average, but the work to get those average grades felt like turning my brain inside out. I couldn't figure out a way to focus on numbers and equations and scientific principles and names of old dead white dudes because, truly, who cares? Sitting at desks, trying to listen to teachers drone on, felt physically painful at times. The second I dropped my white-knuckled attempts at focus, my brain would strap on a pair of Rollerblades and zip away, frolicking into fictional lands and dancing around words, my hands somehow keeping pace with the random ideas by scribbling ferociously in notebooks.

More than once a teacher called out my mental wandering, successfully humiliating me in front of the class by asking if I'd like to join everyone on this planet instead of whichever one I was currently inhabiting. The inevitable hiss of laughter from my classmates always felt like a thousand tiny needles being poked into my skin, mortification and shame prickling out of my pores.

It was, to put it delicately, absolute ass.

The only time I hadn't felt tortured was during AP Lit. I'm always able to lose myself in the works of others. That's how I know I want to be a writer. I want to hop along similes and revel in hyperboles. I want to make people feel and experience and live through the stories I tell.

I also want to avoid going to college to do so.

But explaining that to my parents generates a more horrified reaction than if I told them I kick kittens as a hobby. It's made worse by the fact that perfect Mona went to a perfect university and graduated at the top of her perfect class and blah blah blah. Mona set an educational bar that I can't even skim with my fingertips, no matter how hard I jump and struggle.

We finally pull off the highway for the airport, and when we roll up to my terminal, I scramble out of the backseat like a puppy at a park. I can't stop the little bounce in my legs as I take in the movement around me, the rumble of suitcase wheels along the sidewalk and the *whoosh* of the automatic doors sliding open and closed as people take their first steps to their next destination. It's so exciting I could puke.

"Try to stay organized at each hotel," Dad says, pulling my overflowing bag out of the trunk and handing it to me. "Don't dump out your suitcase and have things everywhere or you'll forget something in each country."

"Okay," I say, accepting my backpack from Mom and grabbing my suitcase from Dad. I do feel a pang of sadness at leaving. As much as my parents drive me bonkers, I will miss them.

"Leave Tornado Tilly in the USA, please," Mom says, pulling me into a hug. "We don't want you to lose anything important."

A tiny hole is popped in my bubble of excitement. With that fabulous moniker, I feel a little less sad about leaving.

"I love you," I say, giving Mom and Dad one more kiss on the cheek before turning and marching toward those sliding glass doors that are the entrance to my grand adventure.

"Don't lose anything!" Mom repeats as I step through the doors and am smacked by the cold AC.

"I won't forget a single thing!" I say over my shoulder with a wave before heading to security.

Chapter 3

Failure to Launch

I forgot my luggage at security.

I swear, it wasn't my fault, but between the crush of bodies and trying to keep track of my shoes and my backpack and my phone while also being swamped by the echoing chaos of the airport and being so damn excited about everything, I may have made the oh-so-small mistake of leaving my suitcase at the security checkpoint.

"It rolled straight from my hand!" I say to the TSA woman who's giving me a bland look. "There I was, walking along, palms all sweaty because, truly, is it always this hot in here? And then *poof* my bag slipped from my grip and I'm not sure if this airport was built on a tilt or what but it rolled right back here and that's why—"

"You left it on the belt," the woman says, jerking her head toward the X-ray machine.

"It . . . uh . . . have you heard of levitation?"

The woman rolls her eyes. "Come over here."

I follow her, and she stops me in front of a large metal table, slinging my overstuffed bag on there like it's a slab of meat.

And then, she proceeds to do the unthinkable.

She snaps on latex gloves, unzips my bag, and starts pulling things out.

For all the world to see.

She begins, of course, with the underwear. There really is no other option for her. She pulls out handful after handful of my cotton panties, setting them down on the table next to my hot pink suitcase. The mountain she creates is so big, I want to absolutely die. An endless stream of people walk by, and we get more than a few double takes at the undie Everest growing on this table.

And next, oh joy, is my supply of tampons. Box after box, she pulls them out, creating a small barricade around Mount Fruit of the Loom.

After what feels like hours of her digging through my possessions—she inexplicably is able to leave all my T-shirts and sundresses in the suitcase while my underwear creates a massive beacon of attention—she lets me go with a stern warning not to leave my suitcase unattended again. After that experience, I'm tempted to travel without luggage for the rest of my life.

I barrel to my gate like a bat out of hell. This is not the classy-ass airport experience I envisioned. I wasn't able to stop at an overpriced restaurant and buy spinach-and-artichoke dip like a mature adult. I don't have an iced coffee in hand as I stroll up to my gate looking cool and sophisticated. I didn't peruse the airport stores and buy glossy fashion magazines to breezily flip through on the plane. I haven't thrown my head back and laughed intriguingly at something a gorgeous stranger said *once*.

Instead, as I bound up to the ticketing counter at my gate, I'm sweaty and frazzled and at risk of missing my flight because

I sprinted in the wrong direction for fifteen minutes before realizing and circling back.

"Take a deep breath, dear," the ticketing agent says, giving me a terrified smile. "We had a little delay, so you're right on time."

I breathlessly thank her, chest still heaving from my run, as I scramble through the door and onto the jet bridge.

When I step onto the plane, a beautiful flight attendant with dark red lipstick and a glorious British accent greets me. I can't help feeling a swell of excitement at knowing my destination will have me surrounded by pretty voices.

I make my way toward the back, jamming my suitcase into the overhead bin with my last reserves of strength after running a marathon through the airport. I collapse down into the window seat of row twenty-seven.

I take a deep breath, trying to calm down my buzzing system.

Then I grin.

This is it. The moment of all moments. The one that will change my life forever.

I press my forehead against the window, heart thumping in excitement. I can't wait to take off. I can't wait to leave the ground and my old life and my problems behind. I can't wait to—

"You're in my seat."

My excited loop-de-loop thoughts are cut off by a crisp, British voice. I whip my head to the aisle and find myself eye level with a long pair of legs in tailored black pants.

I frown, instinctually not trusting anyone who wears non-elastic pants on a plane. Monsters, every single one of them. But, as my eyes trail up an equally tailored black button-down to a face so gorgeous I think I might die, I decide this lovely stranger is an exception. Someone this pretty must be an angel.

If angels wore all black and had sharp noses and chiseled jaws that could cut glass and stern, disapproving frowns. Fallen angel, then.

"What?" I manage to choke out, eyes wandering round and around his handsome face. I'll be honest, my silly heart and head have always conjured up heated tension with literally anyone remotely close to my age in an airport, but this boy . . . well, cute doesn't even cut it.

Hot Guy—wait, would it be Hot *Guy*? Or would the British call him Hot . . . Chap? Bloke? Lad? I'm trying to be more cultured, after all.

Hot *Lad* has dark auburn hair falling in waves across his forehead. His light brown eyes, the color of honey, are framed by a sweep of dark lashes. His long fingers tap against his leg in a steady beat as he stares in the vicinity of my left shoulder.

"My seat," he repeats. "You're in it."

"Oh." I chew on my bottom lip, hoping to look charming and endearing. I would have sworn I had a window seat. And by sworn, I mean I didn't check but assumed because what's the point of flying if you can't look out at the clouds and completely lose yourself in daydreams?

"Would you be interested in switching?" I ask. "I'm really into window seats."

Hot Lad's eyes flick to mine for a split second, then land back on my shoulder. "No." Pause. "Thank you."

I blink at him, mouth falling open. Well . . . that's the end of *that*, I guess. Cool. Cool cool *cool*. Gorgeous moody boy in all black does not play when it comes to seating assignments and is really not fun about it at all and is actually killing my total freaking travel vibe and now I have to sit next to him for ten hours. Love it.

I scramble up from the seat and scooch to the one next to it, dragging my backpack up from the floor and snagging it on every corner humanly possible in the awkward process. I try to squeeze myself against my aisle seat to give Hot Lad room, but he waits, fingers still tapping.

After what feels like an eternity of awkward standing, we both make a little hand wave for the other to move through, me toward his seat, him ushering me into the aisle. I think we're both caught off guard by the gestures, because we then make jerky movements toward and away from each other like pecking chickens.

His eyes go wide like he's being confronted by a feral cat, and I scowl, embarrassment heating my cheeks. I charge forward into the aisle to give him more room, but, at the same moment, Hot Lad takes a definitive step into the row of seats.

And my forehead smacks against his ridiculously chiseled jaw.

"*Agghrrrhhjh*," he groans, head jerking back.

My knees give out and I slump into the aisle seat, head cradled in my hands.

Cut glass? That jaw could bust open my damn skull holy crap that hurt so bad.

It feels like the plane has gone silent, everything frozen as I hold my throbbing head and Hot Lad towers over me with what I can only imagine is a look of unmitigated horror.

He finally squeezes past me, folding his long limbs into the window seat and putting his black backpack on the ground at his feet. He turns slightly away from me, both of us still mildly panting from the chaos.

"That really hurt," Hot Lad says at last, frowning as he looks out the window, rubbing his chin.

I stare at him in gaping disbelief. He says it like it's my fault.

"Oh, really? Because my head feels *great*," I snap. "Thanks for asking."

He turns to me, blinking like he forgot I'm here. I do get a small rush of satisfaction when his cheeks redden and his look turns sheepish.

"It looks like you have a bump forming," he says, eyebrows furrowing as he leans in to look at my forehead. "You should probably ice that," he adds matter-of-factly, sitting up straight again. He gives a small, definitive nod like he's just solved all my problems and turns back to the window.

My jaw has plummeted through the floor of the plane at this point as I continue to stare at him.

Umm, what fresh hell is this? He thumps me on the head with his sharp and gorgeous chin then tells me to *ice* it? He didn't even ask if I'm okay. Hot Lad? I'm sorry, more like Hot . . . *Wanker*. Or . . . *git*! Or whatever other words mean *jerk*.

I huff, crossing my arms over my chest and looking at the cracked pleather of the seat in front of me.

Call it clairvoyance, call it intuition, but I have a feeling this is about to be a very, *very* long flight.

Chapter 4

Eye Contact and Other Hard Things

OLIVER

I keep feeling the eyes of my peculiar seatmate on me. I can always feel when people look at me, and, more often than not, it's horribly uncomfortable. There are a handful of people that I've never had an issue making eye contact with, like my mums or my sister, and even fewer people I've built up comfort with over time. But, generally, locking eyes with a stranger makes my skin crawl and my soul feel like it's being pulled out of my body it's so intense.

Teachers used to try to get me to hold their gazes, saying it was good practice for me to build social skills, and I'd always end up crying, squeezing my eyes shut and clutching my chest like my heart would punch out of it.

Mum and Mãe put a stop to that as soon as they found out.

"They don't have the right to make you feel uncomfortable to fit their ideas of what's proper," Mãe had told me, holding my cheeks between her hands. "You don't have to look at anything you don't want to, amorzinho," she'd added, kissing me on the cheek. Although she moved from Lisbon to London years ago, her Portuguese endearments always roll richly and readily off her tongue.

So, following Mãe's advice, I avoid eye contact most of the time. And interacting with people feels all the more comfortable for it.

I continue to focus on the view outside my window as everyone on the plane bustles about. I'm actually rather sad to be leaving Cleveland. As much as I'd doubted Ohio's offerings before my trip, my two weeks spent interning with the Cleveland Art Museum's curators and exhibit designers were incredible.

The background hum of the airplane grows as we start to taxi across the runway, and I grind my teeth together. This is the worst part about traveling. I don't know how neurotypicals so easily ignore the deafening drone of electricity in spaces like planes or kitchens or . . . pretty much anywhere, when I feel like the dissonance is cutting my nerve endings open. My leg starts bouncing, fingers tapping at my side, focusing that jarring energy into my movements.

I reach for my backpack, pulling out my headphones and slipping them on, my brain breathing a sigh of relief as the din is muffled. I can still hear some of the static hum, but it's better, and I fix my eyes outside, peacefully drowning in all the colors.

I quiz myself on their names, my favorite way to calm my buzzing brain. The large poles down the runway are Pantone 15–1360, Shocking Orange; the vests of the people moving across the tarmac in small vehicles are 13–0630, Safety Yellow. There are calmer colors, too—sooty blues and gentle browns— all creating a soothing harmony through my limbs.

The plane turns and picks up speed. I watch the black

slashes of tar blur into a beautiful flow against the gray asphalt as we barrel down the runway.

We take off, and I press closer to the window, watching the world change from large and imposing to a soft palette of color.

The roads turn into a miniature web as we go higher, the veins of the city weaving until they give way to blocks of lush-green and golden-brown fields. It's one of those perfect days for flying, where I can see the landscape spread beneath me like a colorful quilt that doesn't disappear until we reach the misty clouds.

Everything goes white as we soar into the cloud layer. I always hold my breath for this part. It's mesmerizing and ter-rifying to be surrounded by the culmination of every hue; the intensity of everything that makes the world colorful combin-ing into the brightness and sharpness that is white.

And then, just when I think I'll get lost in the clouds—lost in that endless ocean where every color exists all at once—we pop out into a brilliant blue. Today, the sky matches Pantone 2190. A soft blue. Delicate. Deep. I decide I like it.

I grab my phone, taking a picture of the vast sea of sky with soft puffs of white cushioning the world beneath us. I'll post it when I land.

"Damn, your phone has a nice camera."

I jump out of my skin, the closeness of the voice and the breath sliding across the back of my neck jolting me from my thoughts and plunking me back into my seat. My phone shoots from my hand, and I fumble for it, batting at it as it arcs through the air. The corner of it lands smartly on the bridge of my nose, and I groan, cupping my hands over my face and hoping there's no blood.

"Oh shit, my bad," my seatmate says, panic in her loud

voice. She leans closer to look at me, invading my space even further. "Are you okay?"

Her words are muffled through my headphones, but the pitch of her voice somehow travels through. I tug them down.

"I'm fine," I mumble, trying to blink back sharp pokes of tears at my stinging nose.

"You sure? Sounded like your nose crunched when your phone hit it."

I'm tempted to tell her that I'm thoroughly concerned I won't make it off this flight without being permanently maimed by her, but I have a feeling that isn't the politest way to phrase it, so I grunt in response.

There's another pause, and I feel her stare on me again.

"You're sure *sure* you're okay?" she whispers. "Because I can track down some ice."

"Please stop asking," I grind out, glancing up at her.

The girl flinches like I smacked her. She blinks at me, and, oddly enough, my gaze gets caught on her eyes. I wouldn't call this eye contact though. No. It's more of an . . . analysis. Her irises are a fascinating shade of gray, the color charged like the underbelly of storm clouds illuminated by a streak of lightning. Pantone 536, I think.

"What's your name?" she asks.

My eyes finally unhook from the intensity of hers and land safely on her cheek.

"Oliver," I say. There's a pause.

"Oliver." She repeats it like she's trying out how it feels on her lips. "Well, Oliver, I'm Tilly. And I think *maybe* we didn't have the greatest start to this trip."

I don't say anything in response because, yes, that's rather obvious. I notice splotches of pink rise on her cheeks as the silence stretches on. I'm probably supposed to be filling it with small talk. I'd, quite literally, rather dump a boiling pot of tea on my head than expend the energy small talk takes.

"Anyway," she says, her hands fluttering up and hovering in the air. "I guess we both need to . . . er . . . *keep a stiff upper lip on this one there, right-o?*" she says in a horrible attempt at what, I think, is supposed to be a British accent.

"Sorry, what?"

Tilly's hands land on her throat like she's trying to stop the babble of words coming out, but the accent continues.

"*Right. Cheerio. Just taking the piss,*" she continues, slipping into something that's close to . . . Cockney? What the devil is she on about?

"What the devil are you on about?" I blurt out. I don't understand this conversation. At all. "I don't think any of those phrases mean what you think they mean."

Tilly's face falls. "*Oh, bugger,*" she says, dropping her head back against her seat and crossing her arms over her chest.

"That one actually worked," I say after a moment.

Tilly blinks, then turns to me, a smile breaking across her face. I can't seem to hold my own back. It's at this moment that I realize this odd stranger is actually rather . . . fit.

She's a study in muted colors. Dusky pink lips. Olive undertones to her skin. Strong slashes of dark eyebrows. Upturned nose with a rosy tip. All of it complemented by inky black hair piled into two messy buns at the top of her head.

But what I find most fascinating is a cluster of three birthmarks at the top of her left cheek. I can tell each one has a slightly different pigment, and I want to lean in and identify them.

But I also know, to a stranger, that would be weird and massively inappropriate for me to do, so I check the urge and pull my headphones over my ears, turning back to the window.

I stare at the sky, enjoying the quiet. Absorbing the blue. Searching its nuances.

Less than a minute later, I feel a tap on my shoulder. I turn, Tilly looking at me with those wide, owlish eyes. I pull off my headphones.

"Alright?" I ask.

"Your headphones seem nice," she says.

This is . . . true?

"They are, thanks," I say. "Noise canceling," I add before slipping them back on and turning to the window.

I'm barely back into my lull before I get another tap on the shoulder.

"Yes?" I say, just lifting one ear this time.

"Umm, if you need to use the bathroom or anything, just let me know," Tilly says, waving toward the aisle. "And I'll . . . uh . . . move."

"Right." What else would she do? Block me?

Headphones on (again), I turn to the window (again).

And, two seconds later. There's a tap on my shoulder. Again.

This is going to be a long flight.

Chapter 5

Flight from Hell and Satan's My Seatmate

TILLY

Here's a fun fact: ten-hour flights and ADHD do not mix. It's hour five of this torture, and I feel pretty close to totally losing my (nonexistent) cool. I forgot how *loud* planes are, but in that, like, weird quiet way. There's this constant hum and throb of complex noise that sets my teeth on edge and makes my entire body fidget and bounce. It's the kind of noise you don't register hearing, but it worms its way under your skin.

After two hours of attempting to start conversation after conversation with Oliver to help drown out the background noise, I finally gave up. The whole thing felt like the verbal equivalent of pulling out my own teeth.

Damn you, Hot Lad! Engage me in conversation so my brain doesn't collapse in on itself from lack of stimulation! Also, you're really good-looking and it would be a modern tragedy if we both leave this plane without creating a love connection that inspires a Netflix original movie.

But, alas, I couldn't get him to take those headphones off

long enough to charm the pants off him. Literally and figuratively, of course. I was able to nap for about an hour after that, but now I'm wired and squirmy and it feels like my brain is doing somersaults around my skull I'm so bored.

Thankfully, in-flight meals are being served, and I'm absolutely starving. The flight attendant moves down the aisle, stopping at our row. "Shepherd's pie or cheeseburger, dear?" she asks, giving me a warm smile.

"Burger, please," I say. "And a Sprite. Extra ketchup, too, if you don't mind."

The attendant nods, handing me the black plastic meal tray, my drink, and two packets of ketchup.

Oh, honey.

"Could I have a few more ketchup packets?" I ask, accidentally interrupting her as she's about to ask Oliver his meal choice.

She blinks, looking at the two she handed me. "Of course," she says, grabbing one more packet from the cart and handing it to me.

One? *One* extra packet? Do they have a shortage?

"Sorry," I say, my voice rising two octaves so it comes out as a squeak. Asking for anything related to a meal makes me want to break out in hives, but I'm also apparently incapable of going without whatever I'm asking for. "Could I have a few more?"

The attendant fully frowns now. "Okay . . ." she says, drawing out the word. And handing me ONE more. I'm sorry I'm a monster that needs to basically only taste ketchup on my burger and fries but hot damn, why so stingy? A few means at least three, right?

I open my mouth again, but she cuts me off.

"Really?" she says, eyes wide. "*More?*"

"I'm sorry," I say, sweat trickling down my neck. "Just . . . I don't know. Can you give me a big handful? Or like . . . a small dish of them? I know it's an obnoxious amount of ketchup but like . . . are there explicit rationing rules? Do I need to pay for more? I'm sorry to be such a pain. I just . . ."

She grabs two handfuls of ketchup packets and places them on my fold-out tray. "That enough for you?" she asks, her accent seeming to grow stronger as she shoots me a dirty look. But . . . do I deserve that look? Granted, it's a metric ton of ketchup I'm asking for but also . . . who cares? All of it swirls into embarrassment that presses at my cheeks and chest.

I nod. "Thank you," I whisper.

"And you?" the attendant says, looking at Oliver, who's observing the scene with a tilted head.

Oliver blinks. "I'll have the burger, too," he says.

"Need extra ketchup, do you?" she says with thinly veiled snark.

Oliver looks like he's seriously contemplating her question. "Would you mind if I took one or two of those?" Oliver asks me.

I pause for a moment, ready to feel offended at this ridiculously blown out of proportion ketchup debacle, but I realize he's not mocking me. He's genuinely asking.

I nod, passing him a fistful of the bright red packets and slouching lower in my seat.

When the Keeper of Ketchup finally moves past our row, I straighten, ready to dig in. I open packet after packet, squeezing the contents onto my burger and fries.

I take a big bite, glad for something to do.

Eating sometimes feels like a hobby. Yes, I need food for nourishment, but, more than that, it's fun. Eating holds my attention, calms my constantly spinning thoughts. I would try to sneak snacks during classes to stay focused, but teachers would always lose their shit over it. I might as well have been doing a striptease on top of my desk for how outraged they'd be over me having a tiny carrot stick.

The burger is pretty gross with a subtle sliminess that runs a real risk of making me gag, so I add one more packet of ketchup to the patty to try to get it down.

On my next bite, a wet, squelching sound precedes the feeling of something plopping on my chest. I squeeze my eyes shut, praying that what I think just happened didn't just happen.

I force one eye open and, sure enough, there's a fist-sized blob of ketchup trailing down my chest, leaving a vicious red smear across my white T-shirt.

I let out a Moira Rose–worthy shriek of horror, nearly up-ending my meal tray in the process. I feel Oliver jump beside me at the noise, and I turn toward the aisle as though I can hide the massacre of my shirt.

"Mother fuuuuuuhhhh," I growl, grabbing the world's thinnest napkin from my utensil pack and dunking it in my Sprite. That's what adults do, right? Dip the edge of their napkin in a clear drink and go to town scrubbing at a stain? The problem is, the sheer amount of ketchup that landed on my chest turns the whole thing into a red puddle embedding itself farther into the fabric.

"Sonofabitch," I say as the napkin dissolves in my hand. Getting desperate, I look at Oliver. He's staring at me with wide-eyed horror, a look I'm far too accustomed with for only knowing him a few hours.

"Can I use your napkin?" I say, already reaching for it and opening the plastic packet with my teeth. I move to dunk the square inch of tissue that they're trying to pass as a cleaning tool in my Sprite, but a bump of turbulence causes my arm to swing wildly forward and spill my cup (and my burger and one thousand ketchup packets and also somehow invade Oliver's space and spill all his stuff, too) onto both of us.

"Oh, Christ!" Oliver bolts to standing, catching his knees on his tray and banging his head on the ceiling in the process. A dark wet drink mark is spreading across his shirt and crotch and I stare at it like I'm watching a train crash.

"Excuse me," he says gruffly, bear-crawling over me to get out of the row. Once he's untangled himself, he reaches back across me—accidentally punching me in the boob in the process and getting ketchup on his arm—to grab his backpack and pull it to him. He makes a mad dash to the bathroom a few rows back, the door rattling with the force of him slamming it shut.

I'm frozen for a moment, the pure chaos of the last minute looping through my skull like a swarm of aggressive gnats. Then, I groan, burrowing my face in my hands as the ketchup stain spreads like blood across my shirt, which, at this point, is virtually see-through and plastered to my body.

I consider trying to grab a change of clothes from my bag overhead, but I'd have to, yet again, unpack my ridiculous amount of underwear in a very public forum.

If this were a cartoon, the thought-bubble hovering over my head would be filled with bold punctuation and an aggressive use of the letter *F*.

A few minutes later, Oliver's legs appear in my peripheral vision. I sneak a quick peek at his crotch—purely out of altruism to see how his wet spot was drying—and realize he'd changed into . . . a nearly identical all-black outfit? Maybe he really is a lovely-looking Lucifer.

I take a deep breath. This moment is important. We can either allow the madness to be common ground and laugh this off, or we can sit in stunned silence at how horribly freaking wrong everything has gone.

I glance up to his face, and he has a resigned look and tired eyes. I sigh, then stand, and he shuffles past me and plops into his seat.

Silence it is.

We both stare straight ahead for a while, then I catch Oliver glancing at his watch.

"Four hours and twenty-seven minutes left," I whisper.

Oliver nods. "This might be the longest flight of my life."

"*Keep calm and carry on, right, mate?*" I say with another weak attempt at a British accent.

His eyes close slowly, like he's searching for strength, then he grabs his headphones, slips them on, and turns fully away from me.

Chapter 6

It's the Puke for Me

OLIVER

The end is near.

Not in the apocalyptic sense, despite how many times I've wished for it on this flight, but there's only ninety minutes before landing. The worst has to be behind us.

"We must be getting close," Tilly says, stretching her arms out in front of her and twisting her wrists side to side. "I can't wait to get out of this seat," she adds, squirming some more to emphasize her point. "Are you from London?"

"Surrey," I answer, fiddling with my headphones. "I take it you're from Cleveland?"

Tilly nods. "They call it the London of the Midwest. Our giant, red Free Stamp actually rivals Big Ben in landmarks of cultural significance," she says, referencing a humongous forty-nine-foot statue of a rubber stamp with the word FREE printed on the bottom that sits in a random park in Cleveland.

The designer I reported to for my internship showed it to me on a tour around the city. When I politely asked her what the giant red eyesore was supposed to symbolize, she didn't have an answer for me.

"Right," I say, nodding. "I actually had an art print of the stamp hanging on my bedroom wall growing up. That was the sole reason I visited Cleveland."

Tilly's eyes twinkle as she picks up on my attempt at sarcasm. Which is rather terrifying. I don't usually joke or talk with strangers like this, preferring the safety and comfort of people I know well and can trust to understand me.

"I hope you at least got to see our river catch fire while you were there. Also of huge Cleveland cultural significance."

I blink at her. "What?"

Tilly snorts, waving her hand. "Sorry, that was very niche. Our river caught on fire in the sixties or something, and it's contributed to our 'Mistake on the Lake' status. It's probably better not to globally spread that nugget of information."

"Probably not," I agree. "Is this your first time visiting the UK?"

She gives a haughty sniff and pretends to flip her hair off her shoulder. "I'm quite cultured and well traveled, I'll have you know." Tilly follows it up with an exaggerated wink.

"Right. Your sparing use of ketchup really exemplifies your European disposition," I say, pressing my lips together to hide a smile as I glance at the jarring red stain on her shirt. Tilly drops her head into her hands and groans, then laughs. I laugh, too.

And that's when it hits me how . . . *weird* this is. I'm actually enjoying myself? Talking to someone? Perhaps I'm sick. But I decide to keep going. "What brings you to Lon—"

My words are cut off by a guttural wet noise a few feet from us, followed by a panicked "Uh-oh . . . I think . . ."

Our heads twist in unison toward the noise like wild animals hearing the approach of a stealthy predator.

A green-faced boy, probably about nine or ten, doubles over in the aisle a couple rows ahead. I can no longer see his face, but there's no mistaking the earth-shattering sound of someone puking their brains out.

Tilly gasps, her hand flying out and clutching my arm. Our eyes swivel to each other, both of us too afraid to look at anything else.

The smell hits me next, and it's like every nerve ending in my body starts weeping.

"Oh no," Tilly says, eyes wide, a sheen of sweat breaking out across her forehead.

It takes me a moment, but I realize what that *oh no* signals.

"Tilly," I say, my voice a raw plea. "No. Please, no."

Tilly starts shaking her head rapidly. "There's no stopping it. I'm a goner."

"Resist! Resist!"

"I can't!"

Christ. Here it comes.

Eyes stuck on me, Tilly starts dry-heaving.

"Absolutely *not*," I say, leaping up from my seat. In a blur of jerky movements, I thrust my hands under her arms, lift her like a rag doll, and spin her to face the aisle, charging out of the row of seats and toward the restroom behind us.

With little couth or grace, I push the man vacating the bathroom out of the way, ripping the door wide open and giving Tilly an oh-so-subtle shove inside before slamming it shut again and pressing my back against it as I pant.

I should probably feel guilty about the manhandling, but as the echoes of her vomiting rumble through the door, I'm just grateful for my timing.

I compose myself by tapping my fingers at my side for a moment, then walk back to my seat, aggressively jamming the overhead attendant call button.

After what feels like an eternity, the attendant from earlier appears with a sour look on her face. "This better not have anything to do with condiments," she says, before noticing Tilly's empty seat.

I shake my head, pointing weakly at the vomit spot. "Someone had an accident," I say, trying not to breathe. The attendant's eyes flick to Tilly's seat again. "Not her," I say, gesturing next to me. "Some kid."

The attendant lets out a loud sigh through her nose, closing her eyes. "Be right back," she says.

A few moments later, I watch her and another attendant huddle around the puke. They've put on face masks and rubber gloves, and are aggressively whispering to each other as they point at the spot.

It seems like one of them loses the quiet argument, and bends over, using a single paper towel to wipe at the mess. Seemingly satisfied with that sub-par scrubbing, the other opens a silver package and sprinkles coffee grounds over the remaining smear. They then grab one of the thin airplane blankets, fluff it out, and drape it over the whole mess like it's a dead body.

Gathering up their trash, they turn and move toward the back of the plane.

"Is that all you can do?" I ask, standing up and hitting my head on the ceiling. Again. "A blanket? Where's the . . . I don't know? Airplane carpet cleaner?"

"We don't have everything we need to clean it properly right now," the attendant says, shooting me a bland look. "We're landing soon anyway. It'll be fine."

Fine? *Fine?* Absolutely no part of this circle of hell parading as an international flight has been *fine*.

I'm scrambling for words to keep arguing, but they walk away before any of the thoughts can form. Slouching back into my seat, I slowly bang my skull against the headrest.

After a few more minutes, Tilly drags herself down the aisle and crawls into her seat.

"Are you okay?" I ask, eyes glued to the window and my fingers tapping away at my side.

She clears her throat. "Not to be dramatic," she says, her voice quieter than it's been the entire flight, "but I imagine there are exhumed corpses that are in better shape than me."

I glance at Tilly, and I can't say she's wrong. Her twin alien buns are skewed, spiky black hair sticking out every which way. Her eyes are red-rimmed and skin a grayish green. I reason that agreeing with her verbally could potentially offend her.

Choosing the safest, most comfortable option, I stay quiet the rest of the flight.

Chapter 7

Ugh

TILLY

We finally touch down and my body/spirit feels like I've sprinted a marathon. This was not how I expected to start my grand European adventure.

When the plane comes to a stop and the overhead speaker dings with the OK to unfasten our seat belts, I hop up, wiggling out my legs and arms. Oliver is slower to unfold his long limbs from his seat, and I watch as he stands and stretches his neck from side to side.

Damn. He really is cute—tall and gangly with a soft but vibrant energy that has me believing countless thoughts are swirling under that quiet façade. Or, more likely, I'm just romanticizing the hell out of him as my too soft heart tends to do.

But I'm disappointed this tortuous flight did not a romance make. I don't know why, but my brain is always hooking on to random people, wanting so badly to find a connection with someone, even when there's no logical reason for one.

I've always had trouble relating to my peers, saying or doing the wrong thing no matter how hard I tried to be like them— observing the way they interact with each other and trying to mimic it with very little success. It's exhausting trying to make friends while pretending to be someone you're not.

As people toward the front of the plane slowly start to trickle out, I squeeze into the aisle, wrestling my suitcase down in the limited space, then duck back into the row.

I look at Oliver again, and he must feel my stare, because he glances at me.

And he tentatively smiles.

Ugh, that quick flick of his lips slaps my silly heart around my chest.

Something in me shifts. Determination, maybe? A hopeless need to make something monumental out of the disastrous flight? The past ten hours have been so bad, they literally couldn't get worse, right?

Should I do it?

I think I should do it.

I'm gonna do it.

What's the point of this summer if I don't take my life into my own hands? I'm no longer the person squeezing herself into shapes and molds that don't fit. I'm bold and brazen Tilly Twomley, and I will shoot my shot with hot airplane strangers, so help me God.

"CanIhaveyournumber," I say (yell).

If words could sprint, mine would have just won an Olympic medal. I almost blow out my back with how hard I wince.

"I beg your pardon?" Oliver says, eyebrows arched.

I take a deep breath, squeezing my hands into tight fists at my sides. *Calm*, I tell myself. *You can do this.*

"I was . . . I wanted to know if I could have your number. Phone number. Or like . . . WhatsApp number or whatever . . ." Dead silence. "Since we're in like . . . Europe. Or whatever."

More silence.

Holy *shit* this is a lot of silence.

This silence is, quite possibly, worse than the complexity of airplane noise.

Oliver's eyes go wide and his lips part, but in this painful, slow-motion type of way that forces me to watch him process what I said. He's looking at me like . . . well, like he can't quite believe I spoke those words out loud.

And, as the silence continues to destroy me, I do the only thing I can.

I whip around, accidentally whacking Oliver with my over-stuffed backpack, and bolt.

Dead. Ass. Run.

I barrel down the aisle, hurdling over the puke puddle like an athlete, knocking people out of the way, rolling over toes with my ridiculous suitcase, not even caring about the brutal chaos I leave in my wake.

Screw being bold. Screw being brazen. That shit is for the birds, and I will absolutely *never* take another risk again.

Even when I'm off the plane, I continue sprinting through the airport, my suitcase and backpack banging around behind me. But I can't slow down. If I slow down, people might see my embarrassed tears. If I stop to catch my breath, Oliver might accidentally catch up, that horrified look still on his pretty face. If I don't get out of here as quickly as humanly possible, I might see him at customs or while I'm waiting for Mona.

And the last thing I ever want is to see Oliver again.

Chapter 8

Give Me Caffeine or Give Me Death

TILLY

I managed to get through customs and find Mona without any further disasters (incredible, I know). I was so jet-lagged from the flight that I barely took in the fact that I was in London freaking England when she picked me up, and I crashed immediately on her couch.

"Morning, sunshine," Mona greets me as I blink awake to the sound of her espresso grinder running at full force.

"Morning, Mo-Mo," I say through a yawn, propping myself up on my elbows.

I look around, finally registering her posh and modern (read, angular and sparse) apartment. Everything is a different shade of white or gray with minimalistic furniture, and the walls hold a few hanging mirrors and sharp metal artwork. Mona is the only streak of color in the barren place, strutting around the apartment in a deep red blouse and matching trousers.

I roll off the couch, scurrying across the artfully aged

wooden floors to the large window. I stand, throwing back the curtains with a flourish to welcome in the beautiful, vibrant . . .

Depressingly gray skies?

I frown, then shake myself. This is *London* gray, and is therefore superior to all other shades of gray.

Pressing my face against the glass, I take it all in. A row of beige stone buildings line the street. An older woman walks a fluffy white dog while chatting on her cell phone and . . . oh . . . holy shit . . . be still my heart, is that a literal red freaking phone booth on the corner? I'm about to swoon.

"Mom's upset you didn't call her when you landed," Mona says, coming up behind me and disrupting my very special moment with the red phone booth.

I roll my eyes. Of course she's mad at me. She's always finding some reason to have a hissy fit over something I do.

"I'll call her in a minute," I say, turning to Mona. She's holding a tiny espresso cup slightly away from her body. I grin and reach for it.

"Yeah, right," she says, furrowing her perfectly manicured thick brows. Damn her for figuring out her brow shape and actually maintaining it. "I'm scared to see you caffeinated," she adds, taking a sip of her espresso. "You can have herbal tea."

I frown. "You should be more afraid of an uncaffeinated me," I say in my most menacing voice. Mona isn't impressed as she takes another dainty sip.

"Please?" I beg, switching tactics by making my voice high-pitched and whiny. "It helps my ADHD."

This is actually true. Dr. Alverez had told me my intense coffee habit I started freshman year of high school is likely a form of self-medicating to help with my focus. Whatever it is, the fact remains that I need coffee or I will, quite literally, perish in the most dramatic and crankiest way possible.

Mona purses her lips, looking me up and down, and I squirm under the appraisal.

My sister is objectively gorgeous: short with full curves and thick black hair that hangs in perfect shiny layers around her contoured face. But her beauty is amplified by a certain cunning sharpness she exudes, like she could bring even the strongest person to their knees with three artfully chosen words and a well-timed arch of her eyebrow.

"We'll compromise with black tea," she says, turning and heading back to her small but sleek kitchen.

"You're the best," I say, galloping up behind her and wrapping her in a bear hug.

"Get off. You know I'm not a hugger." She pushes me away and I shoot her a goofy look to mask how much I wish she were a hugger.

She preps my tea and I dump so much sugar in it that I'm sure my dentist cringes from across the pond.

"Call Mom," Mona hounds me, pushing my phone toward me. "I don't want her pestering me every four minutes to ask how you are."

I roll my eyes and sigh. "Sorry to be such a tremendous burden."

It's Mona's turn to roll her eyes. "Don't be dramatic. But this is first and foremost a work trip, and I can't be fielding her calls all day."

"I mean . . . Your priorities are your priorities, but I plan on having *fun* this summer," I say, shooting my mom a quick text, telling her I'm safe and miss her, blah blah blah.

Mom immediately responds with the world's longest list of questions, none even coming close to: *Are you having fun?* Or *How was the flight?* But instead: *Have you taken your meds this morning?* and *Did you lose anything?* and the lovely *I think Mona should hang on to your money so you don't impulsively spend it all, but it's your call. What do you think?*

I *think* I'm going to choose to ignore her.

Mona takes a final sip of her espresso before rinsing out the cup. "I actually wanted to talk to you about that and what Amina and I expect from you as our intern."

I groan while my stomach drops. "I'm pretty sure it's illegal to exploit child labor," I say, blowing on my steaming tea.

"I'm pretty sure you're eighteen and getting a free trip across Europe," Mona counters, tilting her head in a way that reminds me of Mom. "And I promised them I'd make this as much of a résumé builder as I can for you."

"I don't want a résumé builder."

Mona wipes down the immaculate white counters with a hand towel. "Well, welcome to adulthood. You'll be doing things you don't want to do for the rest of your life. Enjoy."

"So this conversation is good practice then?" I shoot back.

An emotion flashes across Mona's face—something that looks close to . . . hurt?—but she turns away before I can fully read it.

A trickle of guilt twists my stomach, but I push the feeling away. There's no way I hurt Mona's feelings. She gave up on feelings when she became a professional business lady.

"For the most part, you won't have to do much," Mona says, her voice cool but defeated. "Actually, the more you stay out of the way, the better, come to think of it."

"Nice."

"*But* I'll need to use your hands. To model the polish for my Instagram and Twitter and TikTok pages," Mona says, turning and glancing at where my fingers are thrumming on the counter.

A grin breaks across my face. "Aw. Like when we were kids."

"Yes," she says, shooting me her own soft smile. Mona has been painting my nails since I was in diapers.

I spread my fingers in front of me, looking at them. I'm not gonna lie, these are some hella beautiful hands. I have long fingers and well-shaped nail beds. I've always liked my hands, which is why I put in a tremendous amount of mental work to break my nail and cuticle biting habit in middle school. Another stimming thing. Now I roll my toes if I get a surge of electric energy I need to get out. It makes sense Mona wants to use my hands. They're so pretty. Ideal. Dare I say perfect?

"I couldn't budget for a professional hand model, so you'll have to do," Mona says, bursting my bubble. "It will be good marketing to have you showing off the polish at different sites we travel to. I'll be meeting with various store buyers at each location, and it will be a nice touch to show the polish in familiar territory. It's an idea my new design intern actually came up with."

"Design intern?" I ask, despite my bruised ego.

Mona nods. "He came on board about two months ago in a part-time virtual role as he helped us strategize. He's coming on the trip. Should arrive any minute," Mona says, glancing at the clock. "Same with my partner. I'm surprised she's not here by now, actually."

"You're dating someone?" I ask, sniffing out a romantic interest like a bloodhound. Mona is a lesbian and I'm desperate to inherit a sister (in-law) that I actually click with.

"*Business* partner," Mona snaps. Way too aggressively for there not to be something there if you ask me. "I've told you about Amina a million times."

I'm about to open my mouth and push the matter when a husky woman's voice calls out from the door.

"Hello, darlings," the woman says, walking into the kitchen. And holy shit is she a stunner. Sharp, high cheekbones, amber skin, and coffee-black eyes. Her locs are draped over one shoulder and a pale pink dress hugs her curves. The probability of Mona not having a crush on her "business partner" is diminishing by the second.

"You must be Tilly," Amina says, shooting me a wide smile and walking toward me.

Oh my God, is she going to hug me? She might just be my favorite person ever if she hugs me. I can't tell if she's actually going for a handshake at the last minute, but I don't care, I stretch my arms out and give her a hug.

She hugs me back, rocking side to side in what I choose to believe is excitement. "It's so lovely to meet you!" she says, pulling away and holding me at arm's length, giving me a once-over. "We're excited to have you on for the summer. I've heard so many wonderful things about you."

I can't stop the automatic, skeptical glance I shoot at Mona. Amina laughs like I'm a stand-up comedian, squeezing my shoulders kindly before releasing me and moving to the kitchen.

"Our other intern here yet?" Amina asks Mona, bumping her lightly on the hip to gain access to the espresso machine. Is that a blush I see on Mona's cheeks?

"No, but I'm not expecting him till nine thirty," she says, looking again at the clock, which ticks to half past right as she speaks. There's an immediate knock at the door, and we all blink in surprise.

"Punctual chap," Amina says, smiling as she takes a sip of her drink.

"An excellent sign," Mona says, heading to the door. She turns out of sight, but her voice carries. "Hi! I'm Mona. So lovely to meet you in person."

I take a sip of my tea as their footsteps approach around the corner.

And, next thing I know, I'm spraying out my drink like an

overzealous bathing elephant, showering myself (and Mona's white throw rug) in hot brown liquid.

"Jesus, Tilly," Mona says, stepping in front of her intern as if to protect him from a bullet.

I start hacking up a lung as I stare at my worst nightmare, dressed (once again) in crisp black pants and shirt.

Oliver's dark eyes bounce up and down my braless, retainer-wearing, really short pajama bottom–clad form like a rubber ball. He squeezes his eyes shut then opens them again, looking at me in horror for a beat before dropping his gaze to his shoes.

"Shit," I groan. "Why does it have to be you?"

Chapter 9

This Can't Get Worse

OLIVER

I'll be the first to admit that I regularly and spectacularly miss social cues, but Tilly's utter despair at my entrance is not a sentiment easily misconstrued.

I'm not exactly thrilled to see her, either. After creating the most physically unsafe in-flight experience of my life, she then proceeded to scream a pickup line at me, and before I could even process what she was saying and how I should respond, she sprinted away. I've replayed this bizarre scene over and over in my head and all I can figure is that she did it as some sort of rude joke to make fun of me. She wouldn't be the first.

I clench my jaw, staring at my shoes. What is she doing here? Why is she in . . . in what appears to be her knickers? Or are those supposed to be pajamas? It's half past nine, put on some trousers for God's sake.

"Why are you being so rude?" Mona, my boss, asks Tilly.

"Why is he here?" Tilly counters, gesturing at me like I'm the antichrist. God, this girl really knows how to make spectacular welcomes.

"I'm here," I snap, my patience worn thin, "because I run a

highly successful Instagram page on modern design and color applications, and was asked to basically start from scratch on establishing a brand for this nail polish company. So, I think the better question is, what are *you* doing here?"

Amina, who I've met a few times over Zoom meetings, sucks in a breath. "I wouldn't call it starting from scratch . . ."

"Ruhe's business page has one hundred and thirty-four followers on Instagram and seventy-two on Twitter. Last I checked, I believe it was four on TikTok," I say, eyebrows furrowing. "You don't view that as successful market penetration, do you?" It's a genuine question. We've had a handful of virtual planning sessions and emails in preparation for the summer, and I want to make sure I understand their goals.

I can tell by the way Amina's and Mona's mouths hang open that I must have been too blunt.

Sigh.

I'm apparently always too blunt. I try to be mindful of it, I truly do, but why say something in fifty "gentler" words when the point can be made in a dozen concise ones?

"Isn't he the charmer," Tilly says, eyebrows raised.

"Sorry. That came out . . . er . . . badly."

Mona blinks at me for a moment before straightening her shoulders. "Okay. Pause. It's only been five minutes and this entire thing feels like a derailed train shooting off a cliff."

"That was beautiful, Mo," Tilly says.

Mona shoots her a dirty look. "Oliver," she says, turning to me with a smile. "Let's start over. It's wonderful to finally meet you in person."

"We're so thrilled to have you on the team," Amina says, walking over and shaking my hand.

"This is my sister, Tilly, and she's sorry for being so abrasive," Mona says, glancing at Tilly with a warning look. Tilly crosses her arms over her chest. "She's our other intern this summer. My parents and I agreed it would be a good opportunity for her to get some life experiences before she starts college. She'll also do some modeling of the lacquers while she's with us."

There's an energy shift, like Tilly is physically dimming at Mona's words, her shoulders curling and arms sliding down to hug around her middle.

"Where are you going to university?" I ask, trying my best to offer an olive branch of small talk despite how much I hate it.

Tilly frowns at me like I just shat on her shoes. "I'm not."

Mona glares at Tilly, and Tilly glares back, something sharp and biting that I can't read being said with their looks.

"And what school will you be attending, Oliver?" Mona asks, eyes still glued on her sister.

"University of the Arts," I answer, that huge swell of anticipation shooting up my spine and down my limbs, making my fingers tap in excitement. "They're allowing me to design an accelerated dual-degree program merging photography and digital media curation for businesses, all with an emphasis on color theory and psychological applications in marketing and advertisements. You see, it will take the fundamentalist concepts of art and design applied to marketing, but with studies into broad appeal versus regional and cultural implications of color psychology. Because even Pantone, this massive authority that has created a universal language on color, chooses their color of the year, right? And that color then influences everything from smartphones to fashion on a global scale. But can we really do that? Find a single color, maybe two, that should be implemented into global design? Is that truly the *best* branding strategy for a company? Or should they look on a more micro scale when executing their goals? You see—"

It's at this point that I realize I'm rambling like an absolute git, so I slam my mouth shut. I can tell by the deep furrow in Amina's and Mona's brows and the way their eyes are bouncing back and forth like they're chasing after my words. Cubby, my twin sister, helped me learn this cue and advised me that, when I see it, I've probably lost everyone.

"Well?" Tilly says, her voice quieter than I've heard it before. I glance at her. Her jaw is hanging slightly open, eyes wide and focused on me. "Should they?"

"W-what?" I ask, caught off guard.

"Should they implement a more micro perspective?"

I blink rapidly then open my mouth, excited words bubbling up my throat as I'm about to tell her my theories on the effect, but I stop myself. Part of having autism means, for some of us, that we can't read what people actually mean versus what they say.

There have been so many humiliating times where I mistook sarcasm for genuine interest, excitedly infodumping about something only to realize the listeners are having a laugh at my expense. It was particularly awful in primary school, being branded as some weird freak for talking nonstop about my latest obsession, but I've learned to mask it in most situations, usually only letting go for my mums, Cubby, or my best friend, Marcus. I don't know why I just slipped up so dreadfully in front of these three women who are virtually strangers.

"Never mind," I say, running a hand across the back of my heated neck. I risk another quick glance at Tilly, and her face falls into a frown. Like I've disappointed her.

I can't understand why.

"Anyway," Mona says after a moment, clapping her hands together and moving so we're all in a small circle. "Today marks the official start on our sales tour, and I truly am glad to have both of you here." I catch Tilly shooting a skeptical glance at Mona.

"We leave for Paris tomorrow for our meeting with Toussaint's," Mona says, thumbing through her phone.

Toussaint's is a boutique chain with locations scattered across Paris and a few locations in London. A cursory Google search told me it's popular with both locals and tourists, and Mona CC'ed me on a briefing that detailed how important getting an account with them would be. I don't really have a stake in Ruhe—I'm using this as a minimum-wage résumé builder—but there are few things I hate more than losing, so I'm invested in their success.

"I'd like for us to dedicate today to stocking up on social media posts," Mona continues, looking at me. I nod. I've already thought of some decadently colorful spots across the city we can use as a backdrop for photos. "Oliver, you and Amina can discuss ideas while I paint Tilly's nails."

"Go team," Tilly says with lackluster enthusiasm, following Mona across the room.

"Want an espresso?" Amina asks me, already preparing one.

"Please." I'll need an IV drip of caffeine to keep up with Tilly. She slides the cup across the kitchen bar, and I sip it.

"Alright, Oliver, let's hear what you've got."

A buzz of excitement hums across my system, and I can't stop my smile. This is the kind of thing I live for.

I fill Amina in on my ideas, mapping out the best route for the day and pulling up a few sample photos of sites to give her a better idea of what I'm thinking. Amina scrolls through them, taking her time to analyze each carefully.

"Brilliant," she eventually says, shooting me a wide grin. "I love the Gloucester Road station idea in particular. Ornate but a touch gritty, all with the polish highlighted . . . it'll be perfect."

I smile, fingers tapping at my side. "Exactly. You get it. Glad the idea translated."

Massively relieved is more like it. It's so hard to morph the swirls of my concepts into actual words, and when I try to articulate them, I often get too excited and dart around from idea to idea. Then I realize how circuitous it all gets, which makes me hyperaware of my talking and it all ends up making my tongue feel thick and awkward and like my throat's choking on the rambling sentences.

Such fun.

"Are you excited for fall term?" Amina asks.

I clock this as a segue into getting-to-know-you talk and shift my brain for the new topic. This is a conversation with a colleague, so I remind myself that I need to keep it interesting, but surface level enough that no one feels uncomfortable.

"Thrilled," I answer honestly. "A bit overwhelmed, too, I guess. There's so much to learn, and I'll finally get to focus on what I'm actually interested in instead of wasting time in things like maths."

Amina gasps, pressing a hand to her chest. "I'd be careful, intern, you're saying such blasphemy to an engineer, mind you."

Oh no. I fucked up. I blink rapidly, trying to figure out how badly I just offended my boss, but she smiles again, patting my shoulder.

"Oh Christ, I'm only joking. Don't look so worried."

My tense muscles sag in relief.

"I remember the summer before I left for university," Amina says wistfully, moving around the kitchen to get a glass of water. "I was so nervous. But you meet loads of people right away. You'll make some of the best friends of your life." She flicks a quick glance at Mona across the room.

I shrug, finishing off my espresso. Making friends is the least of my concerns when it comes to school. I can't really be arsed to put in all the work, if I'm being honest. I already have my best friend, Marcus, who I'm sharing a flat with, and my twin sister, Cubby, who texts me enough to be worth five friendships. My world is small, but I like it that way. Making new friends requires so much brainpower—figuring out how much to tell people without infodumping, constantly missing social cues, second-guessing every interaction—and I'd rather channel all of that into exploring the endless influences of color.

"This is the blandest nail polish I've ever seen," Tilly says from across the room, interrupting us as she holds up her hand, looking at the sandy-beige color from various angles.

I'm tempted to open my mouth and tell her how wrong she is; that it's a beautiful beige that likely will elicit sensations of calm and luxurious relaxation in wearers, but I decide it's not worth whatever biting disagreement she'd subject me to.

"Thanks," Mona says sarcastically. "It's called Bae-ge," she adds, emphasizing the *bae*.

"At least the name is clever," Tilly says. "But do you really want a bunch of pictures with this polish as the focus?"

"I have my MBA," Mona says, straightening her shoulders. "So I won't be taking advice from you." There's a pause as Mona studies her own nails. "And Oliver said he can Photoshop different colors over it."

Tilly gasps like Mona just told her the pope is toying with Protestantism. "But that's a lie!"

"No. It's an efficient way to get photos without dissolving your skin with an enormous amount of nail polish remover between locations."

"You are ever the loving and considerate sister," Tilly says, uncurling her long legs and standing up from the floor.

Amina tries to hide a giggle behind a cough, then claps her hands. "Alright, let's get a move on, darlings," she says. "Time is money, blah blah blah."

"You aren't planning on wearing that, are you?" Mona says,

gesturing wildly at her sister and confirming that I'm not the only one ... um ... distracted? ... by Tilly's exceptionally tiny cotton shorts.

"I like to embrace showing my whole ass," Tilly says, walking to her suitcase. "Literally and figuratively."

"Tilly."

"Obviously I'm changing," Tilly says, shaking the clothes in her fist at Mona. "Would you chill?"

"Don't smudge your nails," Mona says, eyes bugging out of her head. "And don't talk to me like that, I'm in charge of you." Mona stomps after Tilly as she heads toward the bathroom.

Tilly says something back that I can't make out, but I'd be willing to guess it was snarky and sarcastic.

Amina chuckles, putting a hand on my shoulder. "Gonna be a lively trip, isn't it?"

I swallow, eyes still stuck at the corner Tilly disappeared behind. "I'm not sure any of us will make it out alive."

Chapter 10

It Gets Worse

OLIVER

We take the tube to Westminster, and Tilly's head darts around like an excited pigeon's the entire time, her eyes wide as if she's trying to memorize every crack and crevice of London.

It's a bit distracting, really. The way she's so . . . in *awe* of everything. I can't seem to stop looking at her looking at everything else.

She decides to break the peaceful silence between us as we make our way over the bridge to the opposite side of the Thames.

"So, you run a famous Instagram account?" she asks, focus still bouncing around the city like a rubber ball. She stops to lean perilously over the edge of the railing to look at the murky water. Mona and Amina keep walking, and it feels like my brain is being tugged in opposite directions. Do I follow my bosses or do the polite thing and engage in a conversation?

I clear my throat, something about her tone making me feel prickly and awkward. "I wouldn't say it's *famous*."

"That's good," she says, popping back to vertical and

continuing to walk. "Only fuckbois proudly claim Instagram fame. Glad to see you have a humble head on your shoulders."

I think she's complimenting me, but I'm not sure. "The account has garnered a decent following, though," I say, feeling like I should keep talking. I don't know why, but I have this odd need to . . . impress her?

"Mayhaps I spoke too soon," Tilly whispers to herself. In that awful British accent, I'd like to add.

"But a lot of that came after *Architectural Digest* featured it on their 'Design Inspiration Accounts to Follow' post," I say, words tumbling out of me.

Tilly audibly groans. "Yup, I definitely spoke too soon."

I take it I've officially solidified myself as a "fuckboi" to Tilly. Whatever. I'm not going to downplay the excitement of an international design authority recognizing my page. I've just never really had the inclination to sort of . . . brag about it before. It's like my head's on backward I feel so turned around.

"What's your handle?" she asks.

"OliverClarkColors."

"Wow. How witty and creative."

"What's yours? KetchupPrincess04?"

Tilly's mouth slams shut so loudly I hear her molars clang together. A blush rushes to her cheeks, warm and startling. Pantone 16–1720, Strawberry Ice. It rather suits her.

Her lips twitch as she eyes me, and I instantly feel bad. I'm not *trying* to be a prick to Tilly, but she seems to bring out the worst in me.

"I'm annoyed that that was actually an excellent burn," she says at last, rolling her eyes. "But, kudos, or whatever."

The nervous breath I was holding whooshes out of me. This girl is going to give me an aneurysm with how hard it is to figure her out.

Tilly pulls out her phone and starts typing as we walk.

"Holy *shit*," she says, eyes bugging out of her head. "You have over one hundred and twenty *thousand* followers." She stops in the middle of the sidewalk. Again. Mona and Amina are going to be a kilometer ahead of us at this rate.

Her finger flies as she scrolls through her phone. She holds it out, showing me one of my more popular posts.

Like all my posts, it's a collage of four seemingly dissimilar images; swiping to the left reveals the Pantone code of the shared color that threads them together, the subsequent images showing where the color exists in the four photos.

The one Tilly has up features the *Mona Lisa*'s famous smile; a browning leaf with the veins magnified from a raindrop; Mum's calico cat, Luna, stretched out in a triangle of sun; and a coastal slice of Valencia, the tiled roofs outlining the aqua water. This is for Pantone 7566, a vibrant brown with a depth of orangish hues that pull you in. Captivate you.

The caption reads:

People often associate brown with muddy. Bland. Dull. That is, objectively, false. Browns are the backbones of some of the most beautiful moments. It's the curve of Mona Lisa's lips. Nature's celebration of autumn. Fluffy splotches of a cat's fur. An architectural complement to the stunning blue of Spain's seas. Brown is bold and devoted to emphasizing the vibrancy of other colors around it. It's one of my favorite hues. How does it make you feel?

There are hundreds of comments where people talk about how the color gives them a sense of calm or makes them feel cozy, while others say they hate it or it's boring. A few argue over if a different spot on the cat's tail is also the same shade or actually has more influences of red.

I live for these comments.

I'm always asked what I want *to do* with my rather niche

field of study. The truth is, I don't have a concrete answer. But I like what I'm doing now so much, why wouldn't I pursue it?

I once asked my mums if I should consider myself directionless because I didn't have a job title at the ready when an adult asked me what I wanted to be when I grew up. They told me it's okay to not know exactly where I'm going, as long as I'm happy where I am.

What I do know is that there are conversations happening out there right now about color and feelings and design and influence, and I want to be a part of them.

Tilly stares at me like she expects me to say something.

"Do you expect me to say something?" I ask. I'm not sure why she's showing me my own photo.

"You wrote this?" she asks, jabbing her finger at the caption. Her tone seems . . . accusatory?

"That's generally how social media posts work."

"Like, those are your ideas? You noticed those colors?"

"Well . . . yeah. Why?"

She's quiet for a moment, eyebrows furrowed as she studies me. "It's very insightful and . . . lovely." Her frown deepens.

"I'm sorry?" I say, looking for clarification.

"I forgive you." Tilly sighs, looking back at her phone and scrolling further.

She starts walking again, and I trail a step behind, feeling like a needy puppy when I ask, "Does my work offend you?"

"No. The fact that your pompous attitude is justified by how good you are at it does."

"Oh," I say slowly. "Thank you. I think?"

After a few minutes of blessed silence, we catch up to Amina standing outside a Pret. Mona emerges a moment later with four drinks in hand.

"Sorry, Oliver," she says, handing one to me. "I didn't know what you liked, so I went with black coffee."

"Thanks," I say. "That's usually how I take it."

"Same for me, I'm assuming," Tilly says with a tinge of desperation as Mona hands her the next to-go drink.

"Again, not happening. It's herbal tea," Mona says. "And don't drink it yet," she adds, the rim already halfway to Tilly's lips.

"Why? Did you poison it?"

"It's a prop for the photoshoot. It will look obvious by the way you hold it if it's totally empty."

Tilly rolls her eyes and takes a defiant sip. My gaze bounces between the glares Mona and Tilly are giving each other.

"Take it this one's for me, then?" Amina says, breaking the silence.

Mona blinks, then looks at her business partner. "Coffee, no cream, two sugars."

Amina winks at Mona before taking a sip. I glance at Tilly, who's watching the entire interaction with a massive grin.

"Right," Mona says, giving herself a little shake. "Oliver. You're up. What do you want her to do?" she adds, thrusting her thumb at Tilly.

"If she could stand just there—"

"*She* has a name," Tilly cuts in with a growl.

I let out a deep, controlled breath. *If she could stand there and stop being so damn combative, maybe I wouldn't want to ram my head through a wall,* I want to say.

But instead opt for "If *Tilly* could stand right about there . . ." I take a few steps toward the spot along the river walkway. "And lean her forearms on the railing at an angle, I think we could get an excellent shot of her hands holding the Pret cup with Westminster in the background. Might as well get the big landmarks out of the way."

"Love it," Mona says, giving Tilly a little shove closer to the railing.

Tilly looks out over the Thames, eyes zipping around the sites across the river. "I can't believe you *live* here, Mo," she says, turning and grinning at her sister. "It's so beautiful I want to scream."

"Yes. It's great. Can we focus, please?"

"Like, do you ever think about how you live in a foreign freaking country?" Tilly continues, her words coming faster. "Cleveland who, amiright? You don't see stuff like *that* in Ohio," she says, pointing at Big Ben across the way. "I seriously can't get over the fact that I'm here. It's just so cool and everything is so—"

"Tilly!" Mona claps her hands together so loudly both Tilly and I jump. "For God's sake, shut up and focus."

Tilly's mouth slams shut, her face falling.

That seemed a bit . . . harsh. But I'm also not going to contradict the person cutting my paychecks.

Tilly's eyes glisten. Oh Christ, is she about to cry? I absolutely cannot handle it when people cry. She blinks a few times then shuffles over to the railing, stiffly propping her arms like I had explained.

She's not looking at us, her head turned toward the river, shoulders hunched around her ears.

Mona's phone rings, and she pulls it from her bag, glancing at the screen. "Gotta take this," she says, without looking at me. "Go ahead and get started. Amina, did that email come through?"

"Looking now," Amina says, walking away toward a bench with Mona, their eyes glued to their phones.

I set my coffee on the ground, then pull out my camera, taking a moment to adjust the settings before looking through the viewfinder. The angle's off.

"Tilly, would you mind moving a bit to your left?" I ask.

She takes a small step backward, eyes still firmly on the river.

I check again, but it still isn't right. I let my camera hang around my neck, grab my coffee for another sip, and walk over to her.

"Mind if I . . ." My hand hovers over her wrist. Her head turns slightly, and a teardrop rolls down her cheek to land on her arm.

Damn. I absolutely don't know how to handle this. I'm supposed to be taking pictures, not comforting crying people.

I panic.

And drop my hand to her skin.

"The city is . . . er . . . cool," I say. Which is possibly history's greatest platitude. London is amazing. It's bursting at the seams with colors and details. Every street offers a new, decadent surprise for my eyes, and it makes me happier than a kid in a candy shop.

Tilly nods rapidly, still not looking at me. I take the rather obvious hint that I'm not really helping.

Okay. I can't do this. I have literally no clue what comforting words to offer.

I grab the cup from her grasp, and she looks down at her hands, eyebrows furrowed. I place my own coffee between her palms.

"Little boost," I say, trying to ignore the wide-eyed stare she gives me. "Now, set your hands . . . yes. Perfect. Stay like that."

I move back to my original spot, bending my knees and angling the lens to center her grip, Big Ben and Parliament standing proudly behind her.

I get a few great shots that instantly spark ideas on how I'll edit them to highlight the colors of the background, tie them closely with a polish color in the foreground.

"How's it going?" Mona asks, Amina beside her as they rejoin me.

"Excellent," I say, scrolling through the photos.

"Love that one," Amina says, pointing at a shot with a double-decker bus crossing Westminster Bridge.

I nod then glance up from my camera display. And find Tilly's eyes on me. Slowly, she lifts the cup to her lips and takes a sip, then shoots me a small smile.

My own lips kick up at the sides, wanting to mirror the gesture, but I resist the urge.

I'm not about to set myself up to be embarrassed again by her.

For the next ten weeks, we're colleagues. Probably not even that. We're cordial strangers on a business trip.

It'd be best not to get any wires crossed.

Chapter 11

Portrait of a Blur

OLIVER

We end the day in Shoreditch, an artsy part of East London with blocks of street art and graffiti. The entire area hums with color and I'm, quite simply, in heaven.

We're stopped in front of what's probably our fifteenth mural to use as a backdrop for photos. This one spans the side of a four-story brick building, massive flowers exploding across the rough canvas. It's painted to look like streams of color are dripping from the tips of petals—the soft and chewy green of Pantone 13–0443, Love Bird, from the point of a calla lily. Pantone Ultra Violet falling (fittingly) from a posy of violets. Radiant Yellow from the curled edges of dahlia petals.

It's miraculous.

And is providing endless hidden gems for my personal Instagram posts with all the tiny details.

"Take a picture, it will last longer," Tilly says over my shoulder as I snap a shot of a small brick that has both Pantone Blue Grotto and Cool Gray on it. "Oh, wait. You've already taken nine thousand." Tilly snorts.

"What a clever and not at all overused decades-old joke," I say, straightening and turning on Tilly.

"Leave him be, Tilly," Mona snaps. "I imagine it's a constant job to create content for your page," Mona adds, turning to me. Tilly rolls her eyes, and, at this rate, I do worry they'll be stuck back there soon.

The day hasn't been a total disaster (you know, no major risks to my life or limb this time around), and we've definitely gotten some excellent shots, but every time I lose myself in my own world, stopping to snap photos for my page, I catch Tilly staring at me, this odd . . . frown on her face. At least, I think it's a frown. I originally assumed it was annoyance or the standard level of confusion I've gotten my whole life whenever I dip out of the "real world" and lose myself to whatever special interest is making my brain glow with happiness.

But I realize her look almost has a tinge of, I don't know, sadness to it? Whatever that look means, it's hard for me to decipher. She does snap out of it as soon as she's realized I've noticed and at least has the decency to look a bit sheepish for staring.

"Alright, kittens, let's wrap this up," Amina says, snapping her fingers with a kind smile. "Happy hour's on and I've got a date with a pint."

"Got a date with anyone else, Amina?" Tilly asks, sidling up to her with a sly look.

Amina's laugh is deep and husky and warm. If it were a color, it'd be the rich caramel of Pantone 723.

"Depends on who's asking, love," Amina says, tapping Tilly on the nose.

"Well . . ." Tilly says, glancing around. Her eyes linger a beat on her sister. Mona mouths the words *stop it* to Tilly over Amina's shoulder.

I can tell I'm missing some sort of hidden meaning in all these, er, pointed looks, and I'm a bit bored standing here like a clueless git.

"We really better get on with it," I say, clearing my throat. "While we still have good light."

Mona grabs Tilly's hand, jerking her to stand in front of the wall. "Go for it," she says, pointing at me then walking out of the shot.

I turn on my camera and adjust the setting.

"Uh, I know I've been doing this all day," Tilly says, "but I literally have no idea what to do with my hands for this shot."

We've had Tilly holding various props at the other locations, but I don't have a fresh idea that would flow with this background.

"Just act natural," I say, pulling my camera up to my eye and adjusting the lens.

Tilly scrunches up her face, slowly raising her hands so they dangle from limp wrists about shoulder height. She looks like an uncomfortable T. rex.

"This work?" she asks. I almost laugh.

"No, it doesn't work!" Mona says, letting out a groan. "Stop messing around and let's get the shot so we can all go home."

Color floods into Tilly's cheeks, and she starts gnawing on her lower lip, looking panicked.

"May I?" Stepping closer, I reach toward her still-dangling hands. Tilly nods. I circle her wrist, turning her so her back is to me. "Now lift your hands and do a peace sign, or something."

Tilly looks at me over her shoulder. "Oh my God. What am I, nine and taking a Facebook profile pic?"

"I don't know," I say, squeezing her wrist a bit. "Just . . . it's better than whatever you were doing before."

Tilly rips her wrist from my grip, flinging her hands into the air. "How dare you?"

"That's perfect. Stay like that," I say, tripping over my feet as I scramble backward to catch the shot.

"What?" she asks, swiveling her head even more to look at me.

"No, no. Don't turn around. Keep your arms up like that. It looks cool."

Tilly raises her eyebrow and gives me a skeptical look for a moment, but does as I asked, facing the wall and stretching her arms overhead.

The *click click click* of the camera shutter shoots a surge of electric creativity through my arms.

"Tilt your head back a touch," I instruct, and Tilly does.

Her hair falls like an ink spill down her back, the wind gathering up little wisps and curling them around her. Her arms are still flung to the sky and hands spread wide like starbursts. I snap away, the light hitting so the rainbow of color glows between her fingers.

"These look great," I say, as I take a new angle. "Do something new. Something fun."

Instead of giving me hell like she's done for 90 percent of my direction toward her, Tilly does as I ask, curling her wrists to new positions. She keeps going, practically dancing, and it isn't long before she's giggling.

There's so much energy in the way she moves, the way she holds herself, that, for a moment, I think the vibrant colors are coming straight from her palms.

By the end, she even throws in a few peace signs for me. And a middle finger, but I delete that one immediately.

"Being a hand model is exhausting!" Tilly says, collapsing dramatically against the wall when I announce I think we've gotten plenty of good shots.

"Tilly? More like Twiggy," Amina says, reaching out a hand and helping Tilly up.

Tilly blinks at Amina. "Like a tree? I'm barely five-four."

"You're joking," Amina says, cocking her head to the side. Tilly continues to stare at her with that wide, owlish gaze. "The famous supermodel? Fashion icon? Twiggy? Please tell me you know Twiggy."

"Oh wait," Tilly says, head perking up, "is she the one that's friends with Bella Hadid?"

Amina's jaw drops. "Christ, love, please don't make me feel so old."

Mona scoffs. "As if you look a day over twenty."

"You dirty flatterer," Amina says, shooting Mona a wink. Mona's cheeks erupt in red. Tilly lets out a tiny gasp, eyes flicking between the two women like she's watching an aggressive game of tennis.

I clear my throat, feeling like I'm intruding on a moment I don't understand. "Right, so I'm going to head out," I say.

Mona blinks, shaking her head and squaring her shoulders. "Yes. Of course. We should all get going. Big day tomorrow. We need to get organized and get a good night's sleep."

"Good work today, Oliver," Amina says, patting my shoulder as she, Mona, and Tilly start walking in the opposite direction I need to head.

"Yes. Excellent job," Mona says, scrolling through her phone. "We'll see you tomorrow morning at Heathrow? You got the itinerary, right?"

"Yup," I say, holding up my phone and giving it a shake. "See you then." Turning, I start down the block.

"Wow," I hear Tilly say. "Bye to you, too, I guess."

I whip around, stumbling over my feet and almost crashing into the storefront next to me.

Shit, was I rude? Was the conversation not done? Cubby,

Marcus, and I have a running joke about my frequent notorious "autistic exits" where I either mentally check out or fall so far into my own world that I walk away from a conversation before it's finished. We've always laughed about it, but I know that people generally see it as rude and something I need to be hyperaware of. As if the list of social niceties isn't long enough.

The three women are walking away from me, and Tilly doesn't turn back around so I can try to read if she was serious or not. In all likelihood, it wouldn't have done me much good; I'm not great at rectifying situations, either.

My shoulders slump as I continue my walk, deflated.

Today was exhausting.

For the most part, I've gotten better about not masking my autism—my mums have always encouraged me to express myself in whatever way feels most authentic—but sometimes the mask slips on unintentionally. Especially in professional or academic environments.

Primary school wasn't exactly a breeze socially, and I'd started tamping down stims and rehearsing conversations, mirroring my peers, to avoid bullying and feeling like an outsider. But an experience of autistic burnout at way too young of an age had me, Cubby, and our mums in therapy with Dr. Shakil. I'm very lucky that my family created a safety net around me to encourage me to stop hiding the things that made me more comfortable, but I still catch myself mirroring others' behaviors or monitoring my own reactions to make people feel more comfortable.

Today was one of those days.

It's not that Mona and Amina aren't welcoming and understanding new bosses, but I don't know them well. It's hard to trust new people to accept you as yourself when the world at large doesn't tend to accommodate you.

And then there's Tilly.

Thinking on it, I haven't really masked around her, but I spend an enormous amount of mental energy trying to figure her out. She doesn't seem to follow the normal social scripts I've observed in others, and some weird part of me finds that fascinating.

Which is rather ridiculous.

But replaying the day and trying to unravel the anomaly that is Tilly Twomley is the mental equivalent of driving a car uphill when you're out of petrol—lots of gear-grinding and minimal progress. I redirect my thoughts to something far more comfortable: colors.

Pulling out my camera, I scroll through today's pictures as I walk, each step taking me further into my own happy bubble.

Halfway to the tube station, the immediate need to edit the photos overwhelms me, inspiration tugging at me to stop what I'm doing and follow its path.

This happens rather frequently. When the wisp of an idea taps me on the shoulder, I simply have to chase after it; letting it get away isn't an option.

Mãe always smiles when it happens—even if I leave her midsentence—telling me I'm "listening to my muses." She's an artist, so she knows how impossible it is to resist the pull.

I duck into a pub and find a quiet table in a dark corner.

After waking up my laptop, I plug in my camera and launch my editing tool. I cross-reference the master color sheet Amina gave me, making sure I have the color's formula just right as I use Photoshop to paint it over Tilly's beige nails. I toy with the value and vibrancy for a minute or two, making sure it's just right.

It's a brilliant red, deep and poignant, demanding attention. Its vivacity is complemented by the golden glow of Big Ben and Parliament in the background. My eyes wander over the effect, tracing the natural circuit from the dazzling red to the comfort of gold. That red is an anchor. It grounds you in the photo, gives you a starting point before your eyes wander, a safe spot to return to if you get overwhelmed.

My hands itch to post it immediately, to share this moment with the world, so they can bask in the colors, too. Unfortunately, social media is based on algorithms and timing and all kinds of other minutiae that does not bode well for a brain fairly desperate for instant gratification. I generally wouldn't care, much more inclined to follow my whim than cater to social media barriers, but the whole reason I run my account is to bring people joy. Connect with them.

Plus, this is for Ruhe's success, not my own fun, so I force my keen brain into submission with the promise it will reach more people if I wait. Rather annoying, to tell the truth.

When I'm done editing the image, I scroll through other shots from the day. The photos from Shoreditch are remarkable with their bright and delicious colors, and I'm excited to tweak them to perfection. I'm about to decide on the next image to work on when a candid shot makes my excited thoughts screech to a halt, and I get the odd feeling of my heart slamming against my chest.

It's a picture of Tilly, head tilted back and eyes screwed shut while she laughs. The wind is whipping and tangling her hair from every angle, while a stray sunbeam strikes right on her scrunched-up nose. The picture has a subtle blur to it, like her enjoyment of the moment was too dynamic and full to be captured in a still image. I don't remember taking it, or what was causing her to laugh, but her smile is so vivid I can hear the echo of her amusement.

She laughed a lot today, I realize. At herself, mainly. She'd make a goofy move or crack some joke, then cackle like a banshee.

I make the image larger, tilting my head and studying it

from different angles. There are those three freckles again, right below the crinkles of her eye. I zoom in even more.

Damn it, what color is that? Why can't I get this?

I feel myself sort of falling into this image of Tilly, eyes grabbing at little details I hadn't noticed before. It's easier to look at her like this, in the safety of pixels. In real life, she's so much energy and noise and movement, it makes my brain feel like it might short-circuit if I'm not careful . . . But this is ridiculous. I have actual work to be doing. Why am I overanalyzing a blurry picture?

I click and drag the file, hovering it over the trash icon. I don't need this picture. I have no use for this photo of a loud, beautiful girl with a confusing personality and a very obvious dislike for me.

But, at the last moment, my fingers flick away, releasing the file back to a corner of my hard drive.

I slam my laptop shut, feeling . . . off. What's wrong with me? Am I getting sick?

I quickly pack up my things and hustle out of the pub and walk toward home, needing . . . needing . . . Well, I don't bloody know what I need exactly, but I can tell part of it is to move.

The journey home is a blur, and when I get to my new flat, Marcus and his partner, Micah, are cuddled on the couch with *Love Island* blaring in the background.

"Oliver!" Micah says, spreading their arms wide in greeting.

"Hiya," I say, shooting them both a small wave and trying to figure the best way to dart to my bedroom.

"How was the first day?" Marcus asks, not dragging his eyes from the TV.

"Ooh, yes! How was it? Do you like your new bosses? Are you so excited? Come! Sit! Tell us everything." Micah wiggles their bum, and Marcus grunts then moves over, pulling Micah fully onto his lap. Micah pats the open seat next to them.

Christ, I don't want to deal with this.

Marcus is my best mate, and I genuinely, truly like Micah.

But they are so in love it makes me ever so slightly sick to my stomach.

They met online about a year ago, and have been doing long distance. With Marcus and me both moving to London for college, Micah and Marcus are finally able to be together in person. And they're dead set on making up for lost time in the most romantically intimate ways possible.

To put it delicately, our walls are extremely thin, and both Marcus and Micah are extremely . . . passionate. At night. All night.

I am horrifyingly familiar with the details of their sex sounds.

"I probably should finish up some . . ." I wave vaguely toward my door.

"Oh, Oliver, *please* no. Spend some time with us! It's your last night here for months," Micah says, pouting. "Plus, you told us you already finished packing last night."

Damn. Micah has me there.

Reluctantly, I plop onto the couch. I tell them about my day, even showing them some pictures, diving into discussions about color combinations, that little special-interest engine revving up in my chest. Micah asks me tons of questions while Marcus keeps his attention firmly fixed on the show.

Prat.

How could anything be more interesting than color theory?

"She's quite pretty," Micah says, pointing at a picture that has Tilly's smiling face.

I shrug. "She's alright," I say, clicking out of the screen and turning my camera off. I can feel Micah's eyes on me, and I don't know why, but I can tell I want to avoid whatever question is poised on the tip of their tongue.

"Who do we hate this episode?" I ask, nodding at the TV. This finally grabs Marcus's attention.

"Pretty much all of them," he says, and Micah laughs.

We fall down a reality TV hole, watching beautiful people in either bathing suits or clubbing outfits drink and curse each other out for hours.

Glancing over during a particularly dramatic crying confessional, I realize Micah and Marcus have fallen asleep. I flick off the TV, then stand, grabbing a blanket and draping it over them.

They've drifted off holding each other. Something about the way they're cuddled close creates an odd, hollow type of ache in my chest. Like I'm looking at a future I'll never have. One not meant for me.

I've always had this odd feeling I'll end up alone.

It's hard not to when you struggle connecting with people as much as I do. I look at Cubby or my mums or even Marcus, and they all seem to have this ability to . . . *relate* to others. Start conversations. Create moments of quiet connection.

I can't do that.

I'm not sure I want to.

I don't like feeling that exposed, like I have to share bits of myself with others.

It's just . . . being known seems absolutely terrifying. And I don't think I'll ever be able to show myself to someone like that. Like I watch my mums do or Micah and Marcus.

That's why I like being on the internet. I can be in control of the interactions I have. I can think about what I want to say. How I can best say it. I can talk about the things I love without talking about myself. Showing myself.

It's connection without the risk of someone actually knowing me.

I pad to my bedroom, shucking off my trousers and button-down then crawling into bed.

I'm okay, I tell myself, burrowing under my duvet and rubbing a fist against my chest. I'm happy. I have a family that loves me. I have university coming up and a colorful world to explore.

I don't need anything besides that.

Chapter 12

It's About the Yearning

There are few things worse than getting ridiculously excited about something for *months*, then watching it all crash and burn. And that's about how this trip is feeling.

In some sick and twisted sort of déjà vu, Oliver and I find ourselves next to each other on another flight. I'm tempted to ask Mona to duct-tape me to my seat so I can't flail about and do something else incredibly embarrassing.

Okay. No. Everything's fine. My flight from Cleveland to London was *not* my fresh start. This one to Paris is. I refuse to land in another new country and have my fresh start be tainted by any other disasters. I am manifesting the fuck out of good vibes and whatever.

Also, it's Paris. How could anything go wrong in Paris? I'm about to gorge myself on baguettes and ogle hot Frenchmen who I assume wear white-and-navy-striped shirts and berets 24/7 and say gorgeous things like *oui* and *merci* and *voulez-vous coucher avec moi.*

Le sigh.

It's ridiculously early, and the cabin of the plane is dark

and stuffy. I wish I could sleep like everyone else around me. I just . . . can't. I'm not a good sleeper. Never have been, really.

I feel tired all day, but the second I go to lie down, my thoughts start jumping rope and running laps around my skull, keeping me up for hours with restless energy, only to repeat the exhaustion cycle the next day.

Oliver fell asleep about thirty minutes ago, and I keep catching myself looking at him like a weird little creep. I can't help it though. There's something . . . *dynamic* about his face. He's smiled probably twice in the entire time I've spent with him, but something about that crooked grin seared itself into my greedy brain, and I've been hungry to earn more.

Gentle turbulence rocks the plane, and Oliver's head lolls to the side.

And lands on my shoulder.

The firm weight and warmth of the contact has me biting back an obnoxiously loud sigh. I love touch. I need touch like fish need water, and it's not something I get very much of. My parents are caring but they certainly aren't touchy, and I don't really have friends or a boyfriend providing any physical affection. I can't tell you how many times I've been at school—feeling overwhelmed, overstimulated—and wanted nothing more than a friend to hug. Someone to hold me tight, give me a squeeze that reassures me all this zapping energy won't crack my body apart.

Another bump of more startling turbulence tosses us both in our seats, and Oliver wakes up, rubbing his eyes then blinking at me. He shifts away from me, and I pop the silly bubble of disappointment that tries to rise in my chest.

No. Nope. Absolutely not. I refuse to . . . *yearn* over a cute boy that I hardly know and who point-blank rejected my (very aggressive) attempts at talking. Especially not when I'm about to be surrounded by good cheese and French boys.

We touch down about half an hour later, the flight passing without any massive injuries, physical or emotional. After navigating through the buzzing airport, we pack onto a crowded train and make our way to our hotel in the city.

My nose is pressed against the window the entire time. It's mainly gray buildings and trees whooshing by the window but it's trees and buildings and fields that I'm seeing for the very first time. Might never see again. They're so beautiful.

After we get off at the station, the walk to our hotel has me equally gawking, my mouth dangling open as I take in the city. The buildings lean toward each other like plants bending toward the sun. It's gray stone and straight lines and wrought-iron balconies all accompanied by the subtle smell of pee and alcohol on the streets. It's filthy and gorgeous and I love every bit of it.

When we finally get into the lobby of the hotel—which has enough charm to make me want to lie on the ornate carpet and weep in *Parisian aesthetic*—Amina talks to the person at the desk in what I believe to be beautiful, perfect French.

I stare at Mona with a knowing look the entire time while Oliver huddles in a corner.

Mona, emotionless goblin she pretends to be, looks straight ahead. I will go down with this ship.

"All set," Amina says, passing the room keys to Mona before gesturing toward the stairs.

One thing that is actually not at all cool about Paris is that, apparently, these gorgeous old buildings lack elevators. This includes rooms on the sixth floor reached by a staircase that only Tim Burton could have designed in his most twisted nightmares.

"You'll need to get a crane to get me in or out of here," I say, panting and sweating as I lug my suitcase up the final steps, lean over the railing, and look down.

"Always so dramatic," Mona says, sticking a key into her lock. I hold out my hand for my own key, and Mona stares at it for a moment.

"There is one small thing I should mention about accommodations," Mona says, turning the knob to her door.

"Please don't tell me there's a ghost."

Mona scrunches up her face. "Of course not. Ghosts aren't real."

"*Science denier*," I cough into my fist. Mona ignores me, but I do get a decent chuckle from Amina. Love her.

"You two"—Mona points at me and Oliver—"will be sharing a room."

Chapter 13

Big Yikes

U nder no circumstances are you permitted to cross this border during sleeping hours," Mona says as she shoves the final piece of furniture down the center line between our beds.

"What if I have to pee?"

Mona ignores Tilly's question as she adds height to the barriers, stacking lamps on the dresser. "And this door remains *open*," Mona says, pointing at the doorway to our adjoining rooms while giving us a menacing look.

"Why don't you just get us separate rooms, instead of creating this massive fire hazard?" Tilly asks.

I'm not sure if she's ever sat with a thought in her life or if she just blurts everything out in a constant stream of consciousness.

"Because we don't have the budget for our interns to get their own rooms," Mona snaps.

"You . . . don't?"

I don't understand why Tilly is so surprised to hear a start-up is pinching pennies.

"I'm not getting into this with you," Mona says with a sigh, rubbing the heel of her hand over her forehead. "We have enough for two rooms between all of us at the different cities, so this will have to do. But absolutely no funny business. Got it?"

"Shouldn't be a problem," Tilly says, leaning against the doorjamb. "Oliver doesn't possess anything close to a sense of humor."

I feel my cheeks heat and I stare straight ahead at the exceptionally small room with two exceptionally small beds.

"I'm actually quite witty," I say. Christ. Why am I even acknowledging her jabs like an absolute tosser?

"I've never once heard you laugh," she bites back.

I turn toward her, eyes on her cheek. "Well," I say, "I've never heard you say something worth laughing at."

Her jaw drops and a soft swell of satisfaction rises in my chest. But it's quickly replaced by . . . what is that? Guilt?

"I don't think you have to worry about them doing anything, Mo," Amina says with a laugh, bumping her hip against Mona's.

"Maybe just murder," Tilly whispers. I roll my eyes.

"Enough!" Mona snaps at Tilly. "Oliver," she says, turning to me, "get yourself ready, we need to leave for the meeting in twenty minutes."

"Twenty minutes?" Tilly says, her voice rising an octave. "But I wanted to shower."

Mona blinks at her. "Then shower? I don't get your point."

"I won't have time to shower and do my hair if we're leaving in twenty minutes!"

Mona opens and closes her mouth a few times. It reminds me of fish reluctantly trying to survive. "*We?*" Mona says at last. "You know you aren't going, right?"

Tilly's head jerks back. "What? Yes I am."

"Why in God's name would you go?" Mona asks, fisting her hands in her hair.

"Oliver's going," Tilly says, jerking her thumb at me. Oh God, please don't drag me into this.

"Oliver is running our social media and design! He's a contributing member of the team. His input matters."

Tilly flinches, and I stare down at the ugly carpet with its faded paisley pattern. I don't exactly like Tilly but even I can admit that was a bit harsh.

"Yeah, well, as far as I can tell, I'm the only one wearing your stupid polish," Tilly says, flicking both her ring fingers at Mona like she's making a rude gesture. They're painted a canary yellow today, and the color hooks my attention. I follow her hands as they swoop through the air while she continues to fight with her sister. "So maybe I can be a character witness so people actually want to buy the things."

"Tilly, I'm not trying to fight with you right now," Mona says, "but you have literally nothing to add to this meeting. You aren't going."

It's actually rather astounding how quickly Tilly shows emotions; they light her up brighter than a spotlight. And right now, hurt is the most obvious one. Her eyes are shiny, fat teardrops brimming at the pale pink edges while red blotches stain her cheeks, her shoulders hunched close to her ears.

"Charisma."

There's an extended moment of silence, and I'm trying to figure out who said that.

Wait. Was it me? Must've been because all three women have their eyes on me.

"What's that, darling?" Amina asks, tilting her head.

Oh hell. I guess I'm supposed to keep talking. "Charisma," I repeat, coughing at the end of the word. "Tilly has charisma. She should be in the meeting."

Right. What the hell am I doing? Where are these thoughts coming from?

"Are you serious?" Mona asks, her lips tilting into a grimace. She's wearing deep red lipstick. Pantone 19–2429, Plum Caspia, probably. My eyes dart to Tilly for half a second, and all I see is her jaw dangling open before I focus back on the carpeting.

"I believe so," I say, but I'm not actually sure. "She's energetic and charismatic and could add a certain . . . charm, perhaps? If nothing else, she could be an example of penetrating the Gen Z market. Everyone's always trying to figure out how to sell us stuff. *Forbes* writes at least a dozen articles about it a year."

Amina walks over to Mona, placing her hands on Mona's tense shoulders and rubbing gently. "Oliver has a point," Amina says. "Let her sit in, darling. It will be such a great learning experience for her to see how meetings like this work. She is our intern, after all. Plus, she'll be witnessing presentation skills from the very best," Amina adds, giving Mona's shoulders an extra squeeze and shooting Tilly a wink.

Mona's plum lips are pressed into a firm line, and I can't tell what she's thinking.

"Fine," she says at last, but the word sounds anything but. "I have rules, though," she adds, pointing at Tilly.

"Color me surprised," Tilly whispers.

"I don't want you to talk unless they ask you a direct question. No fidgeting. No obscenities. No burping. No farting. No—"

"Wow. You know what? Forget it," Tilly says, crossing her arms over her chest.

"Excuse me?" Mona says, head pulling back.

"Believe it or not, Mo, I'm actually an eighteen-year-old *adult* with feelings and a modicum of self-respect, and your little pep talk doesn't do much to honor any of that. So, yeah. I'm gonna be staying back. And looking into flights away from you."

"Stop being so dramatic," Mona snaps.

At this point, both their voices are raised, and my hands are flapping nervously at my sides. I feel like something is building in the room, an amorphous blob of tension that's going to swallow us whole.

And Tilly's next words tip it all over the edge.

"Then stop being a bitch!"

Chapter 14

Crying in the Bathroom (Taylor's Version)

TILLY

So, here's the thing about a dramatic exit—aka, locking yourself in the bathroom after calling your sister a bitch—you feel a bit like a dumbass after doing it.

Like, cool, I just trapped myself in the smallest space in this hotel room, which also lacks decent cell phone service, and I have to listen to the deep rumble of everyone talking about me through the door without actually hearing what they're saying so of course my brain makes up the meanest things possible.

Go me. Really showed Mona. Huge win.

After what feels like an eternity, I hear the door open and shut and the sound of stillness settle through the room. I wait a few more minutes, hugging my legs to my chest and resting my head on my knees from my perch on the toilet seat.

When I'm confident they're gone for good and won't be popping back in for some forgotten item, I uncurl myself and open the door.

I slink out of the bathroom with every intention of moodily belly flopping on the mattress to have a good cry, but I'm shocked out of my skin to see Oliver sitting at the small desk Mona wedged between our beds. Angled so I can see his eyes sharply focused on his laptop screen, earphones on and back ramrod straight as he clicks around his computer, a picture of my hands blown up on the screen.

The intensity of his focus is palpable, like there's a protective bubble around him telling the world DO NOT DISTURB.

I realize it kind of reminds me of . . . me. Or, at least, me when I'm hyperfocusing on reading or writing—when I drop out of this world and enter one that's totally my own, happy and safe. I continue to stare at Oliver, wishing there was a window to his brain I could peer into and see if what he's feeling right now is anything like what I do when I settle in my special dimension.

I've never been able to relate to anyone about this.

I don't really have friends. I don't mean this in a dramatic, woe-is-me way. It's just a fact. I have acquaintances. I had people I could approach at school and make small talk with (which I tried to avoid because small talk makes my brain feel like it's turning inside out). I didn't eat lunch alone.

But I'm not . . . known.

There isn't a person out there who knows me. Who I truly am. Who I want to be. I've never had that special connection where I'm understood. It always feels like there's a curtain between me and any person I'm talking to, and I worry I'll always feel this separation from the world. Like I'm an extra piece to a jigsaw puzzle, discarded and forgotten under the couch, while everyone else clicks with their matching corners.

My wonky edges won't ever have the luxury of complementing someone else's.

But when I'm writing or reading, I never feel alone. I melt

into the pages, my world morphing into the safety of a story. I feel seen and understood as my eyes dance over lines of text; like I have a chance to be loved. To live and scream and exist just as I am and be the right amount of enough for someone.

Losing myself in my thoughts, I plop onto the edge of the bed. The movement snags the current of Oliver's attention, and he turns suddenly, eyes going wide as he realizes I'm no longer locked in the bathroom.

He jolts to standing, slamming his laptop shut before fumbling with his headphones.

Mortified that he caught me mooning over him, I stand up in an equally erratic way. Which makes the whole thing feel even more awkward because now we're both standing here with lots of ugly carpeting between us, staring shyly at the ground.

After an eternity of silence, Oliver asks, "Are you actually planning on leaving?" He shoves his hands into his pockets and rocks back on his heels.

It takes me a moment to understand his question, and I remember I *did* dramatically declare to Mona that I'm about to become a runaway. I give Oliver a noncommittal shrug, mirroring him and pushing my hands into my dress pockets.

More silence.

"I thought you were supposed to go to the meeting," I say, tracing a swirl on the carpeting with my toe.

"I stayed back."

Well, that's rather freaking obvious. "Why?"

He shrugs like I did a second before, and his response is a mumbled "I dunno," followed by him clearing his throat.

"What was that?"

"I don't know," he says in his crisp, beautiful voice, gaze flicking up at me for a second before landing back on the carpeting.

I narrow my eyes at him. "How do you not know?"

"I don't know that, either," he says, rubbing his thumb across his forehead like this is extremely distressing for him. "I'm experiencing multiple physical reactions to emotions I can't name."

I blink at him, my brain whirring up like a jet engine. "Did you stay back because . . . because of me?" The words slip out of my mouth before I can think better of them.

Oliver's silent, his eyes fixed on my cheek and his jaw tensed before he throws his hands up. It's a mild gesture but I've literally never seen him so flustered. It's very . . . interesting.

History has taught me I should definitely not look for hidden meaning in anything Oliver says or does because it *always* ends with me being disappointed . . . but, like, does that not give the vibes that he's ever so slightly madly in love with me? Am I projecting here? Because that little declaration of unknown-feeling feelings has the ridiculously romantic lobe of my brain convinced that he's smitten with me. Only took me three excruciatingly humiliating days to win him over with my devastating charm.

Okay. I've gotta be cool. Super cool.

"Do you want to go on a walk with me?" I ask, waving toward the cascade of sunlight tumbling in through the dusty window, curling my toes as nerves swirl in my stomach. Wow, that actually wasn't too bad. A neutral activity offered in a calm—dare I say, *intriguing*—fashion. And since I'm pretty sure he stayed back from the meeting for me and we're in the city of love, I'd say my chances are pretty damn good.

Oliver glances at the window, squinting then frowning at the beckoning sunshine.

"No," he says after a moment. Then follows it up with an ever-so-polite "Thank you."

I am going to strangle this boy. Or the whiplash from his

somewhat nice gestures followed by his extremely curt but technically polite rejections is going to kill me first. Time will tell, but I know one of us won't make it out of this alive.

"Whatever," I manage to say without the disappointment cracking my voice. I turn and grab my shoes and my bag, bolting out of the hotel room and clamoring down the stairs.

Out on the street, I start walking.

I walk and I walk and I walk, focusing on my steps, swallowing back the uncomfortable tears that sting my eyes and burn my nose.

Stupid, stupid, *stupid*. I feel so stupid! Why do I keep doing this? Why do I constantly set myself up for failure?

The thing is, I like people so much. I really do. I think people are interesting and good and unique and I have an impulse to know them all. And, with that, I want them to know me, too. I want to be liked. I want to be loved. Screw the moon, I want someone to look at me like I hung the damn sun.

But I can't seem to find that. Not with friends at school. Not with my parents. Not with my sister.

Certainly not with Oliver.

But I also can't help myself from trying over and over again.

I don't know how long I walk, staring at the ground as my feet carry me farther from the site of my latest embarrassment, but, eventually, the sidewalk turns to cobblestones and a soft violin melody draws my head up.

I'm on the outskirts of a bustling square, people strolling through the area, looking around at an endless sea of easels and canvases with artists perched in the open space. I wind my way through the gentle chaos until I find a vacant bench. My leg starts bouncing as snippets of this awful day shoot across my mind. I bury my face in my hands as I try to figure out what to do.

Do I make good on my threat to leave? Do I suffer the

embarrassment of not? If I did leave, where would I go? Somewhere else in Europe? Do I even have the capability to do that?

I'm supposed to be doing some enriching bullshit internship, regularly checking in with my parents to tell them how I'm becoming a perfect clone of my sister; I can't imagine they'd be okay with me abandoning that plan to go somewhere new.

But if I go back to America does that automatically mean going home? Probably, and that idea is more terrifying than the unknown. Mom spent the first seventeen years of my life annoyed and fussy, to the point that I don't recognize her saying my name if it isn't accompanied by an exasperated sigh, and the last year coddling me to the point of suffocation, and treating my ADHD diagnosis like a death sentence. Can I handle being back there?

Figuring out what to do and the order to do it in often feels impossible. My flawed executive functioning skews and tilts and twirls details until I feel dizzy trying to figure out how to accomplish a task.

With a groan, I lift my head and look around me like I can conjure an answer from thin air.

Something about the scene soothes my sprinting thoughts long enough for me to realize how damn picturesque everything is. I have a perfect view of an artist sitting on a stool, head tilted as she studies the watercolor painting in front of her. She's painting the squat buildings surrounding the square, dipping her brush in water then swirling it in paint as she captures the red awnings with big block letters advertising CAFÉ and PÂTISSERIE fluttering gently in the early summer breeze, a gorgeous, domed white church standing proudly in the background of the scene.

She moves with patience, hands careful but confident, and I get lost in watching her work, watching her re-create this small corner of the world on her canvas. As the white rectangle in front of her comes to life with bleeding colors, I start to cry. Her art is so beautiful, it makes my chest ache and my hands itch to make my own.

A daunting and terrifying thought pops into my head, but before I can push it away, I find myself shakily pulling out my phone.

I swipe through the screens until I find the bright yellow app for Babble.

Babble is a social media platform that can be best described as blogging, Pinterest, Twitter, and AO3 having a baby and said weird social media baby displays everything in a grid you could click through: endless rabbit holes of art and writing and conversations.

I haven't opened it in probably three years, but I could never bring myself to delete the app. I made an account in middle school, using it as, regrettably, a very public diary. I had about four rando followers so I didn't think it was a big deal. But, one day freshman year, a girl from school stumbled across my page and told everyone.

It wasn't like I had written anything bad on there—it was 90 percent massive infodumps on whatever latest obsession had me by the throat. I saved my wilder ideas for fanfic, which thankfully was never discovered—but my class for some reason decided it was hilarious and an easy thing to make fun of me about.

In a fit of total mortification, I deleted all my posts and melodramatically vowed never to write on there again.

My finger hovers over the little yellow app now, the sharp sting of the teasing as fresh as when I was fifteen. I start to pull my hand away. I don't have anything worth saying or sharing. Why would I set myself up to risk embarrassment like that again?

I look back at the painter. She's started a new project—the first piece leaning against the leg of her easel—a sharper energy in her posture and movements. Her hand moves quickly, long slashes of pencil on the canvas as her head flicks back and forth from her blank page to a young girl in front of her who's dancing and twirling around the cobblestones with a rainbow of ribbons clutched in her hand. The little girl lets out a screeching giggle as the ribbons tangle around her waist. She quickly unravels herself and keeps dancing.

The artist picks up her brush and palette, her hand moving in a blur as she mixes colors then swipes them across her canvas, eyes focused on the child.

In a few minutes, streaks of watercolors transform the page to a soft likeness of the joyful scene. I want to fall into that painting. I want to feel the freedom of that little girl, the sureness of the artist's hands.

I want . . .

I want . . .

You know what I fucking want? To be myself.

I'm sick of pretending to like things—feel things—less than I do to make other people more comfortable. I'm over lying to myself that I don't have anything important to say. I have so many thoughts I sometimes think my skull will crack open with all of them.

I click on the app.

I scroll through the grid for a moment before hitting the little plus sign in the corner, pulling up a blank slate, fingers hovering over the keyboard.

The urge to edit my thoughts, hold things back, constantly

worry about how others might perceive me is fresh and sharp and tempting to hide behind.

But with a deep breath, I let all of that go.

And I start to type.

The idea of love, almost always, conjures the image of a pair. Two hands entwined. A mother cradling a baby. The mirrored curves of a heart.

I'm in the city of love, surrounded by people and art and centuries of memories, and I've never felt lonelier.

I'm not sure what I expected.

Actually, that's not true. I know exactly what I expected. I expected to enter a new city and find a new me. Step in to some alternative life that fits me better. One where loneliness isn't a constant dull ache in my chest. One where the ghosts of failed friendships don't hover over my shoulder.

I'm crying again as I continue to write, my heart in my hands as I put my feelings into words.

I don't want to surround myself with more people who don't want me. Or who think I'm a burden. If I was looking to embrace that lifestyle, I would have stayed at home in Cleveland.

This trip isn't about Mona or her opinions. Mom and Dad and Mona organized this trip to change me, I think. To entice me into college and business and plans and power suits. But I'm not here for that. Or for them.

I'm here because I want change. I want to get rid of the pieces of myself that others have forced on me, the ones that don't fit. I want to strip away the parts that pinch at my skin and hold my arms tight at my sides. Proudly wear the bits of me that let me breathe. Let me throw my arms in the air and kick my legs and sprint in whatever direction these beautiful cities call me.

I already love the world, now I'm ready to experience it.

I read it over twice, heart thumping and tears drying on my cheeks.

Then I smile as I hit *post*.

Chapter 15

Hate This Journey for Me

OLIVER

This trip is wreaking havoc on my morning routine and I am absolutely not okay with it.

On a normal day, I get up at seven thirty—I don't believe in lounging around in bed; it makes me feel like a dead trout lying uselessly on an ice block at the market. I then shower, brush my teeth, floss, dress, and am in the kitchen starting the coffee maker (which I prepped the night before) by five after eight. Once that's brewed, I check my email and social media, and am ready to leave the house by half past.

Today is not a normal day.

Today, I'm at the airport at four a.m., bleary-eyed, rumpled, and waiting on our flight to Milan.

Yesterday, like every other day I've been in the presence of one of the Twomley sisters, was a disaster. An emotional one to be precise. On my life, I can't say why I stayed back from the meeting. I could tell Mona and Amina were annoyed when

I stated, without much room for argument, that I wouldn't be going with them.

But something about seeing Tilly so upset . . .

Actually, no. That's not quite right. It wasn't something I *saw* so much as *felt*. Hurt radiated off her skin like the sting of standing too close to a fire, and it did something odd to my system, creating a sharp ache in my chest and a twist in my stomach.

Quite annoying, honestly, and it made me shut down in a way.

But Tilly, of course, had to go and ask hundreds of questions that I didn't have answers to instead of us both just sitting in that hotel room in peace. Then she went running off. Again.

She'll be the death of me, I swear.

When Mona and Amina got back a few hours later, they told me that the meeting had been shite and they hadn't secured a contract. They made it clear that they wanted me at the next meeting to drive home different branding and marketing concepts (and also drop my Instagram handle "subtly" as if I have the slightest idea how subtlety works).

Tilly didn't show back up until later into the night when I was already tucked into bed, and I pretended to be asleep when she tiptoed into the room. As she fluttered about with failed quietness, I couldn't stop thinking of exactly where she was in the suite, like a little magnet tugged at my mind as she moved from one spot to the next. I have no bloody clue what that was all about but it certainly made me more alert than tired.

And then when I finally *would* start to drift off to sleep, nonsensical things kept popping in my head like the shape of her hands. The way she always seems on the verge of laughing, like she's enjoying some brilliant joke with herself. And those three blasted freckles on her left cheek, the color I can't quite place taunting me every time she smiles. Absolutely ridiculous.

My virtually sleepless night is what I blame my muddled head on this morning as I go through security and roll my carry-on to the gate.

We board without issue and the flight to Milan is over before I know it.

Squeezing into an overpacked train, we ride the metro to our hotel in a cheaper part of the city, having a few hours to kill before our meeting with a boutique chain called Lumina.

Mona has Tilly and me sharing a room connected to hers again, and I pretend not to internally flip out over this.

Why, why, *why* does it feel so weird to share a space with Tilly? I've shared rooms with my sister before. And Marcus and Micah. My mums even. That was always *fine* but this feels *weird* and I can't pin down the reason.

As soon as I drop my bag on the floor, I make a quick escape to the (extremely small) balcony attached to our room, gulping down air.

Balcony is a generous term—it's more like a rusted piece of metal that I have to stand sideways on so my feet aren't dangling perilously over the edge—but it gets me some distance from Tilly and the peculiar tug she has on my psyche. I lean my elbows on the dodgy railing then bury my head in my hands, letting out a quiet groan.

What is it about this blasted girl that has me so unsettled? Is it because I don't know Tilly well? Because she's constantly bursting with one emotion or another I can't fully grasp?

Her blazing grin flashes across my mind and I shove the image away. Why does that keep happening to me?

Lifting my head, I focus on the colors sprawling in front of me. The shingled roofs are Pantone 7523, a burnt orange . . , a similar hue to the dress Tilly wore yesterday. Which seems like a wholly useless thing to remember. A wispy cloud in the distance is darker than the others. Pantone 651, a soft gray blue. Just a few shades lighter than Tilly's storm-cloud eyes.

What is *happening*? I groan and shake my head, trying to dislodge Tilly from whatever lobe she's burrowed into. I blink a few times then widen my eyes, scanning the horizon with unparalleled focus. It doesn't make a difference. Any color I home in on somehow flows right back to Tilly and my stomach gets this awful falling feeling.

That's it. Time to google.

After searching for medical conditions that explain sleeplessness, ruminating thoughts, stomach upset, flushing, and heart palpitations, I finally pull myself out of an internet spiral that has me convinced I'm suffering from some sort of brain-eating amoeba. With a sigh, I lock my phone and bang the corner of it against my forehead.

I've stalled out here so long my twisted legs are starting to cramp, and I don't have much choice but to go inside.

Tilly is sitting on the floor, back pressed against the dresser and tongue between her teeth as she types furiously on her laptop. She's so engrossed in whatever she's working on, she doesn't notice my reappearance into the room. She's planted herself next to my backpack and suitcase, and I slowly cross the space toward her, leaning down to grab my bag.

I glance at her computer, watching the words fly across the screen.

"What's that?" I ask, nodding my chin toward her laptop.

Tilly jerks in surprise, almost jabbing me in the throat with her shoulder.

"Nothing!" she shrieks, slamming her laptop shut so violently it will be a miracle if the glass isn't shattered. She scuttles across the floor on all fours like a fleeing beetle, leaving me crouched down and, quite frankly, totally bewildered.

"Mind your own business, Oliver," she grumbles, finding safety at the foot of the bed.

I'm not sure why that stings. It's not like I was being nosy. I was . . . well, she has me so damn curious to know more about her and I have no idea why.

"Sorry," I mumble, fiddling with my backpack to keep my hands busy. There's a long silence, and I stand, slinging my bag over my shoulder, assuming the conversation is over.

"I liked your post today," Tilly says, surprising me. She'd seemed so thoroughly annoyed by my Instagram account when I first showed her, I didn't think she'd ever bother looking again.

"Oh. Er. Um. Thank you."

Wow. That was articulate. Poetic, even. Why does my brain go fuzzy and my tongue feel three sizes too big when I try to talk to Tilly?

"It seems like most days you do pictures that all have the same color," Tilly continues, plucking at the hem of her dress. "Why was today's four different ones?"

Every muscle in my neck and back tenses up. Last night while I was angrily lying in bed and blaming Tilly for my sleeplessness, I'd scheduled an Instagram post that was a study of birthmarks: a cropped image showing the mole above Cubby's right eyebrow, Micah smiling as they looked over their shoulder splattered with freckles, the café au lait splotch on Mum's forearm as she kneaded dough, and even my own mole on the left side of my nose.

I'm not sure how I'm supposed to explain to Tilly that I put that collage together out of some sort of weird, artistic spite at being able to name the color of all those marks and not hers. Lying doesn't come naturally to me but I figure now is as good a time as any to give it a go.

"Just mixing things up, I guess," I say, keeping my head down as I walk over to my bed and pretend to look for something in my bag.

The other mattress squeaks as Tilly gets up and starts moving. It's like every cell in my body tries to turn and watch where she's going, but I keep my eyes down.

"You had a lot to say about the color of the freckle above that one girl's eye," Tilly says, invading my periphery by sitting near me on the edge of my mattress. "Is she . . . Do you know her well?" Tilly asks.

"Yes," I say, eyes flicking to Tilly's face before moving away again. But, Christ, my vision gets tangled on her lap, the way the pale pink fabric of her dress falls over her thighs. I slam my eyes closed, but it does little good; I can now picture the curves of her legs in ridiculously vivid detail.

Awesome. Great. First those freckles, then her hands, and now her legs. Wonderful. What other body parts can I add to this obscene fascination my brain seems to have with Tilly Twomley?

Even self-imposed rhetorical questions generate endless responses from my highly literal brain. I start counting backward from one hundred in Portuguese to distract my imagination from wandering any further south than the slope of her collarbones and that small divot at the base of her throat.

Needing space from Tilly and apparently playing into this constant orbiting we do around each other, I stand and shuffle back until my legs hit the edge of the other bed and force me to sit again. She's like an asteroid striking my axis off-balance and sending me spiraling around the room.

"Are you two like . . . a thing?" Tilly asks, but her voice sounds far away through my scrambled thoughts.

It takes me a second to replay the conversation, then I burst out laughing. I look at Tilly, and her mouth presses into a frown.

"God, no," I say, laughing harder. I pull up the photo. "That's me," I say, pointing to my corner of the graphic. "That's my mum's arm, and that's Micah's shoulder. They're dating my best mate, Marcus. We all live together."

Tilly's eyes are fixed on my phone, her hair falling over her shoulder. The way the light slices through the raven strands creates a rich and moving violet. Pantone 19–3716, Purple Plumeria. It makes my breath knot in my throat.

I swallow past it.

"And this is my twin sister. Cubby," I say, hoping I sound normal.

Tilly's eyes go wide and her mouth flashes an electric grin before something a bit more neutral. Well, as neutral as Tilly can be. Even her calmest moments seem to shoot off sparks.

"I didn't know you had a twin! That's so cool. Is it weird? Having a twin?"

I shrug. "No weirder than you and your sister, I imagine."

There's a pause while Tilly blinks at me, and the silence has me worried I said something wrong, but then she bursts out in her signature, sonic boom of a laugh.

"That was a good one," she says, snorting. "Is your sister into . . . uh . . . color . . . curating . . . erm . . . media with . . ."

"Photography and digital media curation for businesses, with an emphasis on color theory and psychological applications," I say, appreciating her effort to remember my university plans. I realize I'm smiling at her.

"Right. That."

"No. Cubby's a musician. She's actually touring with her band right now. We've been texting about meeting up if our cities align."

"That's amazing. I hope I get to meet her," Tilly says.

This catches me off guard. It'd never occurred to me that Tilly might want to meet my sister. I didn't think Tilly had interest in anything to do with me.

"You had a lot to say about the color black," Tilly says after a moment of silence. Actually, she more yells it at me, but I'm starting to come to expect her changes in volume. "In your post, I mean. I had no idea there were so many shades of it. I've always just thought black was . . . well, black."

My head jerks back. "Black is one of the most complex colors out there. It's my favorite."

Favorite is an understatement. I'm obsessed with it. Black is soft and comfortable and chewy and makes the very center of my brain go *ahhhh* in relief every time I look at it.

"It's a common misconception to think there's only one type of black. There're countless," I continue. "I mean, obviously, black is scientifically defined as the total absence of color, but in art black is developed from pigmentation. Think about it; a painter has to mix endless colors together, adding and adding until they get what's supposed to be nothingness. It's like the entire act of producing the color contradicts what it's defined as. I personally think it's a bit contrarian when people correct you for saying it's a color. Like, come on mate, let's not split hairs here. I believe a huge part of the problem is a lack of clarity in definitions. When getting down to the heart of it, yes, there's only one true *shade* of black, which would be pure black. Fine. But there are multiple *hues* of black, and I think that phrasing trips people up.

"You can also get into the various differences between chroma and saturation but Munsell *obviously* would provide a much clearer definition. When it comes to the way colors feel, I tend to take it from a colorfulness perspective. It's less scientific, I know, but color, at the end of the day, is a visual experience, so why not discuss it in those terms, no? And for a color deemed so simple, it's incredibly complex. Varied. It's newsprint and night sky. It's the backdrop to outer space and the dots on a ladybug. It's . . . It's . . ." I glance at Tilly unscrambling all the words clamoring to get out of me.

"It's the spikes of your eyelashes," I say, gesturing at her, my gaze flicking to hers before roaming around her face. "The depths of your dilated pupils when you get excited. Your worndown Converse and that dress with the pockets you seem so fond of. It's . . ."

Tilly sucks in a soft breath, the noise pausing my runaway thoughts. All of which, I'm now realizing, have put themselves in the context of her.

It's at this point I also notice my happy hand stim is moving enthusiastically at my side. I flex my hands then rub one across the back of my heated neck, frowning as I stare at the ground.

Shit. I didn't mean to infodump like that. That's not something I usually do unless it's my family or Marcus.

"I think I only understood about a third of what you said," Tilly whispers. I glance at her, and she tilts her head to the side. "But I love it. I had no idea colors were so complex. I thought they just . . . were."

An overwhelming surge of some unknown feeling pushes at my chest and up my throat. I cough. "Sorry. My delivery might have seemed a bit much. Color theory is, quite simply, the most fascinating thing in the world."

Tilly nods, leaning toward me. "The way you talk about it has me believing that."

I'm smiling again as Tilly and I look at each other. And that's when I realize that we're making something close to eye contact, and I'm not crawling out of my skin about it.

In fact, all of this has felt alarmingly *comfortable* and I don't know what to make of that.

Tilly opens her mouth to say something, and my eyes get caught on the movement. I watch her lips part and her tongue swipe across them. But, for once, Tilly doesn't make a sound. She bites down on her lip, the white edges of her teeth in sharp contrast with the full, tawny pink of her hesitant smile.

An image blazes across my mind, one so disastrous but devastatingly tempting it's hard to believe it came from my own psyche: my mouth pressed against hers. The inky black strands of her hair falling between my fingers as I run my hands through it. The pad of my thumb brushing across those maddening freckles as I cup her jaw.

The idea of it is so overwhelmingly enticing, I feel myself lean forward. Tilly mirrors the movement. Our eyes are wide and, if I'm reading her correctly, mildly terrified at the thick bands of tension cinching us closer together.

Is this happening? What even is *this*? Holy Christ above, why has this girl scrambled my mind? Could the feel of her lips against mine *actually* be as good as my brain has just convinced itself it will be?

We both lean a millimeter closer.

And then . . .

"Ready, Oliver?" Amina says, rapping on the doorjamb as she waltzes into our room. I jolt to standing, breaths short and painful to gulp down past my suddenly dry throat.

"Car should be here in a minute," Amina adds, tapping away on her phone. "Mo is already downstairs."

"Great. Perfect. Yeah. Wonderful. Great."

My extremely smooth and totally normal string of adjectives snags Amina's full attention. She glances up at me with furrowed brows. She's silent for a moment, staring, and it feels like my cheeks will char to a crisp from all the heat that's rushing to them. I can't help being mildly curious about what color they are.

Amina then glances at Tilly, who's still sitting on the edge of the bed looking like a startled owl. Amina blinks once. Twice. Then turns back to me, now with one eyebrow arched, high and questioning, as she takes me in.

"Alright there, Ollie?" she asks, a small smile twitching the corner of her lips. "You're looking a bit peaky."

I'd like to say: *No, Amina, I'm not feeling alright at all. In fact, I think I've gone absolutely mental because I almost just kissed a girl I'm not sure I even like who also happens to be my boss's little sister. In less than a week, she has destroyed my sleep schedule, invaded my brain, and caused me more physical and emotional turmoil than I've ever before experienced. And, wouldn't you know, I still have a good two months of traveling around this bloody continent with her.*

I don't say any of this, of course, instead choosing to cough and then busy myself by pretending to organize my backpack.

Tilly, breaker of all silences that she is, pipes up. "She called you 'Ollie,'" she says, pointing a finger between me and Amina. "I really like that. Can I call you that?"

I make a noncommittal shrug, keeping my eyes fixed on the ugly duvet. I'm scared if I look at her, my face will burst into flames all over again.

"Ollie," she repeats, drawing out the syllables. "Ollie."

Before I can even process the thought, words go flying out of my mouth. "I like the way you say it. Please call me Ollie."

This is true, I *do* like the way she says it—the only person that calls me Ollie is Cubby and she always says it with that exasperated sister-tone that makes me roll my eyes—but I wish I hadn't been so mortifyingly honest about it.

Silence rings in the suite for a moment longer, and I need to get out of here or I'll . . . I don't know, die?

"Goodbye," I say, nodding at Tilly and almost barreling over Amina as I escape to the door. The click of her heels in the hallway tells me she isn't far behind.

Out on the street, I gulp down stale, humid air, dropping my head against the wall of our building. Mona's at the curb, talking on her cell phone as she waits for the car.

Amina's clacking steps come to a halt next to me. I keep my eyes fixed on the pieces of gum spotting the pavement.

After a moment, she chuckles, the sound good natured and husky. I steal a quick look at her from the corner of my eye.

She's grinning at me as she shakes her head. "Oh, darling," she says, patting me on the shoulder. "It's going to be an interesting summer, isn't it?"

Chapter 16

Worse Still

OLIVER

"Chin up, loves," Amina says in the taxi back to the hotel a couple hours later. "We'll get them next time." It's a nice sentiment, but the glumness in her voice has me less than convinced. Based on Mona's scoff, she doesn't believe it, either.

"That was the single most humiliating experience of my life," Mona says, lip snarling as she stares out the window.

"Really? Mine was making a drunken advance on my roommate in uni only for her to tell me she, quote, doesn't like to snack on tacos. Unquote."

"Amina!" Mona slaps her business partner on the arm, her face a violent shade of red, then glances at me.

It takes me half a moment to figure out what Amina means, and then I equally blush to the roots of my hair. Great, this might be *my* most humiliating moment. I pivot my entire body toward the window and stare out.

"Anyway," Amina says like she didn't just thoroughly drop an awkward bomb in this small taxi, "fuck 'em. They were a bunch of stodgy old gits that wouldn't know a good product if it slapped them in the face."

"That's not a bad idea," Mona mumbles.

"But I think we need to regroup," Amina continues. "We take the train to Rome tomorrow, and I say we use that time to zhuzh up the pitch. Reevaluate some metrics and really emphasize the marketing and social media portion."

I can feel Amina's glance, and shame trickles down my spine. I may or may not have totally fucked up my part of the pitch. When it was my turn to speak, my brain was still back in the hotel room with Tilly, and I tripped over every point I had intended to make.

"I'll do better," I say, tapping my fingers against my side. "Sorry I failed you."

"Oh darling, no," Amina says, reaching out and touching my shoulder. "None of that. It's Mona and I that failed *you*. We were fumbling in there for answers to questions we'd never even thought to ask ourselves. You're wonderful. Our Instagram followers have more than doubled already and we're seeing spikes in online orders. We all just need to get on the same page and paint it with a detailed picture for the rest of the trip."

The car pulls up in front of our hotel and we get out, the early summer evening pressing down on us. I shift my camera bag to my other shoulder.

"I know you're probably tired, Oliver, but I'd like us to get at least a few photos around Milan before we leave tomorrow. We still have a few solid hours of light to take advantage of." Mona tilts her head back and looks up at our hotel then pulls out her phone, tapping away. "I'll text Tilly and have her come down to meet us. If I go up there, there'll be no getting me back out tonight."

"Right. Great," I say, fiddling with the strap of my bag. I don't feel ready to see Tilly again after the weird . . . moment . . . or whatever it was in the room earlier. Not like I have much of a choice though, because she comes barreling out of the building a minute later.

"How'd it go?" she asks, looking at each of us with an expectant smile.

"An absolute slaughtering," Amina says with a grin, draping an arm around Tilly. "And how was your afternoon?"

The next few hours pass in a blur of gorgeous architecture and crowded public transit. Mona leads us to various attractions around the city, and we stop to take countless pictures—Tilly holding a bouquet of flowers at an open-air market, stroking her nail across a petal. Her arms raised to the sky, the iconic spires of Duomo di Milano in the background. Tilly's hands wrapped around a large cone overflowing with raspberry gelato. Another where she reaches toward the gorgeous domed ceiling of the Galleria Vittorio like she can touch the cerulean glass.

Her smile is so big the entire time we shoot, I can't help smiling, too.

Tilly even buys herself a half-dozen cannoncini, shoving the cigar-shaped pastries between her fingers and yelling that she's Edward Cannoli-hands. Mona tells her to knock it off, but the sight of her gesturing the pastries at me like cream-filled claws makes me laugh so hard I snap a few photos.

It's late by the time we start heading back to the hotel, and I scroll through the shots as we walk. One in particular snags my attention, and I almost stop in my tracks as I look at it. The echo of her laugh is imprinted in the picture, her head thrown back and hands full of pastries. Like so many photos of Tilly, it's a bit blurry and the alignment is a nightmare, but, for some reason, it feels like a new favorite.

For the Pantone 100c, a buttery yellow, and 7571, a warm golden brown, captured in the cannoncini, of course.

The meeting was awful, but, overall, I think today might have been a good day. For the business, obviously.

"Oh my God, I have to pee so badly I might die," Tilly says, as the four of us climb the stairs to our rooms. She sprints up the last flight. "So, dibs, or whatever," she adds over her shoulder, throwing the door open and dashing inside.

I follow a few steps behind, Mona and Amina walking into their room next door. I slide my camera bag off my shoulder and plop onto my bed, almost sitting on Tilly's laptop in the process. She left it open and propped on my pillows, and the image of her lying on my mattress while I was gone creates an odd, fizzy sensation in my chest.

All the jostling has revved the screen to life, and a web page full of text pops up. I recognize the icon in the corner as Babble, some sort of blogging site Cubby was really into a few years back. My eyes start scanning across the lines.

My family had a cat when I was little. Her name was Smoosh and she was perfect. I loved her so much it used to feel like I would burst with it and, even to this day, I believe Smoosh loved me that much, too. Smoosh would follow me from room to room, her striped tail twitching in excitement every time I'd coo her name.

Someone told me that once you learn how to read, the process is so automatic and involuntary, you can't help reading words put in front of you. I blame that, and not at all a bone-deep fascination with understanding her better, for why I keep reading what Tilly's written.

When I was happy, she'd perch on her back legs and reach her paws toward me. When I was sad, she'd curl up on my chest, purring and licking the tears off my cheeks. It was like we shared a little heart (and the few brain cells between us).

But I also think what was interesting was how she and I would react to the world. When Smoosh got scared, she'd hide. I'd find her in the oddest corners, wedged between bookshelves, tail curled tight and head pressed against the wall like if she closed her eyes and made herself as small as possible, things wouldn't scare her anymore.

I like to do that when I'm overwhelmed.

Sometimes, it feels like the world has so much power to hurt me, I need to—

"What are you doing?"

Tilly's voice slashes like a knife across my senses as I'm pulled out of her words.

"Nothing!" I lie, jumping to stand.

Tilly stomps toward me, snatching up her laptop and slamming it against her chest. "You had no right to read that!" she says, jabbing her finger against my sternum. "How dare you invade my privacy?"

"Your *privacy*?" I splutter. "You literally left your open laptop on my bed with a public website blown up on the screen. How was I supposed to know it was top-secret information?" I say, pointing right back at her

"I—You—I . . . Stay away from my things!"

"Oh my God, why are you yelling?" Mona says, appearing in the doorway. She plants her hands on her hips, the strap of her high heels dangling from her pinky.

"I'm not yelling!" Tilly yells.

Mona arches an eyebrow at her.

"I'm *not*—I—He . . . ugh!" Tilly throws her hands in the air and turns away from everyone. She charges to her suitcase, riffling through it with the force of a hurricane before grabbing a handful of clothes and storming into the bathroom, slamming the door behind her.

The immediate silence has an energy to it, one that makes my skin crawl at the force of it. I glance at Mona. She's staring at the bathroom door, eyebrows furrowed and lip clamped between her teeth.

"You don't have to be so hard on her, darling," Amina whispers, coming to stand behind Mona in the doorway.

Mona opens her mouth like she's about to say something, but closes it, shaking her head and turning, ducking around Amina and moving farther into their room. Amina purses her lips but quickly schools her features, giving me a soft smile before following Mona's lead.

A few moments later, Tilly wrenches the door open, flicking off the lights and heading straight to her bed. She's put her pajamas on and doesn't spare me a glance as she yanks back the covers. Her mouth is a tight line and her eyes are creased at the corners as she lies down. The last thing I see of her is what looks like a tiny, glistening teardrop on her cheek. She scrubs her palm across her face, pulls the duvet over her head, and goes incredibly still.

If the silence before was bad, this is even worse. I'm standing here, feeling like an absolute wanker. I tiptoe to my suitcase, the zipper sounding like a gunshot as I grab my own pajamas. I go into the bathroom and lock the door behind me.

God, Tilly's exasperating. And dramatic. I mean, what's the big deal? What I read was already on Babble. And it was *good*. But she had to go and throw a fit. And why, why, *why* do I care so much?

It's not just me, I reason as I shove my limbs into a black T-shirt and pajama pants. Tilly gets under *everyone's* skin. Mona's exasperation is proof of that. Which is a relief. It's perfectly normal that pieces of her play on a loop in my mind. *It doesn't mean* anything *that I can't get her out of my head*, I tell myself as I brush my teeth so hard it would make my dentist cringe.

And it'll pass. Any day now I'll be desensitized to . . . whatever it is about Tilly that consumes my thoughts like a wretched fever.

I shut off the lights and exit the bathroom, heading to my own bed. The soft sound of Tilly's breath hums quietly through the air as I nestle under the covers and flick off the bedside lamp.

I'm sure by tomorrow, even, things like her breathing, or the soft sighs she makes in her sleep, or the electric punch of her laugh won't faze me at all.

Unfortunately, tonight, they keep me wide awake.

Chapter 17

Going for Gold

TILLY

A gorgeous train ride to Rome isn't the easiest place to be broody and angsty, but I give it my all. I even forwent my designated train outfit (bubble gum–pink dress with a full skirt and a belted waist, all-around perfect) for my most somber look (pale gray maxi dress, white embroidered flowers, billowy top, still dope as hell) to match my mood.

As the train zips along, I press my forehead against the window and stare out at the blur of landscape. If this were a movie, moody instrumental music would swell around me as I contemplate life, some grand realization hitting me, solving all my problems. Or, even better, some handsome Italian stranger would take the seat across from me. We'd share shy glances. A few smiles. Before long, we'd be talking and laughing, and some alt-indie song would come on instead. Then, boom, the movie would cut to a montage of us being gorgeous and happy all around Rome (probably on a Vespa) and we'd live happily ever after.

This, tragically, isn't some rom-com movie. I'm not the

main character. And instead I'm sitting across from Oliver who, granted, is very handsome, but he also sucks and I'm not talking to him right now, let alone smiling at him.

The only person trying to talk to me is my mom, who's playing a fun game where she sees how many passive-aggressive texts she needs to send before I answer.

> Are you being good for Mona?

> Did you take your meds this morning?

> If you go to any museums, make sure NOT to touch anything. No Tornado Tilly ♥

Another message dings through and I stare at my phone like it's a dog tensed to bite me, Mom lighting up the screen.

Our scheduled weekly check-in call isn't for another few days—a fact I cannot forget because my mom sends me reminder notifications every single day—and I can't say I'm looking forward to it. The whole thing feels like a setup for failure. I'll never be able to give a report that satisfies my parents' impossible expectations.

With a sigh, I open the message.

> Haven't heard much from you!
> How's the trip? Missing you xo

My fingers hover over the screen as I try to think of what to say. Honestly, I don't miss being home at all. As rocky as things have been, every day of this trip makes me feel like I can breathe a little deeper. Hold my chin a little higher. Be myself a bit more.

Europe is amazing, I answer back.

Are you enjoying working with Mona?

A small, ironic laugh is pulled from me. Mona doesn't trust me to do much beside stand there with my hands on display while Ollie snaps photos.

It's fine

The entire conversation feels cold. Forced.
And I hate that.
I want to be *excited* to talk to my mom. Share real pieces of myself with her.
I've actually been writing a lot on Babble, I send in a follow-up text. It's felt really good to get back into it.
I watch the text bubble bounce up and down as I wait for my mom's response, dangerous hope swelling in my chest.

I hope you're prioritizing your internship though.
Getting actual work experience.

And *poof* the hope is gone, a trickle of embarrassment left in its wake.
I mean . . . writing is a job for a lot of people, I shoot back, fingers shaky as I type.

Tilly. No. You know that's not a real job.

I stare at my phone, a hard lump forming in my throat.
Real jobs are steady. Stable. You of all people need that in your life! Mom sends in follow-up. I hope you're being realistic about what your future needs to look like.

A minute later, one more message dings through. It's a link to a local Cleveland college still accepting applications.

Two fat, hot teardrops plop onto my lap before I even process I'm crying. I lock my phone and squeeze my eyes shut, trying to press away all the emotion building in my skull. It's embarrassment and frustration and anger and . . . and . . . I don't know, longing? Nostalgia? This bone-achy desperation for a future that I'm apparently not cut out for? One where I have ideas and I share them and I pour my heart into my work instead of forcing my brain into some shape it'll never fit.

I take a shaky breath, trying to calm myself.

Sometimes, I hate feeling so much.

I duck my head and pretend to dig through my backpack as an excuse to let my hair fall over my face and hide all the emotion I'm sure is simmering on my skin. The only way this could get worse is if Mona or Oliver or Amina catch me crying.

My fingers brush against the cool, curved edge of my laptop. A small spark jumps up my arm and straight to my chest. It feels like muscle memory, this delicious, tantalizing reminder that when feelings get big, an open page is waiting to be filled.

Without letting myself think too much—pushing at the doubt that's trying to creep in at the edges—I whip my laptop out and frantically pull up Babble, typing away.

The concept of jobs is so weird to me. Like, we as humans evolved and then said, "Hmm, we get this one life . . . why don't we create these things called jobs and make them the focal point of our entire world, and the major determiner of our lives and ability to survive, and also place moral judgment on how much money we make doing it? Oh, what's money, you ask? It's also this thing we created for fun that will eventually become nothing more than a piece of paper that we assign value to and watch while some people hoard it while others can barely make ends meet! And your entire existence will be centered on these two things! Have fun!"

. . . Woof. Sorry. Unexpected capitalistic rant coming in hot . . . not where I saw this going.

I mean, yes, I'm fully aware that getting basic needs for survival like food and water and shelter takes work. I'm all for work and everyone doing their part. But jobs? We set ourselves up for misery! What the hell is a stock exchange or cryptocurrency or market analysis? It all seems . . . fake. Or, at the very least, not more valid as a job than something like painting or poetry or music like society tells us.

I can tell you, I don't want a job. That doesn't mean I don't want to work. Writing is work. Which is funny because I'm told how it "isn't a real job." But what does that mean? Is it because it's not a guarantee for lots of money? Is it because it relies so heavily on creativity? Because it deals in emotional currency instead of pieces of paper? Putting feelings into words, capturing the intensity of moments, that's hard. That matters . . . to me, at least.

"I'm sorry, but no." Mona's voice slices through my concentration as I read back what I wrote. I glance up.

"Sticking with the staples should still be our approach," Mona says, gesturing at a piece of paper on the small table in the center of our four seats. It's dotted with standard (read, boring) nail polish colors. "These are the most approachable options and have versatility for wearers. Buyers will want that for their customers. Something they can sell that is neutral enough for job interviews or dates."

Amina's lips are pursed as she stares at the sheet. "That's a good point, but I'm wondering if we shouldn't show some of our more unique options." She's quiet for a moment, studying the colors, before she looks at me and says, "What do you think, Tilly?"

My head jerks back in surprise. "Me? I don't know. I have no business sense."

"Mm, you might not have business *experience*," Amina says, "but you're young and fun and have great style. What would you want to buy?"

I close my laptop then knot my fingers in the skirt of my dress, heat crawling up my neck. I feel Mona's and Oliver's eyes on me, but I don't look at them. I keep staring at Amina, who gives me an encouraging nod.

"Those colors are all pretty basic and bleh, honestly," I say. Mona sucks in a breath but I keep going. "I mean, they're nice, but they don't wow me. There's no reason I would take that red over any other of the millions of red nail polishes already out there."

"But the store merchandisers need to know we have a strong handle on the beauty basics," Mona says defensively.

"And you can show them that, but I think you're missing what your *customers* will want," I say, finding the courage to look at her. She's frowning at me but it's not a downright death glare, so I take that as a good sign and keep going.

"Young consumers, like me, aren't buying boring pearly pink polish for stuffy job interviews or because some magazine tells us some specific shade of red is what we should wear on a first date. We're buying it to stand out. To have our own little marker that says, 'Hey, I'm here. I exist and I'm different and I want you to notice, even if I'm not super brave and just showing that in the smallest way possible.'" I wave my fingers, which I've painted a shocking shade of orange, at Mona. "We want to be bold, but in a safe way. It's not always feasible to dye your hair a wild color or have the money to buy a bunch of cool clothes, but nail polish is accessible. It's something we can make our own. And you're already showing that with the types of pictures Oliver takes, so why not present it that way in these meetings?"

The group has gone silent, and I squirm then sink into my seat, tracing the flower print of my dress instead of looking at any of them.

"That's absolutely brilliant."

My eyes flick to Amina, who's grinning at me. "I-it is?" I ask, chewing on my lip as a nervous smile stretches across my mouth.

"I love it," Amina says, looking at Mona. "Don't you love it, Mo?"

Mona's staring at me like she doesn't recognize me. "Which colors would you show, then?" she asks, each word slow and thoughtful.

I glance at Oliver, and his eyes are locked on my mouth, like he can't take a breath until I say what I think.

"Why not all the jewel tones," I say, the suggestion sounding more like a question.

"For summer?" Amina asks, tilting her head. "Wouldn't that be better for fall or winter?" She looks to Oliver for confirmation, but his gaze is still laser-focused on me.

I shrug. "I guess traditionally they are, yeah. But do you really need a season to want to deck yourself out in colors of gemstones? Feel like a million bucks with the rich purples and bold emeralds? Then finish off the samples with the real show-stopper. Be bold. Go with gold."

Mona's mouth falls open, eyebrows furrowed as she continues to look at me.

My heart thumps so hard it crawls up my throat as I wait to hear what mean thing she's going to say. The seconds tick on and on as she stares.

"I absolutely love that," she says.

Now it's my turn to have my mouth hanging open like a dead fish. Was that . . . holy shit was that *praise*? From my *sister*?

"Oliver," she says, a new excitement in her voice. "Do you think you could edit some photos? Get the jewel tones highlighted and add them to the slide deck?"

Oliver's head is a blur as he nods, already pulling out his laptop and waking it up.

"This is going to be *fabulous*," Amina says, scribbling notes in her notebook.

Mona starts throwing out business terms to Amina that I don't recognize or care about, and the two fall into an excited discussion, leaning toward each other as they talk.

A warm glow fills my chest, tendrils of happiness flowing down my arms and buzzing in my fingers. I turn back to the window, smile huge as I stare out the glass for the final hour of the ride.

When we finally arrive in Rome, we all unfold from our seats, grabbing our luggage from the overhead racks and squeezing down the aisle.

Amina and Oliver are already off the train when Mona reaches out her hand and taps my back.

I look at her over my shoulder, and a light blush covers her cheeks. She clears her throat.

"Thank you," she says at last, tucking her hair behind her ears. "What you came up with is very clever. And I'm just . . ." She bites on her lip for a second then does the last thing in the world I'd ever expect. Mona reaches out and pulls me into a hug.

It's awkward and a bit stiff and super uncomfortable because I'm still facing forward and she's kind of hugging my back and jamming my nose into her shoulder and the aisle doesn't leave us much room, but it might just be the best hug of my life.

"Thank you," she repeats. "I'm glad you're here."

I pause for a moment, swallowing past the flood of emotions that clog my throat. When I trust myself not to cry, I say, "I'm glad I'm here, too."

Mona releases me then clears her throat. "If you're, um, interested, I'd love for you to join us at the meeting."

I blink rapidly as that thought tumbles around my brain. "Really?"

Mona nods then smiles, using her hands to usher me forward. I chew this over as I squeeze my bag between the aisles and off the train. Do I want to go? If I'm being honest with myself, the only reason I originally wanted to go was because Oliver got to go. But in reality, business meetings sound like an adult version of being in a classroom. In other words, one of my personal circles of hell.

On the platform I turn to Mona. "I don't think I do want to go," I rush out.

Mona's smile wobbles into a frown, and her body tenses. She's about to get defensive and she opens her mouth.

"Not because I don't believe in what you're doing," I say, cutting her off. "But I just don't think it's the best way I could be helpful. And I want to help. So badly."

Mona closes her mouth and tilts her head, inviting me to continue.

"If, er, you want, I'd love to do more stuff like what happened on the train. Talking with you and Amina. And Oliver, or whatever. That was fun. And I liked it and I think with time I could get better at it. But I'm not interested in the meeting aspect of it. Does that make sense? Is that okay?"

Mona's face softens. "I think," she says, adjusting her blouse, "that makes perfect sense. And we could benefit creatively from your perspective."

Without thinking, I rocket into her, giving her another hug. She staggers back for a moment, tense, then relaxes. Minimally.

"And in return for my sweat equity, I'll accept fifty percent ownership of the company."

Mona laughs through her nose then pulls back. "Wishful thinking, Til."

I beam at my sister then shrug. "It's what I do."

Chapter 18

Runaway Brain Train

TILLY
___

Hullo." Oliver's voice is soft, but it startles the ever living fuck out of me and I screech.

Oliver, Amina, and Mona had dropped their bags at the hotel then headed straight to their meeting. After finding the closest café and gorging myself on espresso and enough slices of tiramisu that I should have just ordered the whole damn cake, I dragged myself back to the hotel and I've been in hyperfocus mode for . . . three hours, if the time on my phone is correct. It could have been three minutes for how lost I got in my head.

Oliver is quiet as I resurface to the real world, something gentle about the way he sets his bag down then sits on the end of his bed. It's a stark difference to how my mom reacts.

My hyperfocus usually makes Mom flip out.

She always barges into my room, telling me to be aware of my surroundings, freaking out at me for forgotten school assignments or chores. Yelling when I'd get caught up in my head, losing hours and hours as my brain got stuck on a useless task like online shopping for a bathing suit or doing a deep dive on some very niche conspiracy theories involving Pete Davidson.

Mom acts like I'm choosing to disappear, when, really, I'm physically unable to rip myself away from the task. Sometimes, hyperfocus lets me create something beautiful or something I'm excited about, like my writing this afternoon. Other times, it holds me hostage until it's 3 a.m. and frustrated tears are streaking down my cheeks.

"How'd the meeting go?" I ask, rubbing my fists against my eyes.

Oliver and I haven't talked much since our fight yesterday, and he shoots me a surprised glance at my question that morphs into a shy smile that devastates me a tiny bit.

"Pretty well, I believe," he says, schooling his features and rubbing his palms back and forth across the black fabric of his pants.

"That's all you're going to give me?" I say, shutting my laptop and leaning toward him. "The three of you have been coming back from these meetings like whoever ran them shoved bamboo shoots under your fingernails, but all you're going to say is *pretty well*?"

I say the last words in a mimic of his accent, and I don't miss the way his lips twitch up at the corners, that smile ready to burst out and ruin me all over again.

"Fine," he says, shifting toward me. "It was brilliant. Absolutely brilliant. They loved the idea so much they were already brainstorming table displays to go with jewelry and outfits they have."

A noise somewhere between a mating whale and a pterodactyl screech bursts out of my throat, and I jump up, running toward the door joining my room to Mona's.

It's shut, but I burst through it.

"Mona!"

Mona screams when the door bangs against the wall, and I hear her body hit the floor on the side of the bed.

"Tilly! You're supposed to knock, damn it!" she says from the other side of the bed.

"The door is supposed to stay open," I say in singsong. I hear the rustling of clothes and the sound of a zipper before Mona finally pops up.

I let out a low wolf whistle. "Damn, Mo. You got a hot date or something?"

"What? No! What a weird thing to say," Mona says, cheeks crimson. She drags her hands over the short, structured halter dress she's put on, looking like she belongs in a 1950s pinup calendar. She glances over my shoulder, and I look, too, seeing Oliver hovering in the doorway.

"I heard the meeting went well," I say, running then belly flopping onto Mona's mattress. I can almost hear her eye roll.

"It was very encouraging," she says, grabbing me by the ankles and yanking me down the bed so my shoes aren't on it.

"You two kill me," I say, sitting up and pointing between her and Oliver. "So stoic and serious. It's okay to admit that it went frigging great."

Mona rolls her eyes again then walks to the mirror to put on makeup. "Don't say *frigging*."

"Sorry. It's okay to admit that it went *fucking* great."

"Tilly!" Mona says, whipping around mid-mascara swipe to glare at me.

"Where's Amina?" I ask, noticing her absence. She would have gotten a kick out of that one.

"She's, um, out," Mona says, tossing the mascara tube back into her makeup bag.

"Out where?" I ask, watching Mona pop the cap off her lipstick and twist the end.

"Uh. She's. I don't know. Just out. Out getting something."
Mona swipes on the color and uses her finger to fix the edges.

"Why do you have your date lipstick on?" I ask, walking up
next to Mona and leaning toward her mouth. She shoves me
away from her.

"I don't."

"Yes, you do. You only wear red lipstick for dates." Mona is
so type A that, even in high school, she had labeled boxes in
her bathroom drawers with makeup specific to events ranging
from Tuesday debate club meetings to Friday date nights.

"No. What. I . . ." She looks around the room like she's
searching for the emergency escape. Her eyes land on Oliver.
"You two should go explore," Mona says, shooing us with her
hands.

"No, thank you," Oliver says.

"I'd rather rip my own hair out," I add.

Mona frowns. "Really. Go. If nothing else, take some pictures for Instagram."

"Are you asking me to explore or are you asking me to take
photos?" Oliver clarifies. "I need to know if I should record the
time on my invoice."

"You're getting *paid*?" I ask incredulously, sinking in my
heels and resisting the downright pushing Mona has started
doing to get me out of the room. "Why am I not getting paid?"
I add, turning on Mona.

"Because you're on a free trip around Europe!" Mona says,
throwing her hands in the air.

Oh. Yeah. Well, work is still work and I need to pinch
every penny if I'm going to keep consuming pastries and coffee at the rate I am.

"Why are you so determined to get us out of here?" I ask,
eyes narrowing as Mona tries to crowd me out like an Austra-
lian shepherd herding sheep.

"I'm not! It's just . . ."

A knock sounds at the door.

"Hi, gorgeous. You ready for our—" Amina pokes her head into the room, a bottle of wine and two glasses in her hands. Her eyes go wide and her mouth snaps shut when she sees Oliver and me staring at her.

Holy shit.

I knew it!

I freaking *knew* there was something there.

I turn to Mona with a giant, open-mouthed grin. I suck in a breath, preparing to scream out my excitement.

"Don't," Mona says, eyes wide as she holds up a menacing finger.

I choke back the gleeful shriek clawing at my throat, my head about to explode.

Moving slowly, as if I'm a wild animal that she's afraid to startle, Mona backs up to her purse, digging around in the pockets. She keeps her eyes locked on mine, knowing that I will absolutely lose my shit if she looks away for even a second.

She holds out her wallet. "Take my credit card and leave," she says sternly, like I'm robbing her.

Body buzzing with joy and lips pressed tight, I manage to nod slowly and take Mona's card. Then I turn, grabbing Oliver's elbow.

"What's going on?" Oliver asks, eyebrows furrowed as I pull him toward the door.

"I'll explain on our outing," I say, shooting Amina a giant grin and wink as we move past. She's still rooted to the spot, but a second later, she grins back.

"Right, but am I being paid for these hours?" Oliver asks.

I groan. "I'll pay you to stop talking," I say, continuing to drag Oliver with me. I hear the door shut behind us, and my smile grows. "Do you accept gelato as currency?"

Chapter 19

When in Rome

Rome is what I would call a sensory nightmare. The heat presses on my shoulders and neck with a physical force, sucking the energy from my muscles. The crowds are so thick and noisy as we try to navigate around Trevi Fountain, I feel like I'm being swallowed whole by the masses of bodies and won't ever have room to breathe again.

And the noise. Holy fucking hell, the noise. There're motors and shouts and dings and water and chatter and bird coos and baby cries all combining in this grating hum that tunnels under my skin and darts up and down my spine with razor-sharp pain.

I become so overwhelmed by it all that I stop walking, breaths short and tears poking at my eyeballs. I feel Oliver stop, too, but I can't bring myself to look at him. If I look at him, I know I'll do something mortifying like start crying or burrow my face against his chest. He'll probably ask me why I stopped walking, or what's wrong with me, or give me one of those cold looks of his and it will be mortifying and impossible to explain that my nuclear reactor is ever so slightly imploding in on itself in the most catastrophic way humanly possible.

And that I'm flipping out.

In public.

A light tap on my thigh draws my attention down, and I see Oliver's fingers tapping away at his side in jerky movements. I risk a glance at his face. His shoulders and neck are taut with tension and a muscle in his jaw tics as he stares up at the sky. Is he . . . could he be hating this, too?

In a flash that makes me jump, those endless brown eyes land on me. He must be able to read the misery on my face because he reaches out, his long fingers lacing with mine.

"Come on," he says, tugging my hand. He turns, pushing against the crowd. Pulling me with him.

Ollie's never touched me for this long before—any physical contact is the briefest of adjustments to my hands: whispers of touches. It should feel foreign and weird and make my nerves jostle around my body that his fingers are intertwined with mine. But, somehow, all it feels is safe.

And just a tiny bit perfect.

The grip of his hand is firm and steadying and tight enough that I know I won't dissolve in all the stimuli around me. Ollie creates space for me as he leads us.

I don't know where we're going, but for some reason, I trust that he'll make sure it's better than here. I keep my eyes pinned on the spot between his shoulder blades, channeling all my focus on the threads of his black shirt, the way the fabric pulls and moves with every step he takes.

We finally pop out on the outskirts of the most congested area, and he tugs me down a narrow side street, the air cooler from the shadows of the rough stone buildings. Ollie's head darts back and forth as he walks, peeking down alleys and alcoves, the explosive noises of the city draining behind us the deeper we wind into Rome's hidden labyrinth.

We fly past a narrow opening between the buildings, and,

out of nowhere, he stops in his tracks. I plow into him, nose squishing against his back.

It pains me to admit this, but he smells ridiculously good. The bastard.

First there's his outrageously handsome face, then his annoyingly beautiful descriptions of colors, and now I have to live with the knowledge that he holds hands like a pro and smells like a god? He makes it so hard for me to hate him.

Ollie spins around, pulling me between the buildings after him.

"Whoa," I say, my jaw dropping as we step farther into a hidden courtyard. I blink a few times as my eyes adjust to the lower light of the area. The surrounding buildings are tall and lopsided, leaning comfortably against each other. Lines with billowing laundry flap overhead, and small balconies overflow with plants.

And the silence.

I could weep in appreciation for the silence. It's soft like a blanket, none of the mayhem of Rome invading this safe little space.

I shuffle a few steps farther into the courtyard, then, without thinking, plop down onto the cobbled ground, the nervous energy draining from me in the peacefulness of this corner.

"Are you alright?" Ollie asks after a moment.

His gaze is like a caress I can feel across my face, and I nod, pressing my cheek against my shoulder, angling my eyes away from him. "Yeah. Sorry. That was just . . . so much." I nibble on my lip. "Really sorry," I repeat.

"There's no need to be sorry." Ollie clears his throat. "I, um . . . I understand. I understand how you're feeling."

I snort. "Okay. Sure."

There's a long pause, and I can still feel Oliver looking at me. "I think you're being sarcastic, but I don't understand why," he finally says.

With a sigh, I press the back of my head against the wall behind me, blinking up at the patch of blue sky hovering over our hideout. I try to pluck at the jumble of words in my head, but it's hard to find ones that will work. Why does admitting this to people always feel like I'm stripping myself naked?

"I have ADHD," I say, continuing to look up. "And while I know that no one particularly *likes* crowds like that, what we experienced pretty much makes me short-circuit."

Oliver is quiet in the tiny pause I leave, and I decide to push forward. Open the vein. Lay it all out there.

"The world has this misconception that ADHD is as simple as not focusing or some quirky personality trait, but it's so much more than that. It's like—God, how do you even explain it?—it's like every single thing around me is screaming for my attention, clawing at my brain and ripping it in one hundred different directions, all with equal force. And my body can't figure out how to process any of it. Crowds like that"—I wave vaguely at the direction we came from—"make my nervous system feel like it's being ripped apart. Like my brain will never stop humming, never catch up to everything begging for its attention. Life is just—I don't know—so fucking much. It's hard to do anything. Figure out the order to do anything. Remember to eat or take care of myself. And . . . yeah. It all kind of makes for gloriously embarrassing meltdowns."

I trace the stones beneath me, trying to swallow past the raw vulnerability building in my throat. Poking at my eyes. Even before I had a name for it, I've been judged for the atypical way my brain works, even by people like Mom or Dad who are supposed to love me the most.

It took a global pandemic, torturous online schooling, and me breaking down in furious sobs on a daily basis when I couldn't get my wandering brain to cooperate for my mom to take me to a child psychiatrist.

Dr. Alverez had explained to us that I wasn't scatterbrained or lazy or undisciplined (like I'd heard far too often throughout my life), but my executive functioning was virtually nonexistent. It wasn't that I lacked attention, I just couldn't regulate it.

But even with my diagnosis, they didn't *get* it. It would be ridiculous to think a random almost-stranger like Oliver somehow would.

"I'm sure you have some sort of inevitable follow-up question like 'Isn't ADHD just for boys or little kids?' so go ahead and shoot," I say, continuing to let my fingers wander over the ground.

I still can't bring myself to look at Oliver, but I hear him take a step toward me. Out of the corner of my eye, I see him crouch down, using his palm to dust off a spot on the ground before sitting beside me.

For some reason, his silence, the warmth of his arm next to mine, is so much worse than if he'd said something shitty like I'm expecting.

"Can I tell you something?" he asks after a moment.

"If you must," I say, trying to be flippant while I oh-so-subtly wipe my eyes and nose on my sleeve.

"I believe we're much more alike than you think."

Chapter 20

Neurodivine and Feelin' Fine

How so?" Tilly asks, her thunderstorm eyes staring up at me with wide vulnerability.

"I'm . . . well . . ." I cough a few times, searching for the right words.

It's hard to trust people to know what to do when they find out I'm autistic. They act like it's some big *thing* instead of a simple fact about my brain.

It's "well-meaning" aunts saying softly to my mums that I don't *look* autistic, or telling my peers at school and having them stare at me in horror like it's catching. It's primary school jokes where I'm called Spock or teachers staring at me with the expectation I'm some sort of savant, when, in actuality, I'm nothing more than myself.

It's not a shame thing that makes me hesitant to tell people—feeling shame over the wiring of my brain would be an utterly pointless waste of energy—more that my autism is a piece of me, and sharing any of my pieces with others is a wholly uncomfortable experience. It's handing another person something they can either treat kindly, or twist and reshape to hurt you.

I swallow, tapping my fingers together at my side. "I'm autistic," I say, staring at Tilly's shoulder. "And I understand your sensory processing issues. I have them, too, but with complex noises and strong smells. Totally scrambles my brain and makes me stim."

Tilly is quiet for so long—for her, that is, in reality, it's like, two seconds of silence—that I risk a glance higher than her shoulder.

She's still staring at me with those wide, gray eyes, but she has a smile on her mouth.

"Oh," she says at last, and something about that single syllable reverberates gently down my spine like the calming effect of a plucked harp string. "So you *do* get it . . . Why didn't you tell me sooner?"

I shrug. "I know you don't particularly care for me, so why bother you with details?"

"Don't . . . what? What makes you say that?" She leans toward me, and a gentle breeze whispers through her hair, the soft and sweet smell of her surrounding me.

I shrug again, my eyes retreating to the safety of those three damn freckles on her cheek. "You regularly get frustrated when we talk and end up storming off. And you always stare and frown at me when I'm taking photos or working on edits or drafting up a post. You've made it clear you find my habits rather intolerable."

Tilly scrambles up onto her knees, shifting so we're at eye level again. I get stuck on those eyes of hers.

"Ollie. No. That's not it at all."

"Then it's my personality that elicits such blatant dislike?"

"Oh my God, *no*. And stop talking like a historical romance hero. It's making my brain fuzzy."

"I don't know what that means."

Tilly blows out a breath, scrubbing the heels of her palms against her eyes. "Fine," she says at last, throwing her hands up. "I'll admit it. I'm kind of . . . *jealous* of you."

I blink rapidly at her. "Jealous of *me*? What the devil for?"

"Because you're perfect! You're annoyingly good at the thing you love to do. You don't flounder or second-guess yourself or even think twice about stopping in the middle of the freaking road to take a picture of a puddle because you're that dedicated to what you do. And you know how to do it. I don't have that. I don't know what I'm doing. Ever. And even when I *am* doing something, I feel like I'm doing it totally and completely wrong and I'm letting everyone down."

I pause for a moment, processing what she's said. "Tilly, those things . . . that's hyperfocus . . . It's not the same as perfection."

Far from it. It's this impulse. This absolute need to analyze color. Play with pictures. Share it with others in the only way I seem able to share anything with anyone.

"Well I didn't *know* that."

"Knowing that I'm autistic and hyperfocusing would have changed how much you disliked me?"

"Yes! Wait, no. That's not what I mean. It's . . ."

"What?" I prompt, nudging her with my knee. She looks down at my leg and smiles.

"It means that you get it."

"Get what?"

Tilly chews on her lips for a moment before they stretch into that smile that seems her default setting. "Get the struggles of navigating a world not designed for you. Get the confusion and frustration and achy chest that comes with trying to connect with people but never getting it quite right, but saying fuck it and being yourself anyway."

Tilly looks at me, and I look back, a weird, fluttering sensation growing in my chest and spreading down my arms to my fingertips. It's kind of . . . nice.

In this moment, I feel *close* to Tilly, like we're sharing a warm blanket that's keeping us both comfortable. I don't know that I've felt this with anyone before.

"Do you ever feel . . ." I clear my throat. "I don't quite know the words . . . but in social situations you . . ."

"Have absolutely no clue what you're doing?" Tilly says, leaning even closer to me and laughing.

"Yes," I say, smiling back at her. "That."

Tilly throws back her head and cackles like a witch. "Ollie. All the time. Every interaction I have feels like I've randomly showed up at some theater, am told I'm the lead in a play, then am shoved onto the stage. Everyone else got a script and knows what to say, and I'm somehow supposed to know the lines, without even knowing the plot. It's a nightmare."

This pulls a laugh from my own throat. "I like that analogy. A lot."

"Thanks, it came to me from stress dreams."

"I've always felt like it was more of a thick glass wall," I say, tapping my fingers on the cobblestones. "I can see other people, observe them, but it's never quite right. It's a bit morphed somehow. And sometimes there's an awful glare that leaves me blinded altogether. And the wall distorts sounds. Screws up what I'm trying to say. Or blocks the coded meanings of others. It always leaves me a little lost. And alone. I think that's why I give so much of myself to my Instagram account. Posting on there—shrinking my world down to a screen the size of my palm while I deep dive about color and the way it moves the world—allows me to feel closer to people than actually being in their presence. It's the only way I've figured out how to really connect."

Tilly sighs, and I look at her, worried I upset her or lost her somewhere in my talking. But . . . no . . . she's . . .

"Why are you smiling?" I ask. Wait. Christ. Is that . . . Oh no. "Why are you *crying*?" My hands make a weird fluttering motion like two flailing birds in her general direction.

Tilly snorts out a laugh then covers her mouth and nose with her hand. She literally flickers through the entire human spectrum of emotions in a second flat. I can't keep up with this girl.

"I, um, I guess I'm feeling really overwhelmed with some really big feelings and . . ." She blows out a breath, lifting the hair swooping across her forehead. "And, right now, I'm just really glad to know you."

A few very terrifying things happen to my body when she says this: my heart skips a beat, squeezes painfully, then pounds double-time in my chest. All the while, a weird surge of electricity shoots across my nervous system all the way to the tips of my toes and fingers, making them prickle. To top it off, my breath gets caught right at the top of my throat, and I'm fairly certain I'm about to die.

I jolt up to standing, doing what I can not to, er, you know, die. I manage to suck in a breath. Then another. And I think my heart is going to be okay, but I'm also going to call my mums tonight to ask if I should seek out a cardiologist to be on the safe side.

I glance down at Tilly, and she's still doing that horrifyingly interesting soft crying/smiling thing while she looks up at me. That's when I realize I'm smiling back.

She pushes herself to standing, too. It's quiet for a moment, and then I clear my throat.

"Would you like to look around Rome a bit more? We could try to find some spots that are more—"

"Neurodiverse friendly?" she says, arching an eyebrow.

"Yes. That."

Tilly nods. "I'm down. Plus, I want to make sure we give Mona and Amina enough time to . . . well, do whatever it is they need to do so they can stop pining after each other already and start dating. The yearning is actually killing me."

"I still don't understand how you picked up on any of that," I say with a skeptical look. "They seem like perfectly platonic business partners to me."

"Expert on sapphic love, are you?" she asks, giving me a lascivious wink. I feel my cheeks burn.

"Fair point," I mumble, dragging my palm across the back of my neck and staring at the ground. When I glance back at Tilly, she's giving me a smile broader than the horizon.

I turn, ready to find us another sensory-safe spot in Rome, when Tilly clears her throat.

"Ollie?" she says, voice soft.

I spin back around.

She clears her throat again. "I . . . like . . . I *totally* understand if this is a no, and no pressure *at all* but would it be okay if I maybe . . . umm . . . hugged you?"

My head tilts to the side as I look at her, and a brilliantly warm feeling fills my chest. If the feeling had a color it would be Pantone 176. A pale pink. Bright. Soft. Safe.

Suddenly, a hug from Tilly sounds like the most wonderful thing in the world.

"Actually, never mind," Tilly says, eyes going wide and cheeks flushing at my silence. "Please forget I asked. Seriously. That was weird. I didn't mean to be weird. I'm just feeling the teeniest tiniest bit ripped open and raw from this afternoon and I think I—"

I'm not sure what comes over me, but, next thing I know, I'm grabbing Tilly's hand and pulling her against me.

She's frozen for a moment—we both are, quite frankly—

but then she just . . . *melts*. She presses closer, wrapping her arms around my waist while mine fall across her shoulders, palms resting on her back. She squeezes me tight, nuzzling her head against my chest. I wonder if she can feel the way my heart is violently rioting against my sternum.

That's it, I'm definitely finding a cardiologist.

Chapter 21

Death by a Thousand Passive-Aggressive Texts

TILLY

The next week is a whirlwind of planes, trains, and automobiles as we wind our way across Europe. Ruhe hasn't struck a deal since Rome, and the initial high has worn off, Amina, Mona, and Ollie alternating moods of superb pessimism with disgusting cheeriness.

For my part, I'm having an absolute blast. Mona and Amina tasked me with writing fun and poppy taglines and descriptions for colors, and I've been slowly pushing the boundaries of weird and outlandish in the descriptions, adding things like "the perfect color to wear to the funeral of your no-good third husband who tragically passed in a sudden and mysterious way. Better Off Red tells the world you're feeling oh-so-forlorn at inheriting his millions."

Mona is always hesitant, but some aggressive puppy eyes from me and Amina have caused her to cave more often than I could have hoped for.

I still don't go to any of the Ruhe meetings—I like to spend those hours alone, wandering and writing. So much writing.

One of my more personal posts has blown up a bit, and my brain feels like an oversaturated sponge as I weed through the replies and DMs.

. . . A neurodivergency diagnosis seems to be taken as a burden to everyone but the owner of the brain in question. When I was told I have ADHD, it was like a map had been handed to me, showing the path of my circuit boards and looping wires. Do I still get lost up there? Of course. But at least now I approach it with a sort of . . . peace. I know that my makeup is different. Not wrong. Just different. I'm not lazy or undisciplined or defiant—things I've been called my entire life—I don't have the tools of executive functioning. It isn't that I lack attention, I don't know how to manage it.

While to me, my diagnosis felt like freedom, my mom cried like I'd been given a week to live. She went from exasperated sighs and outbursts of annoyance at my forgetfulness or voyages into hyperfocus, to coddling me to the point of suffocation, lamenting how hard it is "for the whole family" that I have ADHD.

Why is it that when we talk about neurodivergencies, it's always in the scope of the neurotypical's perspective? Any suggested reading is about a mom who overcame her child's this, or a spouse that dealt with their partner's that. Why aren't these guides from the voices of people living with the conditions? Why do we care more about the supposed burden family and friends feel they endure being in proximity to an ADHD person, instead of the experiences of the people actually dealing with it? Why do we talk about it in hushed whispers instead of joyous celebrations of what different brains can offer the world?

My brain isn't broken. I don't need a cure. I just need compassion.

Pretty much overnight, I went from a few hundred followers on Babble to thousands—which is simultaneously terrifying and exhilarating. The more vulnerable I get in my writing, the more people connect with it.

A lot of people are telling me about their experiences with ADHD, or how they've been made to feel like their experiences living with it don't matter compared to others who talk over them. The post hasn't been spared from ableist assholes talking about how ADHD is overdiagnosed, some people even claiming it's some sort of fake, political propaganda. But others are quick to stand up and shut that down. It makes sharp and wonderful emotions swell in my chest when others with brains like mine waste no time defending what I wrote.

All of it has me feeling exposed and alive. It's kind of . . . a lot. But in a good way. A way that jolts my fingers into dancing across the keyboard. Exposing myself in the hopes that it makes one more person feel seen.

And, of course, everything I write is influenced by how damn romantic Europe is.

I fall in love with every city I see. Brussels. Zurich. Luxembourg. Amsterdam. I cry when we take off for a new spot, never ready to depart, no matter how many hours I've spent in the current one. I leave a little piece of myself in each, marking them all as a tiny home for my needy heart.

Ollie and I have also come to some sort of truce. We bicker as frequently as ever, but there's an undercurrent of understanding there. We get each other, at least a bit.

But we're also keeping our distance. And, at least on my end, it's intentional. I'm trying to check every dangerous impulse I have to cling to Ollie like Saran Wrap.

Getting too close to him would be a mess. Ollie is buttoned up and tidy and organized and has a plan. I'm restless and directionless and don't know what I'm doing when my tourist visa expires in about a month and a half. It would be pointless to get attached to someone so different from me. Someone so set and sturdy. I'd just be a tornado that whips through and screws things up.

We got into Copenhagen early this morning, and I'm stuffing my feet into my sneakers to go explore when my phone rings. Mom's name flashes across the screen, and I let out a deep breath. I've been avoiding her calls as much as possible, until Mona practically ties me to a chair and forces me to talk to her. But her texts come regularly throughout the day, each one a passive-aggressive nick in my skin.

I glance up from the screen. Ollie's in the corner, headphones on and focusing on some editing project. I could take the call in here, but I decide to scoot into Mona's room. She and Amina are out at lunch with some friend from graduate school, leaving me and Ollie to our own devices.

After flopping dramatically onto the bed and waiting till the last ring, I accept the call.

"Hi, Mom."

"Tilly! How are you? Have you been behaving yourself?"

"Uh . . . good," I say, unsure how to fully answer that. I could have the manners of a Victorian baroness and I'm sure my mom would still be able to find fault in me. "How's Dad?" I manage to ask, the silence stretching way too long for comfort.

"He's doing well," Mom says, in her lovely, crisp voice. "Been very busy at work lately. He's gotten a surplus of new clients that have been keeping him occupied."

"Who doesn't love a surplus?" I say, as if I have any clue what she's talking about.

There's that silence again.

"How's the trip?" Mom asks. "How's Mona? It sounds like

she's had some incredible meetings with investors of late. I imagine you're learning a lot."

Mmmmm I wouldn't exactly call any of her meetings incredible. And they definitely weren't with investors. But I'm not about to correct Mom. "Yeah, Mona's doing great. I'm pretty much obsessed with Europe at this point. Everything is so freaking gorgeous and historic and just . . . *amazing*. Every time we get somewhere new I'm like, 'I don't wanna leeeeeeave.'"

The conversation halts. Again. I'm actually not sure I'm capable of surviving any more silence on this phone call, yet I persist.

"Well, it's wonderful that you're having fun, but I hope you're being realistic about the trip," Mom finally says, only sort of easing my suffering.

"What's that supposed to mean?"

"I hope you're being serious about your future and not looking at this like some big free vacation," she says. "This trip is supposed to show you the benefits of hard work, not some free-for-all. Mona's success wasn't handed to her, she worked for it. And you'll need to work for yours, too. This summer wasn't supposed to send you further into Tilly-La-La-Land but show you how important it is you go to school and get a practical degree."

Now this silence? It's on me. Because, really, what am I supposed to say to that?

"Are you still there?" Mom asks after a minute.

"Yeah," I squeak out. I feel incredibly small, like my chest is caving in on itself, my shame a black hole that I'm disappearing into.

"Do you have anything you'd like to say?"

I shake my head then realize she can't see it. "Not really."

Mom's sigh sounds tired.

"I've been keeping up with my writing." Which is a silly thing to admit, but I'm that desperate to prove to my mom that I can stick to *something*. "Been connecting with a lot of people on Babble through it."

Mom sucks in a breath through her teeth. "I'm glad you have your hobby, but journaling does not a career make. Not a steady and lucrative one."

I wish the tears slipping out of the corners of my eyes and trailing down my cheeks could dissolve me. Could ease this feeling of awful, aching failure in my chest.

"You can't avoid growing up, Tilly," Mom says, voice softer now. "The sooner you accept that, the better. You need to get a plan. At least tell me you'll seriously start thinking about it over the next few days and we'll revisit the topic on our next call."

"Okay," I whisper. It's a lie and we both know it.

"Talk to Mona. She's a wealth of information. Look at all she's accomplished. That could be you. If you applied yourself."

The hurt morphs into an angry monster at the base of my throat, snapping its jaws. Apply myself? All I ever do is try. I try so hard I'm practically turning my brain inside out from it. But the results don't look like those Mona has delivered and are automatically wrong.

"I have to go," I say, voice cracking.

"Tilly—"

"Love you. Bye."

With the world's most aggressive click, I end the call and chuck my phone to the foot of the bed. I then proceed to have a teeny-tiny tantrum, kicking my legs into the mattress.

Is this how it's supposed to be? Is every conversation with my mother supposed to make me feel like shit? Am I supposed to spend my life as Mona's lackluster comparison? Live in the shadow of a person people can point to and say, *That. That right there is what your potential could have made. Shame you wasted it.*

Pulling a pillow over my head, I bite my teeth into it and let out a hoarse shriek.

"Are you okay?"

I jolt up to sitting like a vampire awakening from a coffin—very cute and attractive, I'm sure—and find Ollie leaning in the doorway looking devastating in his all-black clothes and his annoyingly gorgeous face.

I blink at him for a moment, his question doing a loop-de-loop around my brain. *Am* I okay? Not really. And it's relatively mortifying how many times Ollie's had to ask me that question. Apparently, I'm never okay. I'm a directionless letdown of a daughter who can't plan for a future and has no motivation outside of pastries, coffee, and validation from internet strangers. Probably not an ideal mental health status.

Years of trial by failure have taught me that people usually ask if you're okay or how you're doing with the expectation that you won't answer them with anything deeper than *I'm good! How are you?* Which most of the time is a bald-faced lie, and it's an exhausting social rule to follow. Yet, it's what I almost say to Ollie. The false words are on the tip of my tongue, but they turn sour as I take in the earnest way he's looking at me, his eyes slowly roaming across my face.

"No," I finally squeak out, shaking my head. "I'm not really okay. But I know I will be."

Ollie's eyes narrow as he studies me, then he nods, satisfied by whatever conclusion he comes to. "Of course you will," he says, straightening his shoulders and fiddling with the cuffs of his shirt. "And it's also okay that you're not okay right now."

My breath catches in my throat as I stare at him. It's one of those terrifying and special moments where someone says something so simple yet validating that instant tears prick at my eyes. That easy but genuine phrase punching right into my chest and squeezing my heart, threatening to crush any walls I have up because I suddenly feel hopelessly safe to fall apart.

I don't know what to say and, for once in my life, I don't blurt out the first nonsense that comes to mind. I'm starting to become more comfortable with the silences that fall between us.

The lack of stimulation used to make me want to turn my skin inside out, but that was before I realized how much there was to notice in the quiet moments with Oliver. The tiny flare of his nostrils with each inhale. The movement of his barely there Adam's apple every time he swallows. The way his charcoal-black eyelashes sweep against the tops of his cheeks with every blink.

Our silences let me learn these crucial details. The ones I'll think about when this summer is over.

"Would you like to work together?" Ollie asks suddenly, and a bit loudly for him.

I tilt my head, mind still hovering between the clouds of my thoughts, shooting him a confused look.

He clears his throat, little splotches of color blooming on his cheekbones. "Obviously, no pressure if you don't want to. I was just thinking you could write and I'll edit some photos."

I laugh way too loudly to feign not knowing what he's talking about. "Write?" I say, unconvincingly. "What would I be writing?"

Ollie tilts his head, mirroring me. "I'm not exactly sure, but I'll admit I'm endlessly curious."

My heart stutters in my chest. I've been hoping myself into delusion that Oliver forgot whatever he read on my laptop back in Milan. The only way I can function is by convincing myself that he doesn't know I've been writing and hasn't read a single word.

But, in classic Oliver fashion, he's boldly and bluntly torn that dream to shreds.

"I write about my brain," I whisper, a secret I didn't know I was going to admit. But something about Ollie and his eyes like honey and the gentle earnestness of the way he talks to me makes me want to tell him everything.

Ollie's gaze travels to my forehead like he can see the organ in question. "What about it?"

I let out a nervous giggle and try not to mess with my hair. "How it's frustrating sometimes. Fun and creative other times. How its wires and circuit boards are different from neurotypicals and that changes how I see the world."

"You talk about your brain like it's a separate entity."

Oh God, I really want to stop with these nervous giggles that make me sound like I'm twelve. "That's how it feels sometimes. Like I have this unruly toddler or creative mastermind renting out a room up here," I add, tapping my temple. "Do you ever feel like that?"

Ollie continues to stare at my forehead, and all I can do is pray I don't have any new zits cropping up.

"I think I do," he says at last.

He doesn't elaborate, but I don't need him to. He's given me enough.

"So, did you, er, want to work together?" he asks after a moment, rubbing his palm across the back of his neck.

"Yes," I practically shout at him, scrambling off the bed and to the doorway. He steps aside as I go through. Scanning my messy half of the room for my laptop, I find it cracked open on the floor between my bed and the wall, and I snatch it up, turning to see where Ollie's going to sit.

It's then that I realize he's rearranged some of the furniture, situating the room's small desk next to a pulled-out nightstand. He's dragged his bed out a bit so one corner acts as a seat he's using now, the desk chair open next to him.

My heart bounces up to my throat as I walk to the setup.

He crams his knees against the nightstand, twisting his lower half so he can fit. So I can have the chair. Why does all of this make me feel like I'm going to cry?

I sit down next to him, opening my laptop and waking it up. I feel Ollie glance my way, and my impulse is to shield my screen so he can't see my messy draft of a Babble post. But I don't do it. I don't hide the thing that makes me happy. The thing I love doing. I let him be a sneaky-sneak and look all he wants.

He reads over my shoulder for a few minutes, and my fingers are stiff and hesitant to write, but it also feels . . . good. Like instead of seeing my words, he's seeing *me*. And maybe, just maybe, he likes what he sees.

Eventually, he turns to his own laptop and we slowly drift into our work, the clicks and taps of our laptops a sweet melody that's uniquely our own. We sit in parallel worlds, the edges of our bubbles gently touching each other.

I'm not sure how long we work for but, eventually, I come to the end of what I was writing, blinking away from my screen for the first time in too long. I smile, an indulgent, satisfied smile, at what I wrote. I talked about traveling, about the stimulation and sensory overload of it. Putting in hints of the chaotic moments Ollie and I have shared on planes or trains. Even though it talks about things that are hard, it feels . . . fun. Like joy was pulled even from the hardest moments.

I look over at Ollie, the intense lines and angles of his sharp profile. I swallow down a small gasp when I see his screen.

He's editing a photo of me, leaning close to the screen, lip caught between his teeth as he slides the mouse around. This shouldn't surprise me; conceptually, I know he takes and edits all the photos Ruhe uses for their social media. But seeing him studying me so intensely, with that powerful focus centered on my face . . .

It has me feeling so much, all at once. Like my chest will crack from every emotion buzzing through my veins. I glance back at Ollie's face to confirm he's still solidly in his own world. Then I type something on my laptop. Something dangerous and scary and disastrous.

I think I like Oliver Clark.

I delete it immediately, but it doesn't matter. The impact still stands. Those six simple words are true and have me tied up in knots.

Any hope of convincing myself that I don't have feelings for Oliver is crumpled up into a little ball and tossed out the window.

Chapter 22

Get the Butter!

OLIVER

Editing photos of Tilly has become a hyperfixation of late. Even when I'm taking pictures of Tilly—I mean, Tilly's nails—my own fingers are itching to get to the computer, to play with settings, manipulate colors. Try to capture then convey the light that Tilly has. I work on edits way more than is necessary, and I'm worried about what I'll do when this summer is over and I have no more reason to spend hours editing images of her.

Luckily, I get paid for this new obsession, and I hope that makes it all look less painfully creepy whenever Mona or Amina sees me working on them, which is pretty much all the time. But having Tilly sit next to me, glancing at me while I work, is a unique sort of meta weirdness even I have the social instinct to feel awkward about. There's no stopping hyperfocus, though, so I carry on.

After double-checking my color master chart, I apply color so her nails are a brilliant red, everything else in black and white. I tilt my head, studying the final result.

Tilly looks like an old Hollywood starlet. Her head is

thrown back, wide mouth in a smile that's impossibly bright, hands halfway to her mouth in a half-hearted attempt to dim the effect of her joy.

I took this picture during our quick stop in Amsterdam. We'd all finished dinner and were walking along the canal back toward the train for an overnight trip, the summer evening cool with the tiniest hints of dusk touching everything with a soft light. Out of the blue, Tilly had made some perverse joke about taking me to the Red Light District, and my subsequent look of alarm and embarrassment caused her to burst out in her endearing screech of giggles and snorts.

I didn't have my camera ready, but the way she looked, the way happiness radiated out of her like she held the sun in her heart, had me frantic to capture the moment, whipping out my phone and snapping away countless blurry pictures.

They all turned out beautifully.

I'm putting the finishing touches on the color balance when I feel a soft puff of air on my cheek. As she turns, Tilly's face is centimeters from mine, our noses almost brushing. We stare at each other for a moment in cross-eyed confusion, then Tilly jerks back and away from me.

"Sorry!" Tilly says (yells). "I didn't mean to get so close to you and, uh, breathe on your neck . . . Ohmygod. I mean, I got sucked into watching you work. I'm not a creep. I promise. At least, if I am a creep . . . it's in like . . . a safe way? What? Okay no please forget I said that. Anyway."

At this point, she's so frazzled her arms shoot out from her sides, hitting both our laptops and knocking over my stack of color charts and Pantone samples.

We watch in silence as color chips rain onto the floor like confetti.

"Shit," Tilly says at last, slithering out from her seat and under the desk then crawling around the floor, reaching every which way to collect the papers. "I'm so sorry."

"It's not a big deal," I say, moving around the desk and kneeling to help her. "Don't worry about it."

"I'm such a mess. I'm sorry. Did some go under the dresser? Let me . . ."

She lies down on her stomach, pressing her cheek against the carpet and reaching her arm into the tiny crack under the chest.

"Honestly, Tilly, it's not a big deal. You can leave it. Or I'll—"

"Got it!" Tilly says, rolling her neck so she's looking at me. The movement reminds me of the terrifying way Cubby used to turn her doll heads all the way around.

"Shit," she says again, eyes going wide.

"What's wrong?"

"My arm's stuck!" She jerks her body toward me while her arm stays firmly lodged beneath the furniture. "Holy fuck, it's super stuck."

"Okay. Wait. Um. Maybe stop doing that jerking thing?" I say, my voice rising an octave. "I don't want you to hurt yourself."

"Ollie, holy shit. It's really stuck. I don't mean to freak out, but I'm kind of freaking out." Her free hand claws at the carpeting.

"What should I do?" I say, like the completely useless git I am.

"I don't know!" Tilly screeches, her panic flaming my own. "Can you get . . . I don't know, some butter?"

"Butter?"

"To rub on my arm and help slide it out?"

"Where am I going to get butter?"

"I literally can't solve all your problems for you, Oliver! My arm is stuck and I'll probably die on this nasty-ass carpeting!"

"Hold on," I say, scrambling to my feet and rushing toward the bathroom.

"It's not like I can go anywhere!" Tilly yells after me.

I grab the little bottles of hotel shampoo and soap, then dart back to her, kneeling by the dresser. Tilly does that horrifying head swivel thing again.

"This might work," I say, unscrewing the caps and squeezing out the goop from the bottles onto her arm.

Tilly shrieks.

"What?" I shriek back at her.

"That's cold!"

For a moment, I contemplate leaving this contrarian girl right where she is.

"I think you'll be able to cope," I finally grumble, rubbing the goop on her skin and sliding my fingers under the crack to reach whatever I can under there.

"I'm not sure that's true. I completely lack resilience." There's a hint at something in her tone that makes me think she might be enjoying this. Just the tiniest bit.

She has me equal parts panicked and annoyed, but an unintended smile cracks across my lips.

"Let's give this a go," I say, gripping her upper arm with one hand and her waist with the other. It's absolutely awful timing that I notice how soft her skin is. How perfectly the dip of her waist lines up with my palm.

Desperate to push any similar thoughts out of my head, I give her a tug.

I was expecting there to be much more resistance, I really was. But no. She's dislodged in an instant, and the force of it has me falling back, head hitting the floor and the weight of Tilly's body landing fully on mine as she lets out a winded *oof.*

For a moment, I can't breathe, and it's not only because Tilly's elbow landed firmly in my diaphragm.

It's the way her legs are tangled with mine, the warmth of her seeping into me, the soft puffs of her breath against my neck and the tickle of her hair against my chin.

It's . . .

I'm . . .

I don't have names for the odd emotions surging through me, but I feel *everything.* Like my heart is unfolding, expanding further and further until it threatens to burst out of my chest. Like bees are buzzing in my stomach, and warm honey is dripping in my veins.

It's so much all at once, but, for some reason, I hope it never stops.

After a moment, Tilly shifts, lifting her head and looking down at me. And it's like . . . fuck. I don't know. Maybe she's feeling everything, too? Is that possible? I've spent so much of my life feeling disconnected from others, I don't know what to make of this charged, live wire that's suddenly tethering us together.

"Are you okay?" Tilly whispers, and I feel the breath of her words dance across my mouth.

I nod. "Are you?" I manage to ask, my voice hoarse. My limbs apparently no longer belong to me, because, suddenly, the pads of my fingertips are resting on her cheeks.

Tilly nods back. The friction of her skin against mine feels like a sharp zap of lightning up my arm and straight to my chest. The gentlest glow of pink warms the spots I touch. Pantone 12–1305, Heavenly Pink. All of a sudden, I'm convinced the color was named only after Tilly gifted it to the world.

We stay there, suspended in a moment, focused on nothing

but each other. Tilly leans a centimeter toward me. I lift my neck an equal distance up. My head is spinning, and fragments of questions poke at my brain. What is she . . . ? Is this . . . ? Are we . . . ?

Is she going to kiss me?

Then an even more important thought solidifies at the forefront of my mind:

I want to kiss her.

Right as I'm about to close the distance, a booming knock rattles at the door, scaring us both. We jolt so hard our foreheads smack together. Tilly lets out a string of curse words as she rolls off me, and I cradle my head in my hands as I groan.

The second, obnoxious knock creates a pulsing pain in my skull, and I scramble to standing, ready to kill whoever just stole that moment from us.

A third, even louder knock.

I'm at the door in four long strides, and I wrench it open. "What the fu—"

"Good to see you, too, Ollie," the world's most familiar voice says. "You always were one to give the warmest of welcomes."

I close my eyes, then sigh, using my free hand to rub my temple.

"Hi," I say at last, feeling an odd mixture of annoyance and excitement at the surprise of seeing the last person I expected.

My sister.

Chapter 23

Contemplating Sororicide

OLIVER

"What are you doing here?" I ask Cubby, stunned to see her. Despite our texting and trying to coordinate, I didn't think our schedules would line up this summer while Cubby's touring with her band.

"Ollie, truly, there's no need to roll out the red carpet like this to greet me," she says, rolling her eyes then throwing her arms around me in a hug. "I missed you," she adds, giving me an extra squeeze before letting go. "I convinced the bandmates to skip some shithole pub in Odense so I could come see you instead."

I glance over her shoulder for her usual crew of misfits: Darcy, Harry, and Cubby's boyfriend, Connor.

"I left them back at our hostel," Cubby says, reading my mind in that easy way she's always been able to. "We can meet up with them later. I figured you and I could get dinner first and catch up."

I nod, my fingers tapping wildly at my side as it slowly hits me that Cubby, my favorite person, is actually *here*. I tend to be a bit slow to process, and showing excitement doesn't come naturally for me, but I'm thrilled to see her.

Cubby notices my tapping and grins, sliding past me into the room.

I turn to follow her and end up smacking into her back.

"Well, hello," Cubby says, looking at Tilly, who's standing like a frightened owl in the corner. "Who are you?"

Tilly glances at me, then back to Cubby, at me one more time, then down at herself, like she has no idea how to answer the question. Her cheeks are still the dusky pink they were a minute ago when I touched them. When I was hungry to kiss them.

"This is Tilly. She's my . . . no . . . her . . . I . . ."

"I'm Ollie's boss's younger sister slash summer intern or whatever," Tilly says, saving me from my endless sputtering. "Hi."

"Of course," Cubby replies slowly, a smile crawling across her mouth. "Ollie mentioned he was traveling with someone around our age." She pauses. "He failed to mention how ridiculously stunning you are."

There's a fresh beat of silence, and I would like to, quite simply, die. Or murder my sister. Perhaps both.

Then, Tilly lets out a wild boom of laughter while I subtly pinch my sister's arm. Cubby pushes me off and walks over to Tilly.

"It's so great to meet you," Cubby says, extending her arms in a hug.

Tilly hesitates for half a second before stretching out her own arms and hugging Cubby like they're best friends.

"Okay, first things first," Cubby says, pulling away from Tilly after a moment. "We absolutely *must* video call Mums."

Before I can get a word in, Cubby's already stripped off her jacket, made herself comfortable on my bed, and is holding up her phone while a ringing fills the room.

The call is picked up in no time.

"Darling!" Mum's voice trills across the line in greeting.

"Our sweet little cub," Mãe says over her. "What city are you in today, my love?"

"Look who I'm with," Cubby says, grabbing me by the elbow and pulling me down next to her, smooshing our faces together. My parents screech in unison, and it takes all my willpower not to slap my hands over my ears.

"Oliver, our wonderful boy, how we've missed that precious face!" Mum says, and my cheeks heat.

I accidentally glance at Tilly, and she's staring at me and Cubby with a massive grin on her face. I blush even harder.

"Wait, where are you both?" Mãe asks again, leaning so close to the screen that we have a magnified view of her forehead.

"I surprised Ollie in Copenhagen," Cubby says. "Although, based on the less than enthusiastic welcome I got from dear Oliver here, I think I must have interrupted something."

Can you die from blushing? It can't be safe for this much blood to be rushing to my cheeks. Another quick (again, accidental) glance at Tilly lets me know she's experiencing a similar physiologic crisis.

"Interrupting what, darling?" Mum asks, nudging Mãe away from the camera.

"Nothing," I say. Way too loudly. All four women blink at me. Then Cubby bursts into evil laughter.

"I'll explain later," Cubby says, shooting our mums a wink. "But, more importantly, you have to meet Tilly."

Cubby pushes me away and walks straight to Tilly, wrapping an arm around her shoulders.

"Mums, this is Tilly. She's been traveling with Ollie this summer for the internship."

There's a pause before my mums squeal again. I'd like to dissolve into the carpeting.

"My *God*, you're gorgeous," Mãe says. "Isn't she, Lu?"

"It's so good to meet you," my mum, Louise, says, at least slightly calmer than Mãe. "And yes, you *are* lovely."

I drop my head into my hands and stifle a groan. Not sure why everyone is so suddenly obsessed with Tilly's looks. She has one thousand even more distinct qualities. Like cleverness. The ability to start conversations with literally anyone. The energy she radiates every time she steps into a room.

With a bit of strength, I sneak another look at Tilly, trying to gauge how uncomfortable she is. How much she probably despises me and my overly enthusiastic family.

Her gaze meets mine almost instantly and she gives me a dazzling smile that has me dropping my head back in my hands.

"How's the trip been for you?" Mum asks. "I know Ollie's having a brilliant time. He's been texting us about how much he enjoys editing the social media content."

"It's been . . ." I can feel Tilly looking at me. "This trip has certainly been a whirlwind. But I love working with Ollie on the photoshoots. He makes hand-modeling easy. And I know my sister and Amina are so happy with how much growth and buzz he's gained for them on social media."

"Are those your hands in all the pictures, dear?" Mum asks.

"Yup. He does a great job directing me, because otherwise, I'd just have my hands like this in every shot," Tilly says, smiling and holding her limp wrists in front of her chest like some sort of adorable squirrel.

"Well, you've certainly inspired him," Mãe says. "He's sent us *hundreds* of hand photos he hasn't posted yet. Going on about this color or that."

"Truly," Mum chimes in. "So many pictures. So many. I can't figure out how to stop my WhatsApp from automatically saving all of them, so my entire camera roll is basically your nail beds."

Cubby snorts at this and I, once again, am hoping for a timely demise.

"I want in on this 'Pictures of Tilly's Hands' group chat," Cubby crows.

"I'll send you some of my favorites," Mãe says.

"Cubby, I'm ready to leave for dinner," I say, standing and walking toward them. "Mums, I love you and I am giving you the courtesy of letting you know I'm hanging up on you."

Tilly glances at me, biting her lip as she smiles. Cubby cackles, at what I have no idea, then looks back at her phone.

"We love you both," they say in unison before I jab my finger at Cubby's screen and end the call.

"Your moms are so cool!" Tilly says, turning to Cubby.

"They are spectacularly wonderful," Cubby says, sliding her phone into the back pocket of her ripped jeans. "Which makes it spectacularly annoying to try and write angsty songs. How dare they give us a great childhood and steal away potential trauma to make art out of?"

Tilly giggles. "What do they do for a living?"

"Mum is an art curator, and Mãe an artist. Mum met Mãe while working in a gallery down in Lisbon. They fell so desperately in love that Mãe followed Mum back to Surrey from Portugal and never looked back."

"That's so romantic," Tilly says.

"Runs in our blood," Cubby says, punching me on the shoulder. I glare at her for a moment, before noticing how Tilly's eyes flicked toward mine then away. I stare long after her look has left me. But then Cubby jams her elbow into my ribs and I jolt out of my daze.

"We're leaving," I growl at Cubby, marching across the room and tossing her jacket at her. I swing open the door and stare at her expectantly.

"So bossy," Cubby says, raising her eyebrows and giving Tilly a conspiratorial look. Tilly presses her lips together in a failed attempt at hiding a smile. "It was great to meet you, darling," Cubby continues. "We'll see you after dinner for a pint. I'm not accepting no as an answer. Plug your number in."

Tilly nods, accepting Cubby's phone and typing away. "I'll be there."

"Fabulous. My bandmate Harry will be there, too. He's single and artsy and always on the prowl for a new woman to write tragic love songs about so I'm sure he'll be particularly keen to get to know you."

"Cubby. Leaving. Now." I'm not above dragging my sister out of this room with brute force.

"My, my, Ollie, what has you so flustered?" Cubby asks as she passes through the door, making sure to give my cheek a sharp pat. "You look downright feverish."

"I'm fine," I grit out through clenched teeth.

Cubby clucks her tongue. "Always such a closed book. No matter, I have all of dinner to pry it out of you."

Chapter 24

Birds, Bees, and
Other Life Lessons

OLIVER

And I explained to them, even before we left for tour, that Copenhagen was far too happy for my natural disposition and it would be an artistic disaster booking *four* shows here, but do they listen to me? No. Of course not. All they see is free booze and want to sign on the dotted line. Little do they realize that we need to constantly surround ourselves with emotionally stimulating environments to create our nuanced sound. It's like trying to charge an iPad on an Android charger: it doesn't work."

Cubby has been talking for at least thirty minutes about the latest artistic differences she's experiencing with her bandmates, this one centering on how touring in too-happy cities is bad for her creative process.

She's the singer in a jazz-punk nightmare of a band that has exceptionally long song titles like "my last cigarette feels more like home than you ever did anyway."

Apparently, they're quite good.

I literally have nothing to add to this conversation, but I do enjoy listening to Cubby talk, and she seems to enjoy having someone to talk uninterrupted to. She pauses just long enough to take a bite of her pizza and a sip of wine.

"Ollie, are you using protection?" she asks.

I tilt my head as I look at her, finishing a bite of my own. "Against what? Thievery? You told me that my travel money belt was, quote, *absolutely bloody hideous.* Unquote."

"I stand by that," Cubby says, leaning forward and pointing her finger at me. "That belt-wallet-giant-beige-thing *was* hideous. But I'm not talking about protection from pickpockets, you twat. I'm talking about condoms."

I choke on a sip of water. "Cubby. No. This is one of those inappropriate sibling boundaries Dr. Shakil told us about. I can tell."

"We're twins, Ollie. It's different."

"I'd be willing to bet it's not," I mumble, coughing harder into my napkin. "And it's a moot point. I'm not . . . in *need* of them."

Cubby snorts. "That so? Because the way you look at Tilly conveys something very different."

"Tilly?" I nearly yell. "No. No, no. Never. We're . . . We're not even friends. We're just . . ."

"Totally obsessed with each other and spending ninety percent of your time sneaking glances while the other isn't looking?"

"She looks at me?" I ask. My heart does an odd flip in my chest. Is this an arrhythmia?

Cubby rolls her eyes. "Don't be dim. Of course she does. But what's more interesting is the way you look at her."

"No, it's not," I say, automatically. Then, "How do I look at her?"

Cubby laughs. "Do you remember when we went to the Dalí museum in Spain with Mums?"

"Yes." It was one of the best experiences of my life. We spent hours weaving in and out of the playful and bonkers galleries.

"And do you remember how Mãe looked at *Galatea of the Spheres*?"

I nod, remembering every detail of the exquisite painting. The fractured wholeness Dalí had created. The grace of the colors. The tenderness of his wife's face. The way it all nearly moved Mãe to tears.

"Then do you remember how Mum looked at Mãe looking at that painting?"

I nod again, trying to swallow through my dry throat. Mum had looked at Mãe like Mãe was the sun and Mum couldn't believe she had the privilege to bask in her warmth. It was one of many variations of loving looks I've seen on both their faces during my life. It's overwhelming to imagine feeling so much you look at someone like that.

"*That's* how you look at Tilly," Cubby says, as if she hasn't just dropped an atomic emotional bomb on my lap. Lovely sister. "It's obvious you both fancy each other," she adds.

"You've made your assumptions on it quite obvious, thanks," I say tersely, shoving more pizza in my mouth. "But you're, not so shockingly, wrong. Our relationship extends to nothing further than business acquaintances."

"That right? So I take it that it was purely for business that you were acquainting yourself with her mouth when I walked in?"

"I was not!" I nearly shout in outrage, part of which is due to the fact that that's exactly what I was *trying* to do before she so rudely interrupted us. But I'm not about to tell Cubby that.

Cubby's smile turns into something softer, more serious. "It's okay to like her, Ollie. You deserve to like someone. And to have someone like you back."

I shake my head, shoving another bite of pizza into my mouth. "Grenadine!" I say through my bite. It's our safe word. The one we established with Dr. Shakil years ago for when conversations get to be too much. Too intense. Too hard for me to process in real time.

Cubby leans back, respecting the boundary. That's one of the reasons she's the best sister in the world: she'll push me more than anyone, but acknowledge the moment I ask for a break.

And I'd do the same for her. If she ever needed a break from a conversation, that is. But I throw out one random question about her shithead boyfriend, Connor, and she's off like a racehorse with complaints and examples of what a total dick he is.

I'm listening to Cubby, I swear I am, but half of my brain keeps circling back to our previous conversation.

I'm not having sex. Certainly not with Tilly.

. . . Not that I don't *want* to. Hell, the idea has popped into my head way more times than I think would be socially acceptable to admit. It's . . . well . . . It seems so far out of the realm of possibility that Tilly would want that with me. Would feel . . . whatever this . . . this *thing* is I feel toward her.

But that doesn't mean I won't have sex one day. Hopefully. Oh God, seriously, hopefully.

There's a small break in conversation as Cubby takes another sip of her wine.

"How does one, theoretically, buy condoms?" I ask, staring at my plate.

She nearly spits out her wine then cackles so loudly I consider walking away from the table.

"Okay," I say, dabbing at the spots of sprayed merlot that hit me on the cheek, "forget I asked."

"Never," Cubby says, giving me that evil grin of hers. "One, theoretically, walks into the pharmacy, struts to the appropriate aisle, peruses lubricated options ribbed for everyone's pleasure, takes them to the till, pulls out one's money—not from a hideous belted travel wallet, mind you—pays for said condoms, and leaves the store with them."

I nod, wondering if she'd give me hell if I pulled out my phone to jot this down in the notes app.

"Then one goes to one's partner, gets glorious consent, and has protected sex like bunnies in heat, then repeats the process as needed."

"Bunnies don't go into heat," I say, my entire face burning.

"Yes, they do. All mammals do. It's biology."

"Rabbits have an estrus cycle, not a menstrual cycle."

"Oh my God, grenadine! Grenadine!" Cubby cries, slapping her hands over her ears.

"Right. Because the discussion of rabbits' follicular development is so much more inappropriate than you telling me to buy condoms," I say, frowning at her.

"Respect the safe word or I'm calling Dr. Shakil." Cubby pauses, then points at me. "And Mums."

With the threat of all threats hanging over my head, I take the last bite of my pizza and flag down the bill.

Chapter 25

Fanfiction Addiction

TILLY

Okay but for real is there anything more intimidating than going solo to a freaking pub, in *Copenhagen*, to meet up with a girl you desperately want to be best friends with, her bandmates, and a guy you definitely have overwhelming unreciprocated feelings for?

Didn't think so.

I hover outside the entrance for so long, I start to get funny looks from the people drinking outside. But instead of doing the logical thing and actually going in, I decide a few loops around the block would be the better option.

An all-too-familiar voice stops me as I'm starting my fourth lap.

"Tilly?"

I turn, seeing Ollie standing in the doorway of the bar, golden light putting his lean frame in silhouette.

"Hi," I say, giving him a jerky flap of a wave.

"You've circled past at least three times. Is your GPS not working?" Ollie asks, nodding at the phone clutched in my hand.

Oh my God, strike me down now.

"Yeah," I lie. "I guess so. It kept telling me to go five hundred more feet."

Ollie frowns then walks toward me. "We can't have you walking around with a faulty GPS. Would you mind if I look at your phone? Maybe there's a missing update I can help you with."

Since I'm a dirty coward *and* a liar, I shove my phone into my purse, then wave off the question. "I'll have you look tomorrow on the train. We'll have so much time to kill."

Ollie thinks about this for a moment, eyes swooping up and down the street like he's on the lookout for robbers.

"Okay," he says at last, moving so he's ushering me through the entrance. "But I don't like the idea of you wandering around aimlessly in foreign cities."

I'm turned inside out enough by this boy to admit that I absolutely glow at his concern.

"We're right over here," Ollie says, leading me toward a booth in the back corner. "I've had us move four times to find the least overstimulating spot. Wouldn't do for either one of us to go into sensory overload and have a meltdown."

"Yeah, it sure would be awful to embarrass myself in public for the first time in my life ever. Definitely have no idea what that's like."

Ollie glances at me then picks up on my sarcasm, giving me that grin that always threatens to kill me.

I blink away, focusing instead on Cubby in the corner who shoots me a smile and a wave-flick-of-her-wrist thing that looks so effortlessly cool I'm already sweaty.

When we finally squeeze past the sizeable crowd and make it to the table, I'm dismayed, but not surprised, to find her apparent bandmates to be equally cool and moody looking.

"Tillyyyyyy," she sings, standing up to kiss me on both cheeks like we're best friends finally reunited after years apart. "Come. Sit. Ollie, scoot over, my God."

Oliver gives Cubby a bland look but does as he's told, making extra room for me on the bench next to him.

"Tilly," Cubby says, "I'd like you to meet my band, Tongue-Tied."

"I thought your band's name was Rabbit Hole," Ollie interrupts.

Cubby glares at him. "We haven't been called that in ages."

"You were called that four months ago when you made me buy that Rabbit Hole T-shirt at your show in London."

"Right, but shortly after that we realized people started chanting 'bunny pussy' at our gigs thinking we meant a different type of hole," the other girl at the table says, giving Oliver a broad smile.

Cubby sighs. "Regardless. We're Tongue-Tied now. Tilly, these are my mates. Darcy, she's on bass . . ." The girl with streaks of pink in her hair winks at me. "Harry, who's on keyboard—"

"And sometimes sax. When the boss lets me," the handsome guy sitting next to me at the end of the table says, his glacier-blue eyes sparkling as he leans close to shake my hand. He's that alarming type of handsome that every Taylor Swift song has warned me about, and he's packing the extra lethal addition of an Irish accent. My traitorous cheeks flush at the broad smile he gives me.

"And this is Connor," Cubby says, draping her arm around the shoulders of the broodiest member of the group. "My boyfriend. He's on guitar and sometimes joins me in vocals."

Connor barely looks up, offering a grunt in acknowledgment, then shrugs off Cubby's arm, leaning against the wall and scrolling through his phone. What a charmer.

I give an awkward wave to the table. "How long have you been on tour?" I ask.

"What, six weeks now?" Darcy answers, looking to Harry for confirmation.

He shrugs, then subjects me to that smile again. "Sounds about right. Been such a blur."

"Where all did you go?"

"Feels like everywhere," Harry says, propping his elbow on the table as he takes a sip of his beer. "Couple shitholes in London. Few more in Brussels. Some stops in France. Wound our way down to Lisbon even. Cubby's mums joined us for that one."

"Mãe managed to round up all her friends from uni for it," Cubby says to Ollie. "They might as well have hired us to play a reunion for the turnout she got."

"Really great for our image," Connor mumbles.

Cubby glances at him, a hurt cracking her cool facade. "I thought you said you didn't mind that they came," she whispers. Connor rolls his eyes then goes back to his phone, Cubby still looking at him in that wounded way.

It feels like I'm eavesdropping, and I start bouncing my leg, hoping Darcy or Harry will continue talking. But they stare down at their drinks.

Even Ollie senses the tension, his body shifting and back stiffening, fidgeting in his seat like he's trying to identify the source of the change.

Cubby clears her throat, giving me a quick smile. "The tour's been great. Such a blast. Just two weeks left, though. We're already mapping out another."

Harry and Darcy nod enthusiastically.

"This time around Ireland. Isn't that right, babe?" Cubby says, cuddling closer to Connor.

"We'll see if we survive this one first, yeah?" Connor says. "Scoot out, will ya? I've gotta piss."

Darcy and Cubby slide out of the booth, letting Connor out. Instead of heading toward the bathrooms, he walks to the other end of the bar, sidling up to a pretty girl around our age.

We all pretend not to notice.

Well, all of us except for Oliver, who's staring straight across the space at Connor with a look that could kill.

"And what do you do, Tilly?" Darcy says, her voice bright to combat the dark cloud hanging over the table.

I do what I always do to try to defuse the tension, alleviate the pulsing emotions of others that press on my chest like they're my own: I make a joke about myself.

"After initially dabbling in starting small kitchen fires and spilling every drink I ever touched, I've found my true calling as a hand model," I say, batting my eyelashes. "Might try feet next. Heard there's a big foot fetish market on the internet willing to pay tons for my smelly socks."

Darcy and Harry blink at me for a moment before snorting with laughter. Even Cubby lets out a soft chuckle.

"Tilly's a writer," Ollie says, finally pulling his eyes from Connor. My cheeks burst into flames.

"Are you?" Darcy says, leaning forward. "What kind of writing?"

"Death certificates for boys with big mouths," I say, shooting Oliver my most menacing glare. He glances at me out of the corner of his eye then takes a sip of his beer.

"It's nothing, really," I say, tucking a strand of hair behind my ear as I turn back to Darcy. Talking about writing—this vague, elusive thing I want so badly my bones ache—feels like jumping off rocks into a lake: thrilling and terrifying with a really good chance you're going to expose your most intimate bits and bobs in the process.

"She's quite good," Oliver says. "Clever."

Who knew two syllables could make my heart swell like a

hot-air balloon, lifting me right off the ground and setting me gently in the clouds.

"I'm hooked already," Cubby says, and I'm glad to see some of the spark back in her eyes. "Go on."

I suck in a deep breath. I can do this. I can believe in myself enough to tell people about the thing that makes me happy. The thing I lose myself in. Even if nothing will come from it. Even if it's the world's biggest pipe dream. Writing is still something I love, and I'm allowed to love it openly.

"At first, I started with fanfic—"

"As God intended all great writers to start," Darcy says.

I beam at her. "AO3 has me in a five-year choke hold with no hope of letting go. It's both my greatest joy and the bane of my existence. I've been waiting like, fourteen months for the next chapter of this Steve/Bucky fic that left on a tumultuous sexual cliffhanger involving the metal arm. The. Metal. Arm. Who writes 148,000 words and is about to make my laptop melt from the sexual prowess of Bucky freaking Barnes using said metal arm then leaves the public hanging?"

"Oh. My. Gawd," Darcy says, eyes widening as she reaches across the table and grips my hand. "Are you talking about *Bucked by Barnes* written by LexiProse22?"

My mouth dangles open for a solid twenty seconds. "Do you want to be best friends?" I blurt out. Wow. Smooth. Very subtle.

I wait for the awkward look. That signal that I've crossed a boundary or been too forward and made her uncomfortable. It's the usual response when my mask slips off.

Darcy, Earth angel that she is, doesn't miss a beat as she nods and grins. "I think we already are, darling."

"I literally have no idea what you're talking about," Harry

says, giving us a dimpled grin. "But what's this website you mentioned?"

"Ready for some bionic arm smut, are you?" Cubby says, giving him a wink.

"Can't knock something till I try it, now, can I?"

We go on for another half hour, laughing and screaming about our favorite fandoms and ships. At first, I'm worried that I'm being too much. Too loud. That I'm misreading them and infodumping way too hard on strangers. I glance at Ollie, who hasn't said much, nervous I'm being embarrassing in front of his supercool sister. But his eyes are scanning over me, a soft smile tilted on that stern mouth that makes an absurd giddiness rush in my chest. Darcy, Harry, and Cubby seem equally enthusiastic, fighting over some obscure band that apparently has a very heated love triangle.

I can't stop all the excited words tumbling from my mouth, and, for the first time, I feel like what I'm saying in a conversation actually enhances it. That my volume, or the speed I talk, doesn't matter. That I can deep dive or bounce from topic to topic like a rubber ball and the people around me won't give me weird looks, but keep pace. Spur me on.

Maybe it isn't that I've been bad at conversations my whole life, but that I haven't been having conversations with the right people.

"What do you write about now, Tilly?" Darcy asks when we've all finally calmed down enough to think straight.

I shrug. How do you answer that? Everything? Nothing? I want to bare my soul on a page while simultaneously locking away every word that tries to pour out of my heart.

"I guess, at this point, I write about, uh, life? Which I know sounds incredibly vague and kinda dumb but it's true."

"I don't think that sounds dumb at all," Cubby says, reaching across the table to squeeze my wrist. "It's kind of the whole point of writing when you think about it, isn't it?"

I nod. "I just want to write something that makes people feel seen," I say quietly, chewing on my bottom lip.

There's another sentence on the tip of my tongue. I want to be brave. I want to say it. But can I really?

I glance at Oliver, and he's still looking at me. And something about that look makes me feel incredibly brave.

"I have ADHD," I say, curling my toes tight in my shoes.

No one bats an eye and . . . Wow, admitting it so casually feels like throwing back the curtains from a window in my chest and letting sunshine stream through.

"I like writing about how it shapes the way I see the world. How it makes some things harder. Some things more beautiful. I don't know. I'm probably not explaining myself super well."

"Tilly has an incredible blog," Ollie says.

"Do you?" Darcy says, eyes lighting up. "Can I read it? Sorry, is that like, incredibly rude of me to ask? You're just such a laugh and I'd love to see how you put that into writing."

I glance at Ollie, and his look is soft, his smile a gentle push for me to be brave one more time.

"What's your WhatsApp?" I ask, turning back to Darcy. "I'll send it to you."

Chapter 26

Rubber Meets the Road

OLIVER

I t was so great to meet you," Darcy says outside the bar, giving Tilly a hug. "And don't forget to send me that Harley/Ivy fic you mentioned."

"Send it to me, too," Harry says, also giving Tilly a hug. For some reason, watching him wrap his arms around her, seeing her press up onto her tiptoes to squeeze him tightly, sends a sharp feeling through me, my stomach twisting like a wrung-out dishrag.

"Don't worry about Harry," Cubby whispers at my side, putting her hand on my shoulder.

"What?" I ask, brows furrowing.

"Harry's got nothing on you, Oll. No need to get jealous."

I frown. "I'm not jealous. What would I be jealous of?"

Cubby rolls her eyes and smiles at me. "Can I stay with you tonight?" she asks.

"Of course," I answer automatically. "Why?"

Cubby lets out a long sigh. "Another fight with Connor. I've no idea where he's pissed off to, but I certainly don't want to share a room with the dickhead tonight."

"You always seem to be fighting with Connor."

"It's really none of your business, is it?" Cubby crosses her arms over her chest, dragging her toe along the sidewalk.

"You're my twin sister, Cubby . . . I like to think it's at least a little bit my business."

Cubby sighs. "Not tonight, Ollie. I just want to hang with you and not think about all the shitty things. Is that okay?"

I reach out, giving her a quick, one-armed hug. "Of course it's okay."

"I'll catch up with you in the morning," Cubby says, waving to Harry and Darcy.

"Don't miss the train or we'll be forced to leave you in the land of the happy," Harry threatens as he and Darcy start moving down the street.

"Even you aren't cruel enough to subject the innocent people of Copenhagen to that," she calls to their retreating silhouettes. Their laughs echo back to us.

"You don't mind if Cubby stays with us, do you?" I ask Tilly.

"Mind? I'm peeing with excitement. Hold on, let me just text my sister and give her a heads-up."

"You two share a room?" Cubby asks, grinning up at me with wide eyes. I can see pink touch Tilly's cheeks. In the faded light, it looks like Pantone 14–1714, Quartz Pink. It's lovely.

I cough. "Mona books rooms with a connecting door we leave open so it's more like a big suite for the four of us."

"Sure it is."

"Mona says it's fine," Tilly says, glancing up from her phone. "Let's go."

The night is misty and cool, and it does nothing to air out the fogginess of my head, Tilly running laps up there. Tilly and Cubby link arms as we walk, heads bowed close as they laugh and giggle. And it's like—God, I'm not sure of the right words—but it's like my chest is full and my limbs are warm and maybe it's okay for my head to be up in the clouds.

When we get back to the hotel, I'm surprised to see Amina or Mona has closed our joint door, the nightstands pushed between the beds as a lackluster barrier.

Tilly squeals, launching into some whispered conspiracy that Amina and Mona are actually madly in love but too scared to admit it to each other and somehow the closed door confirms everything. Cubby agrees with her every word.

We stay up way too late, the three of us talking. Well, Tilly and Cubby do most of the talking, the pair lying in opposite directions on Tilly's bed. But all three of us are equal in laughs.

I feel . . .

Well, this feeling is happiness. There's no mistaking it.

The next morning, I wake up to find Cubby gone and a text from her on my phone.

> Sorry I left without waking you . . . you know how much
> I hate goodbyes. Love youuuuuuuuuuu

I smile down at my phone. Love you back, I type.

A small noise from Tilly tugs my attention to the other bed. She's curled up, a little lump in the center of the mattress, her inky-black hair a striking contrast to the white duvet tucked around her, like she's sleeping on a puffy cloud.

A startling surge of feelings overwhelms me—a sharp prickle at the nape of my neck, a tightness in my chest, a rush of adrenaline down my arms—as I watch her breathe.

I tear my eyes away, scrolling madly through my phone until I find Marcus's name. I start typing in a moderately frantic way.

> I think I might be dying
>
> every time I look at Tilly it feels like my heart is going to explode
>
> I'm worried I might be having a heart attack?
>
> what does liking someone feel like?
>
> isn't your uncle a cardiologist? Can you get me an emergency appointment with him?

It takes Marcus four minutes to respond, which is rather alarming, seeing as I'm dying and all.

> hey, Oliver. Good to hear from you! I'm great, thanks for asking. How are you?

I blow out an exasperated breath through my nose.

> Glad you're well. I'm fine except for the whole possible heart attack thing

> lol who the hell is Tilly?

I bite back a groan. I don't want to get into the details right now, all I want to know is how I survive whatever terrifying thing is happening to my system.

nvm

I fall back against the pillows, dropping my phone next to me. My fingers tap wildly at my side as I try not to focus on the sound of Tilly's inhales and exhales, a rhythm that's become as familiar as my own.

Another text buzzes through.

the start of liking someone can be so overwhelming it feels a bit like you're dying. But that's only because you're on the precipice of really living

I read this over about seven times then roll my eyes.

what does that even mean? That doesn't make sense. This exchange has been useless

lmao. Miss you, too, mate

Tilly greets the day with a startling and scratchy yawn as she suddenly sits all the way up. Her sleepy eyes are heavy-lidded as she looks around the room, hair sticking out in wonky angles. My heart squeezes.

What the fuck.

"Did Cubby leave already?" Tilly asks, frowning as she looks at me. "I didn't get a chance to say goodbye."

I swallow past the knot in my throat. "That's kind of her way. She likes to pop in and out of people's lives with as much dramatic effect as possible."

"A woman of mystery," Tilly says, fixing me with a smile. I catch myself smiling back.

I continue to look at her, eyes fixed on her mouth, and I'm

surprised to find color creeping up her neck and cheeks like ivy. Pantone Burnt Sienna.

Tilly clears her throat then looks away, yawning again.

"What's that?" she asks, pointing at a plastic pharmacy bag on the dresser as she stretches her arms overhead. An envelope is propped on top of it. "Wait, is that a chocolate bar?"

I squint and make out the colors of a Cadbury dairy milk bar wrapper through the thin white plastic. "Guess so."

Tilly glances at me. ". . . Can I have some?"

"It's seven in the morning."

"Who are you, my dentist?"

"Be my guest," I say, waving at the bag.

Tilly scrambles across her bed like a rabid animal to the dresser.

"Hand me the card, will you?" I ask. Tilly tosses it at me, then turns back to the bag, fingers waggling like a cartoon villain.

I've just broken the seal on the envelope when Tilly screeches, causing me to slice my finger on the edge.

"What's wrong?" I ask, sucking on my bleeding paper cut.

"Um . . . nothing," Tilly says, backing away slowly from the dresser with her hands held up in surrender. "I changed my mind on the chocolate."

"Okay . . ." I say, drawing out the word.

"Okay. Bye." Tilly darts into the bathroom, and the shower is turned on moments later.

Good Lord, she's odd. I pull out the card and flick it open.

Loved seeing you, Oll. Got these to save you the trouble. Mind you, they're NOT to be worn with the hideous money belt under any circumstances.

xo,
Cubby

I kick back the covers and walk to the dresser, digging into the plastic bag. There's chocolate bars in there alright, but there's also something else. A shiny purple box. It takes me a second to read the label.

DUREX X-TRA PLEASURE

I drop the package and dart away like Tilly did moments ago.

Oh God, *Tilly*. She saw them.

Tilly saw the condoms.

I literally can't even imagine what she's thinking. Probably that I'm some creepy wanker who has his sister buy him condoms and chocolate.

I'm not sure this could get any worse.

The one thing I *am* sure of is that the next time I see Cubby, I'm going to kill her.

Chapter 27

Moonwalking Through
the Feels

A DHD can often cause obsessive thoughts.

Sometimes it's things like: *I need to get to a craft store TODAY and buy ALL the watercolor supplies because suddenly I am destined to become an artist but I MUST DO IT RIGHT NOW OR I MAY JUST DIE.*

Or it's: *Hey! Remember that time when you were eleven and you walked into a glass door at the art museum and shattered it and everyone laughed? Let's play that moment on loop for the next eight days until you've cringed so hard you've strained your butthole.*

Often enough, it's the simple and potent: *I am a clingy nightmare and everyone hates me* over and over until you kind of start to hate yourself.

But, for the last three days of traveling, the *only* thought that seems to go through my head is: *Oliver middle-name-that's-probably-delightfully-British Clark has condoms in his bag and I need to know who he plans to use them with.*

It's none of my business who Oliver has sex with. I know this. I can understand the rationality of that thought and why it is objectively true. But I can't, for the life of me, get my brain to listen to it.

I keep conjuring up all these fantasy girls that Oliver is in love with, picturing him kissing and touching them in the ways I want for myself. I break my own damn heart over and over again trying to guess what she'll look like, what she'll be like. Because I never imagine someone like me. It couldn't be me. No matter how badly I wish it was.

I'm nostalgic for a life and relationship I've never even had.

I will give myself some credit though and say, minus my extremely unchill reaction to finding the condoms, I've done a pretty decent job pretending like nothing's wrong. In fact, Ollie and I are getting along really well. And anytime we're working together or he's listening to me go on and on and *on* with some infodump, and the feelings I have for him start to build in my chest and clog up my throat, I've found that moonwalking out of the room is a safe way to exit and cry in private without him following me.

Our lodgings in Stockholm also provide me some space from Ollie. The hotel doesn't have connecting rooms, and because they only had one double and one single left, we've played sleeping musical mattresses and I'm bunking with Mona and Amina.

"I don't get why he gets his own room," I grumble to Mona. She scowls.

"I'm not about to have my eighteen-year-old intern sleep in the same room as his two bosses," Mona says.

She has a fair point.

"Well," I say, unzipping my suitcase, "I'm also your intern."

"You're my sister first and foremost."

My mouth twists up, but a little poke of happiness hits me in the ribs. "You've got me there. But you also shouldn't force your co-founder to sleep in the same bed as you when you could easily share with your sister," I say, flicking an innocent glance at Amina, Mona, and the mattress they're sitting on.

Mona blushes the color of hot tamales and scooches over so her hip is no longer pressed against Amina's.

"I—We—I . . . you thrash in your sleep," Mona sputters out. "I'm trying to make it out of this trip alive."

She stands, crossing her arms over her chest and wandering around aimlessly. I'm fully grinning now as my gaze slides to Amina, who's pressing her lips together to hide a smile. She shoots me a quick wink and I almost scream.

Love them.

Mona's cell phone rings, and she answers in a clipped tone. "Hello." Pause. "Oh. Yes. Hi. This is she."

She's quiet for a few more moments and that's about as long as it takes for me to lose interest and start scrolling through my phone.

My most recent Babble post is getting some traction, which is surprising and weird because it was a big, unedited post about how dogs are stimming masters.

Dogs get so excited they shake their butts into little torpedoes, start whining and hopping, then go grab their favorite toys to show you like they're telling you all about them. And we love that about puppies. Their excitement. Their outpouring of uncontrollable joy, something they wouldn't dare try and control. Why can't we love that about humans who stim, too?

I'm reading a comment from someone saying they're usually embarrassed by their vocal stims, but are going to start looking at them as big puppy energy because of my post, when

Mona screams. My soul nearly leaves my body, it startles me so badly.

"You won't believe this," Mona says, darting to Amina's side. "That was the buyer for Vers, the small chain in Amsterdam. They've been talking and planning for the fall, and changed their minds. They want to put in an order with us!"

"Shut up!" Amina says, gripping Mona's hands. "Are you serious?"

"Yes! They asked if we could come in tomorrow to show a few more of the jewel tone samples before they finalized their order."

"And what did you tell them?"

"Yes, obviously," Mona says, throwing her arms around Amina. "This could be *huge* for us."

Amina squeezes Mona back, rocking gently side to side. They both look so . . . *happy*. My heart swells watching them.

Mona breaks the moment, clearing her throat and pulling away, retreating back behind her Professional Lady™ walls. "We better get travel figured out," she says.

Amina's heart is still on her sleeve and in her eyes when she nods. "On it, darling."

"Let's try and get on the next flight out if we can. And that hotel we stayed at while we were there was relatively cheap, so hopefully they have another room open."

"I'll sleep on a bench near the canals if it means securing this deal," Amina says, pulling out her laptop and typing away. "Christ, the connection in here is awful," she says, swinging her laptop from side to side. "I can't get a site to load. I'm going to run downstairs to the desk and see if they can help." Amina jumps up and bolts toward the door.

"Wait," Mona says as Amina reaches for the handle. Mona glances at me. "Tilly, can you give us a minute?"

"And go *where*?" I ask, gesturing around the shoebox-sized room.

"The hall?"

"No, thank you," I say, sitting primly on the bed.

Mona looks like she's going to pop the vein bulging in her forehead, but she finds her cool. "Fine." She turns back to Amina. "Just get tickets for you and me. Coming back after the meeting tomorrow if possible so we don't need to get a room for two nights."

"Got it," Amina says, leaving the room.

Everything is quiet for a moment.

"You're abandoning us?" I cry.

"Don't be so dramatic," Mona says, moving like a well-dressed tornado through the hotel room as she gathers up her things. "Amina and I will likely be back tomorrow. Do you really think you can't handle one night without adult supervision?"

I straighten my shoulders, trying to look mature and wise and justifiably indignant. "Of course I can."

"Then what's the problem?"

"I just don't get *why* you wouldn't take me and Ollie with you. I really liked Amsterdam. I wouldn't mind going back."

"Hate to break it to you, but this isn't actually about you," Mona says, zipping up her makeup bag.

I give her a haughty sniff. "Well, that's simply not true. I have big main character energy. So what's your next excuse? Is this all a ploy to have a secret rendezvous with Amina? You don't have to pretend like you don't have feelings for her. We all see it."

"Would you stop?" Mona says, voice raised as she slams her handful of toiletries into her suitcase. "Not everything is a joke."

"Oh my God, why are you yelling?" I yell. "It was just a question."

"It's because I'm running out of money, okay?" Mona says, glaring at me. "There. Does that make you happy?"

"You're . . . what?"

"Running. Out. Of. Money," she says through gritted teeth. "My business is *failing*, Tilly. I can't afford to fly you and Oliver back to Amsterdam for the second meeting without going over budget. And I'm sure you can't wait to rub it in. So go ahead, let's have it." Mona crosses her arms over her chest, eyebrows furrowed and a deep frown curling her mouth.

"Why do you think I'd rub that in?" I ask, taking a step toward her.

"I . . . I don't know," she says, staring down at her shiny leather heels. "You act like I'm supposed to be perfect. Like you can't wait to catch me failing. And I'm . . . I'm just not. It's embarrassing."

I look at her, my heart cracking. "Mo, that's not true. Like, at all. You're the most successful person I know, and I love seeing you absolutely kill it. But you know you don't have to be perfect, right?"

Mona rolls her eyes then blinks rapidly, looking off to the side. "It's not that simple."

"What do you mean?"

"There's always been so much pressure on me to be some sort of success. Dad's been telling me I'd make the lists of influential people under thirty since I could walk." She takes a deep breath, using one hand to cup her forehead and shield her expression. "Then going off to Yale was weird. I was surrounded by these wildly high-achieving, rich, successful people and there's this constant undercurrent of competition and no matter how hard I worked, I felt like I was coming in last."

Her voice fractures, and she sinks onto the edge of the bed, shoulders slumped in a protective curve around her ears.

"Nothing was ever good enough. I felt like there was this other person I was supposed to be—someone serious and driven—and the more I leaned into it, the more Mom and Dad seemed happy with me. I don't know . . . sometimes I feel like I don't even know who I really am anymore. If I'm not perfect, if I'm not a business mogul or innovator or whatever else people expect me to be, then what am I?"

"You're my Mo-Mo," I say, reaching out and grabbing her hand. I hold it tight even though her fingers are stiff. "You're my force-of-nature big sister. You're the smartest person in the room. The girl who laughed and sang Taylor Swift songs with me while painting my nails. The person who loses their shit looking at pictures of baby elephants."

Two tears roll down Mona's cheeks, and she gives me a watery smile. "I really do love when they give bottles to baby elephants."

I bite my lip, giving her a sad, watery smile. "But Mo . . . you've got to realize that if anyone here feels like they have no room for error, it's me. I'm the one living in your shadow."

Mona's look cuts me open with its earnest pain. "I hate that you think that."

I shrug. "It's kind of hard not to."

Mona's eyes roam around my face like she can decipher some secret code in my features.

I'm starting to feel too much, too sharply, and I wave my hand to dissolve some of the seriousness. "You probably should keep getting ready," I whisper.

Mona shakes her head then turns fully toward me, gripping my shoulders. "This is more important."

"What is?"

"You, Tilly. Us. I'm done lying to myself that fixing our relationship can be put off until life calms down a bit."

"You think it needs fixing?" I say, a few teardrops plopping down my cheeks.

Mona's smile is devastatingly sad. "I know it does."

"I . . . I miss you, Mo. The old you."

Mona hugs me to her, hard and steady, my muscles melting as she runs her hand over my hair.

My throat squeezes tight, but I decide to be honest with my sister. "I feel like when you left for school, you changed. You . . . you stopped liking me. Or wanting to be my friend. And I don't know why."

"I'm sorry I've hurt you," Mona says. "I'm so sorry I've ever made you feel like I don't like you or that you aren't wonderful exactly as you are."

"It feels like I'm not good enough. Not for you or Mom or anyone. Like I'm an annoyance and a burden you're stuck with. You're the perfect older sister while I'm the family fuckup." My words crack on a sob as I press my face into her shoulder.

Mona holds me tighter, a small, fractured sound coming from her throat. "Being your sister is an honor, Tilly. I hate myself for treating you in a way that makes you feel otherwise."

I let out a deprecating snort.

"I'm serious," Mona says, pulling back to look me in the eyes. She's crying, too. "I can't change Mom or Dad. I can't make them treat you better. But I do understand. I know how hard it is to break out of any role they cast you in. I've folded in on myself under the weight of it."

It's never occurred to me that Mona might feel stuck, too.

"But you're so wonderful," Mona continues, tucking my hair behind my ears. "You're hilarious and energetic and brilliant and can pull a smile from just about anyone. I'm sorry I don't show you enough how amazing I think you are."

I don't know what to say, so I lean in to Mona again, letting her gently rock me from side to side as we learn to be comfortable in our silence.

"I really do love you, Tilly. So much," she whispers against my hair. "I'm going to get better at showing it."

Chapter 28

Risky Business

TILLY

Eventually, Amina and Mona leave, and I lounge in our room for a bit, scrolling through my phone. My emo moment with Mona has me feeling off-kilter: warm and bubbly but also jittery and ready to move.

For a minute, I contemplate going next door and annoying Oliver, but I know he's in his editing zone and it doesn't feel right to invade his bubble.

And maybe I want to be . . . alone? I'm not sure. I can never decide if I want the freedom of solitude or the energy of another person.

I roll off the bed and bear crawl to my backpack for my wallet, deciding I at least need to get out of this hotel room. Immerse myself in this beautiful new city.

The corner of my laptop sticks out from an inner pocket, and that's when I finally realize this zapping spark moving on a constant loop from my brain to my fingers is a want to write. Little thought bubbles and pretty words float through my head, shiny and delicious and begging to be chased down, captured on paper.

I make a mad grab for my backpack, zipping it up and dashing from the hotel room and out onto the sidewalk.

I walk for a few minutes through Stockholm's cobbled streets. Although it's overcast, the city has a cheerful radiance about it—the intricate stonework of historical buildings, the sleek and modern high-rises that reflect the city back to itself, bicycles and tulips and the river—and I absorb all the small details like sunlight on my skin.

My phone buzzes in my pocket, and I fish it out and see it's a text from Darcy.

> Hello, darling! How are you??

I grin. Darcy and I have texted a few times since meeting in Copenhagen, and I like to think we've actually become friends.

> Hi!! I'm good! How are you? What city are you in?

> Some shithole town outside of Frankfurt

> Pray for me

> But listen, I wanted to talk to you about something

> Mind if I ring you?

Half a second after I message sure, Darcy's call comes through.

"Right," she says by way of greeting. My grin grows wider. "Cubby's here, too."

"Hiya, Tilly," Cubby croons in the background.

"We've been reading your Babble posts—truly brilliant by the way, you constantly have us in stitches."

"Very clever," Cubby adds.

"And yesterday after a show, we got to talking with this other band—"

"They were a bit too poppy for my taste," Cubby says.

"Oh, yes. Far too much synth. This isn't 2014."

"And they tried to make a bagpipe moment happen and, like, artistically do I understand the carnal magnetism they were going for with it? Yes. Was it raw and did it create cognitive dissonance that reflected the political climate when juxtaposed with the pop-synth beats? Of course. But, did it work?"

"No," Darcy finishes. "But anyway, lovely people despite their confused sound. And we got to talking and long story short, one of the girls in the band, Hamda, has a cousin that runs this super trendy online magazine—"

"I thought it was Hamda's cousin's friend?" Cubby asks.

"Mmm no. Definitely the cousin."

"You sure?"

At this point, my head is spinning as I try to keep pace with these two, but it's a lost cause.

"Regardless of whose cousin or friend or whatever, Hamda knows the person running *Ivy*."

"Apparently it's like *Cosmo* meets *BuzzFeed* with a touch of *Elite Daily* but less desperately millennial," Cubby says.

"And they're *hiring*," Darcy says. "Looking to hire, quote, unique voices, unquote." There's a pause. "So what do you think?"

I'm silent, assuming Cubby and Darcy are going to continue talking over each other, but they don't.

"Think about what?" I ask.

"About *applying*, of course," Darcy says. "We showed

Hamda your Babble and she thought it was fabulous. Apparently her cousin has ADHD, too. We gave Hamda the link and she sent it to her cousin who said that you should send in your CV and some sample writing."

My stomach pinches. It's that rush again. Of knowing people are absorbing something I've created.

"I . . . uh . . ."

"Oh, Tilly, you *must* apply. You'd be perfect. We're texting you the link right now."

Sure enough, my phone buzzes with the application website. I scroll through it for a moment, reading the editorial assistant job description.

"I'm not sure I'm qualified for this," I say.

"Oh my God, literally who's qualified for any job anymore? You need ten years of experience for an entry level job at this point. Please apply, Tilly, please! You'd be so perfect for it."

"So perfect," Cubby echoes. "We're your biggest fans at this point. We're not above stealing your identity to submit an application on your behalf."

My head feels like it's full of bumblebees buzzing around my skull as I try to process everything.

Is this . . . Is this what having friends feels like? People who encourage you so unabashedly? It's overwhelming in the best possible way.

I'm scared. So scared. It's basically a guaranteed rejection, I'm a nobody with absolutely zero experience.

And yet . . .

"Okay," I whisper, then smile. "I'll apply."

Cubby and Darcy screech. "Perfect. I'll text Hamda to text her cousin to be on the lookout for your application. Do it today! Right now, if you can."

"Okay," I say again, my smile growing.

"Okay, we've got to run, Tilly," Cubby says. "Give our love to Ollie."

"I will," I say. "And, thank you—so much—for thinking of me. I'm really excited."

We end the call and I duck into a café, ordering a coffee and a pastry called kanelbullar, which looks a bit like a cinnamon roll but somehow tastes even better.

Grabbing a tiny table in the corner, I pull out my laptop, gulp my coffee, and, before I can overthink it, fill out the application. I submit samples of my writing, taking a risk and submitting some of my more vulnerable pieces about ADHD. I probably rush through it way too fast, my leg bouncing the entire time, but I want to get it over with, out of my way, before the doubt can fill me up too deeply.

When it's done, I take a deep breath. I feel kind of . . . proud of myself. Like I just did something proactive. Something good.

But I don't want to think about it anymore. If I start to want it too much, it will hurt all the more when a rejection comes in.

Pushing away those thoughts, I open a new tab, take another deep breath, and free-fall onto a fresh, blank page.

A few hours later, I've drunk enough caffeine and eaten enough kanelbullar that I feel my heartbeat in my toenails. I tap out the final lines of my blog post, then collapse back in my worn leather chair to read the final few paragraphs:

I've always thought my sister was perfect. That perfection was woven into her DNA like her black hair or brown eyes. She fits into every space she enters.

And, I've always thought messing up was the backbone of my genetic makeup. I have ADHD. My brain doesn't work like everyone else's. It always feels like my brain and body are being asked endless, probing questions, and they don't have an answer for any of them. I can't process them. And society tells us that means I'm doomed from the start. That my brain's unique way of functioning is a personality flaw. A lack of discipline. No spaces accommodate me, and I don't deserve to disrupt the room and carve out my own spot.

But maybe that's not true. It sure as hell isn't fair. My sister shouldn't have the burden of being expected to dominate every task she attempts. I shouldn't bear the weight of being labeled a screwup before I even try.

So, what if we tear down these boxes we're supposed to squeeze ourselves into? What if we undo the knots that keep us tied to expectations? What if we let each other, and ourselves, just be?

P.S. These are genuine questions. Ya girl doesn't have the answers, sooo . . .

P.P.S. This post was fueled by way too many cups of coffee from Drop Coffee Roasters . . . This isn't a sponsored ad or anything (yet), but we all gotta manifest those dreams, amiright?

I smile.

I really like what I wrote.

I guess I don't realize how heavily some words sit in my heart, and I forget that my hands can lift that weight by clacking away on a keyboard. Writing my feelings doesn't take them away, but it gives them another space to be held. A spot I can leave or revisit as I need to.

With shaky fingers, I hit *publish*. There. It's out.

Writing feels like a paradox. I simultaneously want the world to absorb my words and am horrified at the idea of literally anyone seeing them. I want to be known but not judged. I've liked writing little blurbs for colors on Mona's website, but it isn't the same. It isn't pieces of *me* in those words.

My blog feels like the safest place to put myself out there. It exists, in the Wild West of the internet, but I don't do anything to direct people to it. It's not so much putting myself out there as poking my head through the door. Actually, it's probably more than my head at this point. I've seen a pretty substantial spike in my Babble engagement and followers, which is simultaneously thrilling and terrifying.

I don't exactly understand *why* people care about what I have to say, but connecting and messaging with other neurodiverse people on the app has been one of the most validating experiences of my life. I finally understand what Ollie meant when he said that talking to people on the internet allows him to feel closer to others than actually being in their presence.

I try to dredge up self-control, but I'm me, so I have none, and I start refreshing the analytics page of the post. I hope someone's read it. I hope no one's read it. I hope . . . damn. No views. How does my untagged, non-monetized, personal blog not have four billion views within twelve seconds of me posting something?

I hit *refresh*.

Oh. Oh shit. It says two people have clicked. Okay. Wow. Oh my God. Cool. What are they thinking? Probably that it's dumb and they hate it.

I hit *refresh* again. I want another rush of dopamine like I got when that number changed from zero.

Wait. No. Not doing this.

I slam my laptop shut before the page finishes loading. This has "runaway brain train" written all over it. This obsessive need to click on something with the desperate hope for a virtual reward. The gut-punch of disappointment when there aren't any new likes. Or views. Or comments. That odd, expansive feeling of being so alone in a world of constant connection.

I wrote that post for me. Only me. And it felt *good*. I'm going to protect that, damn it. I do not need external validation on something that brings me joy. Except for the times I desperately do . . . but this summer is all about growth et cetera, et cetera.

I push up from the table, gathering my things and shoving them in my backpack. I leave the café and start walking down the street, popping in my earbuds and letting music cascade down my body. This is the kind of noise I like. It's concentrated and makes sense and I know to expect it. It's so different from the random, nails-on-a-chalkboard noises of crowded areas.

There's something so freeing about being in a new place. Being there alone. I am only in charge of myself. I can eat what I want. Go where I want. I don't have to worry about if someone else is having a good time. If they're bored. If my constant stops to look at the different things that hook my sticky brain are annoying them. I can be totally, utterly, me.

I melt into Stockholm's streets as I keep walking, every step etching a love note into the cobblestones. *Tilly Twomley was here and, God, did she have a good time.*

After a few blocks, I'm in Gamla stan, Stockholm's old town. The tourist traffic is heavier here, but I get why. The buildings are like Technicolor gingerbread houses, tall and thin and pressed tightly together. The edges are swooped in some places, sharp in others, the happy heights smiling down on the narrow streets.

My attention snags on a window display, and I scuttle over to the glass like a moth to a flame.

The storefront display is stacked top to bottom with shoes.

Not just any shoes.

Clogs.

I go ahead and let myself in.

The smell of leather and wood wraps around me like a hug, and I pull out my earbuds, taking in the gentle quietness of the shop.

All my senses hum and vibrate at a happy frequency as I drag my fingers along buckles and clasps while I weave through the shop. I pick up a hundred different shoes, studying them from all angles, admiring the intricacies of the different designs. A pair of wooden wedges with butter-soft leather and small carvings of leaves tempts me to reach for my wallet, but I also know the four-inch heels would likely lead to my demise, and, with as much melodrama as possible, I set them back in their spot on the shelf.

But then I see something that makes my eyes turn into giant hearts.

Bright. Red. Wooden. Clogs.

I approach them slowly like they're a skittish animal about to run away. I drag a reverent finger over the intricate painting on the tops. It's a landscape. Bushels of flowers tucked into a patch of green grass, all set against a perfect blue sky and a windmill in the distance.

I immediately think of Oliver. I wonder what color he'd find in some corner of the scene. What he'd say about the balance. Or the feelings. Or the way his eyes, sharp and intense and wonderfully deep, would roam over and over these bright red shoes.

I snatch them up and head to the register.

"*Hej hej!*" the older woman behind the counter says to me, ringing up the shoes.

"*Hej!*" I say back in greeting. "I love the shoes," I add.

"They are pretty, aren't they?" she says, turning them from side to side.

"And so authentically Swedish," I say, which is objectively the most cringey tourist thing I could have uttered. She gives me a funny smile then hits a few buttons on the cash register.

The price blinks at me, and I suck my lips against my teeth in surprise: 2200 krona. That's like . . . a lot, right? Or is it not?

I can't remember the conversion rate. Isn't it like . . . one US dollar is . . . fifty krona? Or . . . twenty-five krona? I try to stealthily take out my phone and pull up my conversion app without looking tacky and panicky, but I don't have any reception.

Okay. This is fine. Now's not the time to panic. I'm sure the conversion is either twenty-five or fifty krona for every US dollar. So that means 2200 is somewhere between forty-four and eighty-eight dollars. Which is . . . objectively a giant gap and kind of a lot for shoes but then again they're so pretty and authentic and like, when in Rome, right? Or, uh, Stockholm, that is. Whatever. I'm buying the damn things.

Out on the street, I immediately slip off my sandals and slide on my precious new hunks of wood.

What. A. Stunner.

I am, quite simply, the most esoteric bitch in Stockholm right now and I couldn't be more pleased. These shoes are now officially my entire personality.

I start wandering, my shoes clonking on the cobbles. I'm a bit dismayed to feel a blister forming on my heels, but the double-takes from what I imagine are tourists allow me to ignore the subtle throb. They probably think I'm some sort of Swedish fashion influencer and they're amazed at my flawless European style.

After a while, I recognize some of the buildings around me, and I realize I've meandered back to the hotel.

The place we're staying is small, and I take a moment to watch the fading golden light of dusk touch the building. We're on the second floor of the four-story hotel, and Oliver has the corner room looking out onto the narrow side street below us. The dying sunlight creates a glare on his window, and I'm suddenly kind of desperate to see him. To enjoy the calmness of his company.

Is he up? Is he working? Watching TV? Maybe he's on the phone with the mystery girl he has condoms for.

I hate the possibility of that idea and it pulls me forward until I'm standing under his window like the world's greatest heartsick cliché. Barf.

But, if I'm going to be a cliché, I might as well really give it my all. Looking around, I find a tiny pebble on the ground. I pick it up and toss it toward his window. It barely makes a sound when it hits the sill. Frowning, I find a slightly larger rock and chuck it, but I miss his window entirely. I grab the last stone I can find and hurl it at his window.

And . . .

CRASH!

The sound of shattering glass creates a similar sensation in my stomach.

I'm rooted to the spot as the window screeches open and Ollie's head juts out. He looks back and forth down the alley then directly down at me. "Tilly?"

"Hi, Ollie," I say, giving him a limp wave. Like an idiot.

"Are you alright?"

"I . . . uh . . . I was wondering if you were busy."

"You broke the window," Ollie says, stating the painfully obvious as he stares at the glass.

"Yeah. I can see that," I call back.

"Is there a particular reason you threw a rock at me?"

"It wasn't at you . . . just your window."

"I guess that's one way of looking at it," Ollie says.

"So . . . are you busy?" I ask, tapping my clog against the ground.

"Besides now having to figure out how to replace a pane of glass? Not particularly."

My grin is slow, but unstoppable. He's such a sarcastic ass. I hate that I find it so adorable. "Wanna hang out?"

Ollie grins right back at me.

Chapter 29

Death by Clog

TILLY

D o you like my new clogs?" I ask, kicking my feet out and tapping my wooden heels as we walk and eat our ice cream. I try not to wince at the stab of pain that shoots from the blisters straight to my kneecaps. "I'm practically a Swedish local at this point."

Ollie frowns, looking at my shoes as he takes a lick from his mint chocolate-chip swirl. "They're completely made of wood."

"Nothing gets past you, kid," I say with a wink, trying to make my collapse onto a nearby bench look casual and not like my feet are in so much pain they just gave out on me.

His frown deepens as he sits next to me. "But that's wrong, isn't it?"

"What? No." I pause. "How?"

"Well, wooden clogs like that are . . . Dutch, I believe?"

"Please don't stereotype the Scandinavians, Ollie. It's not cool."

"The Dutch are from the Netherlands. Just like that style of shoe. I mean, they even have tulips and a windmill painted on them."

I pause, staring warily at my shoes. He can't be right. "I know you're some sort of ridiculously amazing color-wordsmith-person whatever, but you clearly don't know fashion like yours truly," I say, hooking my hand under my knee and hoisting my leg in the air so my fabulous clogged foot dangles in front of his face.

Oliver pulls out his phone and types for a minute then holds up the screen for me to see. Sure enough, it's a little graphic showing that Swedish clogs tend to be wooden bases with leather tops and the all-wood look with the pointed tip is . . . Dutch. Damn it.

I push his hand away. "Why would they sell Dutch clogs in Sweden?"

"To make sales to gullible tourists?"

I growl at him. "Well . . . whatever. They were a steal and are still my new favorite pair of shoes. I'll probably wear them every day." . . . If they would stop rubbing my feet raw.

"How much did you pay for them?"

"Twenty-two hundred krona."

Ollie eats the last bite of his ice cream cone, tilting his head to look at me. "You consider that a steal?"

Oh no. A small trickle of dread travels down my spine. "Yeah. I think they're handmade. And that's like . . . what? Eighty bucks?"

Ollie pulls out his phone again and types for a moment. "Closer to two hundred," he says, showing me a conversion calculator of krona to US dollars.

My heart sinks.

Holy shit. TWO HUNDRED DOLLARS? I paid two hundred dollars for a pair of two-by-four torture devices parading as shoes? I can't even return the damn things because they're soaked in my foot blood.

"Looks like you can get a pair online for about twenty-five

quid," Oliver says, scrolling through his phone as he pours salt in my (foot) wound. "I'd say you drastically overpaid."

I turn my head away from him, feeling like an absolute idiot. An embarrassed breath rattles my chest, and I want to cry. I can feel Oliver watching me, so I do what I can to keep it together.

He does one of his little cough things that always snatches up my attention. Nope. Not gonna work. I will not be Pavlov's freaking dog to those strangely precious nervous coughs of his. Not me. I'm impenetrable. I'm made of ice. I'm—

"I'm sorry," Ollie says, shocking the hell out of me by reaching out and placing his palm on my upper arm. "I was teasing you. I love your new shoes. Worth every penny."

I turn to look at him, my gaze tracing the knuckles of his hand, up the curve of his arm, to that sharp jaw and big nose and those soft brown eyes. Did I say I was made of ice? Because, at the moment, I'm more like a puddle of warm . . . goo. Or something less gross. But warm. You get the idea.

"The colors are brilliant," Ollie says, leaning forward to look at them. "Controlled chaos at the tips of your toes. Could I take a picture of them?"

And, for some odd reason, that right there makes them worth the embarrassment of my cultural confusion and the devastation to my poorly converted bank account. Or, at least, it does for a second. I really do wish I hadn't spent so much money on them.

Ollie pulls out his phone, snapping a few pictures. He smiles at the screen, then inches toward me on the bench, showing me.

"The lighting is a bit dark," he says, his shoulder brushing mine. "But I think I captured it well enough that I can correct it later. I love the hints of pale pink and yellow to illuminate the scene and draw your eye to the center. I'm guessing it's

Pantone 12–1706, Pink Dogwood, and 11–0620, Elfin Yellow. I actually have the perfect other three photos to go with that pink."

He tilts his head even closer to mine, zooming in on a section of the shoe and pointing out the spot behind the windmill that makes it look like sunlight is shining from my shoes.

I look at him, taking in the devastating swoop of his eyelashes, the excited slant of his mouth, the tiny bump on the bridge of his nose.

After a moment, he turns to look at me, too. His gaze skips from my eyes to my cheek, then traces to my mouth.

We pause, the world shrinking to only us and this park bench and the coolness of this summer night. I want him to kiss me. I want him to like me. I want . . .

I want Ollie. His quirks and his bluntness and his gorgeous brain and pretty face.

And when he looks back at me like this—undivided attention, sharp intensity—it's easy to imagine some alternate universe where he wants me, too.

Which hurts. It's so disastrously painful that he won't ever want me like that. That there's some lucky person out there who's already the focus of his want. Someone else who makes this moment not belong to me.

A chilly breeze pushes through our bubble, lifting my hair and sharpening the pain in my chest until a shiver runs down my spine. Ollie notices. He notices everything.

"You're cold," he says, eyebrows furrowing as he looks around like he's trying to see the wind. "We should head home."

I nod, standing up with him. I wrap my arms around my middle like I can keep together my cracking heart.

Oliver starts walking and, with a deep breath, I move to follow him.

Except, after one step, so much pain erupts in my feet and darts through my body that my knees buckle and I crumple to the sidewalk, letting out a *yip* of pain as I slap against the concrete, limbs landing in odd angles.

Ollie whips around, eyes bulging as he looks at my boneless form.

"Are you alright?" he asks, moving back to my side to hover over me.

Not sure how to explain that if I could die right here and now, I would, I wave limply at him and let out a small grunt. "Yeah. Just have a tiny blister."

Ollie's eyes trace down to my feet. "Tilly, is that *blood*?"

I look across my body and, sure enough, a line of blood is trickling out from the edge of my shoe and wrapping around my ankle.

"I'm fine," I say, trying to move to a more dignified position on the ground.

Oliver bends over me, sliding the back of my left clog down my heel a bit. I have to bite my lip to not scream.

"Oh my God, your feet are massacred," he says, dropping the clog and backing away like I'm radioactive.

"Don't be such a drama queen," I say, finding some inner strength to drag my body up to a standing position. I take a wobbly step as more blood fills my clogs. Even my blisters start to blister.

"Look at you. I've seen butchered meat in better condition."

"Wow. Always such a charmer," I hiss out, continuing my painful shuffle down the street.

"Tilly, stop for a moment."

"I appreciate the concern. I really do," I say, looking at him over my shoulder, sweat prickling my skin. "But if I stop walking there is a very good chance I won't be able to start again. And I'll probably cry."

"Do you have other shoes?"

I blink at him as I hobble along, then pat down my torso like I might find them in some giant hidden shoe pocket. Where *are* my other shoes? "Shit. I think I left them at the shop after I bought these and put them on."

Ollie bites his lip as he continues to watch my feet. "What if I . . . What if I carry you?" he says, stopping me in my (painful) tracks.

"C-carry me?"

"On my back? Maybe? You can't keep walking like this."

I stare at him with wide eyes. That would mean touching him. And him touching me. Wrapping my arms and legs around the guy I'm pining stupid hard for. All of which puts me at extreme risk for doing something absolutely mortifying like . . . sniffing his hair or . . . or *sighing* in his ear. Or, I don't know, groping him and his black button-down.

But, as another slice of pain shoots through my gnarled feet, there isn't really another option. Or, more accurately, there isn't a universe where I would turn down getting closer to Oliver Clark.

"Okay," I say at last, drooping a bit. I plop back down to the ground. I gingerly slide off one of my ridiculous clogs. The drag of the wood and the whoosh of air on my open wounds feels like a knife and I whimper, tears pricking at my eyes as I squeeze them shut.

Breathing in that aggressive, rhythmic way women giving birth do, I pull off the other. A wave of nausea hits me from the pain and my skin gets clammy and gross. This couldn't get worse.

And then, I feel the soft weight of a cool palm on my cheek. My eyes fly open.

And land on Oliver crouched in front of me. He flinches (rather dramatically) at what I imagine is my wild, googly-eyed expression. Ollie's eyes are similarly wide as they slide to look at where his hand rests on my skin, like he doesn't know how it got there. Like he doesn't know how to move it.

"Hi," I blurt out. Really loudly. Like a dumbass. But, truly, what am I supposed to say? Oliver is touching me and I think my system is short-circuiting.

"Hi," he says back, still frowning at his hand on my cheek.

With what seems like effort, he pulls his hand away, eyes still locked on my skin. After a long moment, he stands, reaching out to help me up. I gingerly stand, and Oliver turns, bending at the knees considerably so our heights are more even.

"Hop on," he says, glancing at me over his shoulder.

In a perfect world, I beautifully float onto his back, arms and legs wrapping gracefully around him.

In reality, I'm sweaty and nervous and end up collapsing on him like an overeager linebacker after whacking him in the chest with my wooden clogs gripped in one fist.

He doesn't seem to notice.

Oliver hitches me up higher, looping his arms under my thighs, and I, quite simply, melt.

He starts walking, and every step presses my chest closer into him, and I hold my arms around him a little tighter. I wonder if he can feel the way my heart is clanging around in there.

"Alright?" Ollie asks, his voice the soft opposite to the sonic boom of my racing thoughts.

"Yeah," I say back. Because, yes, my feet hurt and are still bleeding and I'm not sure I'll ever be able to wear shoes again, but Ollie just touched my cheek and is now holding me in his arms and seems genuinely concerned about my well-being and I've never felt so wonderfully alright in my life.

"Only a few more blocks," he says, as if I'm not silently begging for this walk to never end.

All too soon, we're back at the hotel. Oliver stops in front of the steps of the entrance. He turns, depositing me on the second step so I don't have to reach too far down. I might be back on solid ground, but I don't think my head and my heart will ever come down from the clouds after that walk.

Oliver moves past me up the stairs, fishing around in his pockets for his keys. I sling my backpack around to my side, looking for the same. This hotel is old and still uses traditional locks and large brass keys for the rooms and access to the lobby.

My searching has turned a bit frantic by the time Ollie swings open the front door. "Everything okay?" he asks as I rip my backpack fully off and start dumping stuff on the ground.

"I think I've lost my room key," I say, dread dripping down my throat and settling in my stomach as a familiar panicky spiral swirls around my brain. Damn it. Why do I always lose everything?

"Where did you lose it?" Oliver asks. Which is objectively the most useless question ever.

"If I knew where I lost it, I wouldn't have left it there, would I?" I snap, turning the side pockets inside out.

Oliver is still for a moment, watching me spiral, and, for some reason, it makes it all the worse. I don't want to be like this. I don't want to be messy and careless and forgetful and—

"Tilly," he says, his voice soft and touch secure as he reaches out and circles my wrist, pausing my frantic fingers. "It's okay," he continues. "It's just a key. I'm sure they have extras. We can go ask the desk."

I close my eyes for a second, trying to get the courage to look at him, knowing full well the expression of annoyance that'll be etched on his features. It's what's always on someone's face when I screw up.

But, when I finally glance at him, he looks . . . patient. And calm. And not that he's worried about the missing key but worried about . . . me.

"Okay," I say, nodding.

Ollie nods back then unlocks the door to the foyer.

A bored-looking guy is slouched in a plastic chair behind the table serving as the check-in desk, scrolling on his phone and not bothering to look up when the little bell above the door signals our presence. His crooked name tag reads LIAM.

After a moment, Oliver clears his throat. Liam glances up then back to his phone.

"Yeah?" Liam says, barely stifling a yawn.

"Hi. Yes. So sorry to bother you," Oliver says, "but my er . . . uh . . . my . . . friend . . ."

Oliver trips over what to call me so thoroughly that even Liam notices and looks up, assessing us a bit closer. "Yes?" he drawls.

"She's lost her room key and needs a replacement," Oliver finishes, the words shooting out in rapid fire.

Liam looks at Oliver, then me, then my hands clutching my bright red clogs and my disheveled backpack, before finally landing on my feet.

"Do you have identification?" Liam asks.

Oliver and I exchange panicked glances.

"I . . . the room is under my sister's name. Room twenty-seven."

"Are you listed as a guest in the room?" Liam asks, yawning again.

"I don't know. Can you like . . . check? Or something?" I say, waving at the ledger on his desk. "My name is Tilly. Tilly Twomley."

Liam stares at me like I've made his day excruciatingly hard, then glances at the ledger. "That name isn't listed," he says.

"Um. Okay. I do have my ID if that helps," I say, digging into my backpack. "We have the same last name."

"No," Liam says, attention back to his phone. "Unless the person whose name is on the room can show ID, I can't help you. Sorry," he says, not sounding sorry at all.

Oliver and I look at each other again, totally clueless about what to do.

"I'm a guest of Mona Twomley," I say with fake assertiveness, pointing at the spot in the ledger where I see her name. "And I demand access to the room."

"Right," he says with a sneer. "Again, I still can't give you a key without her here and your name not being listed. And I also, quite frankly, don't believe you whatsoever." Liam gives me an obvious sweep from tip to toe, lingering on my shoeless, horrifying feet.

Well.

I do feel a tiny bit less guilty about the whole shattering-the-window incident from earlier after this guy's attitude. But what am I going to do? Sleep on the stoop? I've seen one too many abduction shows to envision that ending well for me.

"You can stay with me," Ollie says, like he can hear my thoughts.

I look at him. "What? No. Okay. Are you sure?"

He gives me a puzzled look before offering a subtle smile. "Of course. Come along."

He turns and heads up the stairs. I give Liam one last look, wishing him massive inconveniences on all future morning commutes, before following Ollie.

"I . . . er . . . shall I sleep on the floor?" Oliver says, as we both stare in shocked horror at the realization that his room has only one bed.

One. Bed.

"No!" I pretty much shout at him. Very subtle. "I mean,

you shouldn't do that. I'm the one that lost their room key. If anyone is banished to a dirty hotel carpet, it should be me."

"You know I can't let you do that," he says after a moment, eyes still fixed on the mattress.

I shrug, swallowing past a dry throat. "I guess we could share?" I wave at the bed that has the presence of a third person in this room.

Oliver's eyes slowly grow wider and wider like he can burn a hole through the comforter. Then he nods. "I guess we will."

We both stand there awkwardly for another minute, not sure what to do next.

"I don't have any pajamas," I say, more to myself than him.

Oliver blinks twice, then nods, opening a dresser drawer and riffling through neat stacks of clothes. I kind of love that he's unpacked his suitcase and found a home for every item despite us only being here for a few days.

"Maybe these will work?" he says, handing me a bundle. I let a pair of pajama bottoms and a large gray T-shirt unfurl in my hands. The fabric is soft, just the right amount of worn, and I can smell Oliver on them already. I don't know why it makes my cheeks heat.

"Thanks," I mumble, barreling past him to the bathroom and shutting the door behind me. I slip on his clothes. The drag of fabric over my skin makes me shiver, something about it feeling simultaneously foreign and like the nicest reminder of home.

What the fuck.

I look in the mirror, trying to have one of those movie moments where a great epiphany comes from staring at your own reflection. Maybe, if I look hard enough, I'll be able to rid myself of this excruciatingly painful crush and get some sense that having a one-sided obsession with a boy I'll be saying goodbye to in about a month isn't a great idea.

Tragically, I get nothing but a slightly sweaty, red-faced girl with wild hair and her heart in her eyes.

Cool.

Love this for me.

There's no way this won't end badly.

Realizing the longer I hide out in the bathroom, the greater the chance he'll think I'm pooping, I flick off the lights and step out.

Oliver's put on a different set of pajamas, and he's sitting on the edge of the bed, scrolling through his phone. He looks so . . . so . . . outrageously adorable. The swoop of his hair across his forehead, the slight curve to his back as he hunches over his phone, the earnestness with which he's typing away on the screen, probably talking to someone about some wild use of the color mauve.

"Ollie, are you dating anyone?" I blurt out. Then slam my mouth shut so hard my teeth rattle.

His head whips to look at me. "I beg your pardon?" he asks.

I let out a sigh. "I . . . uh . . . I wanted to know if you're seeing anyone. Or like . . . *you know.* Because it probably wouldn't be cool for me to sleep with you if you are."

Oliver stares at me for a moment, and I watch as his eyes go comically, alarming wide. "No!" he shouts at me, waving his hands and standing up. "I mean, I'm not. But this is not . . ." He gestures wildly between us then points at the bed, shaking his head.

Wow. Cool.

"I know that," I say, crossing my arms over my chest. "There's no reason to act so horrified at the idea."

"I'm not horrified," Oliver says, sounding horrified. "I'm . . . I'm . . ." He lets out a deep breath, his shoulders slumping. "That caught me off guard. I think what I'm trying to say is, I'm not romantically involved with anyone. I wouldn't share a bed with you if I was. But, like, I didn't want you to think I was assuming . . . What made you ask that?"

I shrug. "I just wanted to check. I don't want to be disrespectful to anyone out there that might be . . . special to you."

Oliver continues to stare at me, the silence pressing against my chest, pulling more words out of me.

"And I saw the condoms Cubby got you. Obviously," I say, my pulse hammering in my throat as the word vomit continues to spew out of me. "So I kind of assumed—"

"Cubby bought those as a joke," Oliver says, rubbing his eyes, his cheeks turning pink. "Some really odd, perverted sibling joke. I'm not currently . . . um . . . using them."

I nod, pressing my lips against my teeth to hide the elated smile that wants to stretch across my face.

Oliver isn't seeing anyone. He's not having sex with anyone. This doesn't change that my obnoxious-as-hell yearning is totally one-sided, but it does loosen the tight knot that forms in my gut at the idea of him with someone else.

"Cool," I say at last, nodding as I walk to the opposite side of the bed.

"Cool," Ollie repeats.

We stand in some weird stalemate on our sides of the bed, waiting for the other to make the first move.

My body is buzzing with energy, my mind whipping around like a puppy chasing its own tail. I can't stay still any longer. I can't.

"Welp," I say, pulling back the covers. "Probably should get some sleep. Early worm eats birds and all that."

"Right," Ollie says, following my lead.

We both sit on our edges of the mattress, then awkwardly swing our legs onto the bed. Half my body is hanging over the side, and I can honestly say I've never been so tense in my life.

Oliver coughs. "Good night," he says, reaching out and turning off the light.

"Night," I whisper, having a total internal panic as we're plunged into darkness.

Oh my god, what do I *do*? I can't maintain this half-over-the-edge pose all night but like . . . what's the alternative? Do we sleep on our backs? Like two . . . I don't know, corpses? I sure as hell will not be sleeping butt to butt. Even the idea of my butt cheek touching Oliver's butt cheek makes me do a full body cringe. Crap. Did he feel that? How could he not have, I just created a small earthquake across this ridiculously tiny mattress. We can't lie on our same sides though because I don't trust myself to not curl around him like a needy koala. I—

"Are you okay?"

"Hm?" I squeak out. Wow. Ariana Grande has nothing on these octaves I'm hitting.

"Are you okay?" Oliver repeats. "You seem a bit . . . fidgety."

I swallow then clear my throat, feeling embarrassed. "Sorry. I'll be still. I don't mean to be so squirmy. But the second I think about being still, my body's like, 'Hey, watch me thrash around!' and then my breathing seems all loud and then it's like I forget how to breathe and I—"

"Tilly." Oliver's voice is soft. Deep. It hits straight to my heart, sending ripples through my chest like a stone into water. Then he turns and faces me. "I really don't mind sleeping on the floor. I don't want you to be uncomfortable."

And, shit. This is one of those moments. The type where someone says something not particularly special, but it guts you all the same. The clarity of the words. The gentleness they're said with. All of it makes my heart skip a beat and my throat close up and tears prick at my eyes because it just feels like someone . . . *cares*.

Not someone.

Oliver.

Oliver cares . . . about me.

I clear my throat, deciding to be brave. "I think what makes me uncomfortable is how badly I want to touch you."

Oliver is still.

Really still.

Like, as still as I wish I could have been two minutes ago so he wouldn't have asked me what was wrong and I wouldn't have OPENED MY GIANT MOUTH AND SAID WHAT I JUST SAID.

"Okaygoodnightbye," I say in a rush, throwing my entire body to the edge of the mattress and burying my head under my pillow. Maybe I *should* go sleep on the street.

I'm barely breathing, mortification swamping my body. Why why *WHY* did I say that? What did I think would happen? What was I—

There's a tap on my back. I pretend I don't feel it. Maybe he'll think I fell asleep in the thirty grueling seconds since I last mortified myself.

Another tap. Oh God.

"Oliver," I whisper. "Please, *please* don't make me acknowledge that I just spoke out loud."

This time, it's not a tap. Oliver gently lays his palm across my back. Okay, now I'm really not breathing. I feel him spread his fingers wider, brushing the edges of my shoulder blades.

"I—" Ollie clears his throat. "I want to touch you, too."

My eyes shoot open. Excuse me, *what*?

A cool, calm version of me would let his words linger in the air. Say something delicate back. Maybe slowly roll over, letting his palm glide across my body as I turn to face him.

Instead, I whip around, crushing his hand under me and accidentally bringing my face two centimeters from his. "You do?" I say. It's a whisper, but it feels like I might as well be shouting.

I hear Oliver swallow, then I feel his nod against the pillow, the dark hotel room making his face nothing but soft shadows and glinting eyes.

Moving slowly, I reach between us, pulling his hand out from under me. I hold him by the wrist for a moment, teetering on the edge of some great big decision I don't even know the question to. Then, I place his palm on my shoulder.

Ollie releases a breath, the warm heat of it caressing my cheek. I feel little pulses and jumps in his fingers. Carefully, he slides his hand up, moving over the curve of my neck to the angle of my jaw. His fingers brush against my cheeks then tunnel into my hair. He lights up every nerve ending in my body as he runs his fingers against the locks, tracing a strand to its end. Curling it around his finger. He repeats the movement like now that he knows what it feels like to touch me, he can't stop. He finally brings his palm to rest at the back of my head, holding me, the slightest pressure bringing me closer. He doesn't have to tell me twice.

I cuddle nearer, and he tucks my head under his chin.

I breathe him in like it's my first taste of oxygen. He's warm and heady and I feel like I could pass out from the smell of him alone.

My own hand starts moving, and I wrap my arm around him, sliding my palm across his waist to his back. My middle finger rests between the muscles on either side of his spine. I drag my hand up, feeling him suck in a deep breath as I do it. My wandering fingers finally stop at the nape of his neck, the ends of his hair curling between my fingers like cool silk.

We stay like this for endless moments, our breaths moving together, our chests touching with each inhale.

I didn't know it was possible to feel this much all at once.

"This is really nice," I whisper into the hollow at the base of his throat. I feel him swallow.

"Incredibly," Oliver says, squeezing me gently in emphasis.

"I don't think I'll be able to fall asleep," I say.

Oliver laughs, soft and silent, but I feel it reverberate straight through me. "I don't think I will, either, but we both ought to try."

It could be minutes or it could be hours, but, eventually, Ollie's breathing turns deeper. Steadier. It sounds like the tide going in and out.

I'm glad *he's* able to sleep. Couldn't be me. No way. Not when Oliver freaking Clark has his arms wrapped around me. I think I'll be awake forever. There's no way I could ever sleep and miss a moment of this. I'm feeling too much. It's all so perf—

I fall into the deepest sleep of my life.

Chapter 30

Just Kiss Already

OLIVER

The next few days are a bit of a blur. Mona and Amina collected us in Stockholm after striking a decent deal in Amsterdam, and the refreshed capital has breathed new life into the second half of the tour, making them squeal with a giddiness I didn't think either was capable of. The only person louder in all the excitement was Tilly.

Mona rented a car in Stockholm, driving us to Hamburg, then Berlin, and finally Prague before we went back to air travel. I usually hate car rides, all the buzzing mechanical sounds for hours on end making my skin crawl, but even a ten-hour trek across the continent wasn't too bad with Tilly crammed in the backseat with me.

We still found things to bicker about every few hours, but it's somehow different than before. Like we're both holding back a smile as we annoy the other. And between the arguing, we'd talk, Tilly listening to me ramble about color, her talking about her writing. Other times, we'd be silent, periodically texting each other songs back and forth in some sort of modern equivalent of a mixed tape.

Ruhe secured another boutique vendor in Prague, and from there we boarded a cramped flight to Granada, Spain.

And, wow, do I love this place. It's hot and dry and gorgeous, every shade of beige and green surrounding the landscape, making me buzz with excitement in the subtle differences.

And, somehow, Tilly makes it all the lovelier with her wide smile and booming laugh as I photograph her through the city.

We've wandered our way to the outskirts of the town, where thick tangles of plants hug the old white stucco buildings.

An intricately carved door has caught my interest, pulling me deeper into the richness of the dark wood and the precise angles of the design.

"It's Pantone 483 I believe," I tell Tilly, whose head is tilted to the side as she falls into the pattern with me. "A rich brown but with obvious rusty red notes. The contrast of it with the white is rather astonishing, isn't it?"

"Hell yeah," Tilly says, taking a step toward the door and dragging her finger over it.

At first, I think she's only humoring me, and the heat of embarrassment swamps me, but then she looks over her shoulder and gives me one of those grins that Shakespeare probably would have written an entire book of sonnets about.

"It reminds me of your hair," she says, looking back to the door.

My jaw falls to the dirt because, now that I think about it, the color is very similar to my hair. But I can't believe Tilly put that together. That she would see me in colors like I see the world. It shoots a nearly painful surge of feeling through my chest and up my throat.

I don't really know what to say, because the emotions swirling through me feel important, but words don't come easily.

Instead, I lift my camera to my eye, capturing Tilly's gaze in profile as she looks with something like delight at a door that reminds her of the color of my hair. The click makes her turn.

"I wasn't ready," she says, scrunching up her face but unable to hide that smile that comes so easily to her.

I take another picture.

"Ollie, oh my God, these are going to be terrible. Stop it," she says, reaching toward me. I dodge her hands and snap a few more.

She's laughing hard now, and I know every single one of these photos will be masterpieces.

"You're the worst," she says at last, choosing a new tactic and slapping her hands over her face to hide from me. I take a few snapshots of that, too.

"I'm sorry," I say, letting my camera hang around my neck. "My finger slipped."

"Four hundred times? Sure." Tilly reaches out and gives me a playful shove. "Let's get serious and take some for Ruhe."

"Right. Because 'serious' is the first thing that comes to mind when I think of you."

"I'm sure ketchup is a close second," Tilly says, and a burst of laughter erupts from me. Tilly turns, looking at the door once again. "We could do something where it looks like I'm pushing it open," she says, placing her hands against the wood.

"I like that idea," I say, holding up my camera and focusing the lens. Her nails are a bit obscured in the position she has them in.

"A bit to your right," I instruct. Tilly leaves her hands firmly planted on the door and shifts the rest of her body sharply to the right until she's making an awkward angle.

"Not your legs. Put your hands—no, not there. Over a bit to—" I put the camera down, moving to her and gently wrapping my fingers around her wrists. A sharp dart of energy shoots up my arm and echoes down my spine. Tilly looks at me like she felt it, too.

Carefully, trying not to create any more . . . sparks, I move her hands and place them against the wall so they're tilted to the side. Her mismatched rings glint in the sun, the small stones and gold creating a glow across her skin.

I stand there, staring, forgetting that I'm supposed to be doing anything but looking at the graceful lines of her fingers, the way the light slopes up her arms and kisses her cheeks. She's . . . she's . . .

Tilly is everything.

"What's wrong?" she asks, her tone quiet.

"Nothing," I say, stepping away from her. "Sorry."

I hold up my camera and click the shutter button a few times then adjust my angles. Everything in me feels shaky, like my body turned itself inside out.

"I think we got a few good ones," I say past my dry throat.

"Noice," Tilly says in a goofy voice. "Wanna keep exploring?"

I nod, and it's all the encouragement she needs to start moving.

We walk for a while in comfortable silence, the day crisp and clear, offering perfect views of our hilly desert landscape. Eventually, Tilly veers off the main road onto a dirt path that heads down into a valley.

"Where are you going?" I ask, trailing after her.

"I don't know!" Tilly says, giggling as she picks up speed down the hill. Dust kicks up at her ankles and it looks like, at any moment, she'll leave the ground altogether. Fly away.

"We don't have a map. And service is spotty at best," I continue, pulling my phone out of my pocket and glancing at the low bars in the upper corner as I try to keep pace with her.

"That's what makes it an adventure." Tilly glances at me over her shoulder, and her grin is so full and vibrant, I almost trip over my own feet.

At the base of the hill, she stops running, and we both work to catch our breath between laughs.

"Come on," she says at last, gripping my wrist and tugging me after her as if I won't follow wherever she goes. "I think I hear water."

"Water?" I nearly shriek. "What do you plan to do if we find water?"

"Honestly, Oliver, do you think I *ever* have a plan?" Tilly says, turning around and tapping me on the nose before skipping down the path. "Being planless and pantsless are my two favorite states of being."

"I beg your pardon?" I choke out. Great. Now, I'm picturing her without pants. Good lord, this girl is clearly trying to kill me.

"Beg away, darling," Tilly says in that awful attempt of a Cockney accent she has.

She cuts left suddenly, squeezing between a thick tangle of shrubs. I stop short, hesitating to dive into unknown flora that could easily give me a rash.

And then Tilly gasps and the sound kicks my heart into overdrive that something bad happened.

I plunge into the plants.

And nearly run Tilly over.

She's staring straight ahead, mouth hanging open. My eyes get stuck on her. The curve of her nose. The white edge of her teeth. The angle of her jaw and the way her shallow breaths make her chest rise and fall.

Tilly is lovely. There's no other way to phrase it.

Without looking at me, she reaches up her hand, placing her fingers on my cheek and swiveling my head so I can see what has her attention.

And, wow, her gasp wasn't an exaggeration.

A cerulean pool—a lullaby for my senses—is shaded by a ring of small trees and shrubs, a gentle stream trickling down rocks and into the basin. Beams of sunlight glint off the surface in little golden triangles, turning the tropical pocket into a kaleidoscope of beauty and color.

I sense Tilly's gaze land on me, and I turn to her. We look at each other in awed silence for a moment, before both breaking into grins.

"Let's go," she says, disrupting the silence in that wonderful way of hers.

Next thing I know, I'm no longer picturing Tilly without trousers on. She's demonstrating the look in real time after kicking off her shoes and peeling away her socks. She rips off her T-shirt next, then stands there for a moment, in nothing but her underwear and sports bra, a square of light making her absolutely glow. She lets out a giddy screech, sprints toward the water, and jumps in.

Bloody. Fucking. Hell.

Tilly's head bobs to the surface, and she raises her smile to the sun.

"Oliver. Get in here. It's perfect." She ducks back under the water.

In a haze, I shuck off my black T-shirt and trousers, shoulders hunching in on myself in awkwardness.

Tilly resurfaces again, looking around then smiling when her eyes land on me. The water has her hair a midnight black, the sun illuminating her from behind.

"What are you waiting for?" she shrieks.

Something about that smile, the unbridled happiness in her voice, has my shoulders squaring and my legs marching straight to the edge, jumping in like she did moments ago.

The water hugs me, muting every sense like a sigh of relief

as I sink. I open my eyes, nothing but a fuzzy Pantone 3025—a deep and fathomless green-blue—surrounding me. When I tilt my head up, slashes of silver sparkle at the surface. Where Tilly is. I kick myself toward her.

"Told you it was perfect," Tilly says, when I find her in the sunlight.

All I can do is smile at her.

We float around for a while, the water gently pushing us together then pulling us apart in its natural rhythm. It's impossible not to feel peaceful in the calm of the water and warm day. This little pocket-sized paradise must have a bit of magic, because it shrinks the great, big, noisy, vast world and its echoes in my brain down to a hum.

Eventually, Tilly holds up her wrinkled fingers and, in a voice mimicking a terrifying old woman, complains of getting pruney. We get out of the water and sit on the sun-warmed rocks.

I pull my black T-shirt back on, then my trousers. I don't really like the way the sun feels on my skin. Tilly apparently doesn't mind, because she stretches out on the rock, rays of sunlight kissing every inch of her. It takes more willpower than I care to admit to keep from ogling her.

"Can I tell you something?" she asks, turning her head and using her hand to shield her eyes as she looks at me.

"You can tell me anything."

Tilly bites on her bottom lip, squinting one eye at me then propping herself up on her elbows to look at the water. She shakes her head, and, suddenly, I want to know what she's hesitating to tell me more than I've ever wanted anything in my life.

"Please," I say softly.

Tilly swallows, still staring at the blue pool. "It's scary," she whispers.

"What is?"

"That I'm going to tell you something, and then you'll know. And I'll probably have to live with you not saying it back."

"Tilly," I whisper. And I can tell I sound a bit desperate. But I don't care. I want to know. *Need* to know.

"I like you," she says at last. "Like . . . *really* like you."

She takes a deep breath, lips pursed and lines of pain around the corners of her eyes as she continues to stare at the water. "I think you're annoying and hilarious and unfairly gorgeous and the most interesting person I've ever met and there's no one in the world I'd rather talk to. And I feel so much of this . . . liking . . . that it's overwhelming. And it's sharp. It has spikes and teeth that dig into me as it grows because I know you won't feel the same way. But I still wanted you to know."

I blink at her, trying to process everything she said.

Wait.

Not feel the same way?

Is she daft? Does she have any idea, any clue, of what she's done to my heart? That it aches and twists when she's hurt? That it swells to discomfort when she so much as smiles or laughs? How does she not know about the absolute havoc she's wreaked on the damn organ? She's turned me inside out with everything I feel for her.

"I—I . . ." Words are, yet again, failing me.

"It's okay," Tilly says, waving her hands frantically. "You don't have to say anything. I didn't mean to make you feel uncomfortable."

"Tilly. I'm not. It's just . . . Well . . . I . . ."

"Seriously," Tilly says, pushing to stand. "It's probably better if we never bring it up again."

"Wait." I stand, too.

"In fact," she says, grabbing her clothes and pulling her T-shirt on backward, "I think we should pretend this never happened." She takes a step away from me. She's talking so fast I can't even think.

"Tilly. Hold on. I need to—"

"Okay. Cool. Glad we're on the same page of this being an afternoon we swam and literally no conversation was had. Think I'll run home. Or to the Atlantic Ocean. Maybe try to swim back to the States." She starts moving.

Grabbing her wrist before she moves out of reach, I tug her back toward me. Her forehead collides with my chest and she lets out an *oof*.

She looks up at me, eyes wide and vulnerable, and I feel a slight tremble in her hands where I hold her. I can't find the words. Can't figure out the names for the feelings. I can't . . .

And then, my lips are on hers. The ache in my chest eases, the frustrating chaos of my thoughts turning back into that peaceful hum I felt in the water. My head feels light, like I'm not getting enough oxygen. And it's somehow perfect.

I want to stay right here. Forever.

But I can't. Because, holy shit. I just kissed Tilly. Without asking permission first. Cubby would absolutely have my head if she knew.

I break away, taking a step back and sucking in a deep breath. Tilly's eyes are closed, and she sways forward. Both our chests are heaving.

When she finally opens her eyes and looks at me, they're wide and wild, a spark turning the gray electric.

"You kissed me!" she screeches.

"No, I didn't."

"Yes, you did!"

"No, I—"

"Do it again," Tilly says, reaching out and fisting her hands in my shirt, pulling me toward her like I have any power to resist. When it comes to Tilly, I'm the tide and she's the moon; I go wherever she wants me.

If I thought kissing Tilly was great, it's nothing compared to Tilly kissing *me*. She presses her body against mine, threading her hands in my hair, waking up a thousand nerve endings in my scalp. Her lips mold against mine, soft and wonderful. I hold her even closer, and the kiss gets deeper. Clumsy. Perfect.

Oh my God, kissing is great. Amazing. Huge fan of kissing. Cannot recommend enough.

Eventually, we become a little less frantic. Taking our time. Memorizing the feel. Because I'm certainly never going to forget this.

If this kiss were a color, it would be a soft, decadent gold pouring from Tilly's lips and radiating through my veins.

When we kiss to the point that we absolutely have to break for air or become serious asphyxiation risks, I rest my forehead against hers, unable to hide my smile.

"Tilly," I say, reaching up and tucking some wet strands of hair behind her ear.

"*Hmmnnnggg?*" she, uh, kind of says, looking up at me, both of us going cross-eyed.

We giggle.

"I, um. Well, I wanted to make it clear that, what you said earlier? I don't want to forget it. Or pretend it didn't happen. Because . . ." I take a deep, shaky breath. "Because I feel the same way for you. Honestly, I feel so much for you, I don't know that I can actually articulate it like you did but I hope you know that."

I must have done a decent enough job getting my point across because Tilly's grin is incandescent.

And then, she kisses me some more.

Chapter 31

Alexa, Play "Toxic" by Britney Spears

TILLY

maybe kind of had a small idea or something," I blurt out at the tail end of a Ruhe meeting.

Mona and Amina have been including me in their weekly briefings. I usually don't have much to add, mainly because I tend to zone out while they're talking, but I've been chewing on a new idea for the past few days and it apparently can't wait any longer to come out.

"Say it with conviction, darling," Amina says, shooting me a smile. "Declarative statements."

I nod a few times, squeezing my toes in my shoes. "Okay. So, uh, Ruhe is special because of your formula, right?" I say turning to Amina. "Like, not only is the polish nontoxic but it's also eco-friendly? And the bottles are even biodegradable?"

"Only spent eight years of my life getting it right," Amina says with a beautifully proud smile.

"So, like, why don't you all talk about that more?" I say. "I feel like you're missing a huge opportunity here."

Ollie, Mona, and Amina blink at me.

"No offense, Tilly, but we do," Mona says, tilting her head. "You haven't been to any of our buyer meetings, but it's definitely a point of pride in our pitch."

"Right, but it could be so much more than that," I say, leg bouncing. "It's not a bullet point but the *entire* point."

"Go on," Mona says slowly.

"You've focused your brand on being for for the modern nail polish wearer, right? Like, your target market is a young person looking to express themselves. Well those are the people who care. Those are the people entering adulthood in the midst of just like, total shit. But they *care*."

More of that blinking.

"Sorry, I'm all over the place." I blow out a breath, lifting my bangs as I search for words. "What I'm trying to say is, your target market is a generation of people who care about the planet. They care about what goes in their bodies. What goes on them. They care about how they're sold things and the messaging that goes into it and where their dollar goes and how their products are packaged. They care about those things because they *matter*. And your nail polish is aligned with that."

The silence in the room is overwhelming, but I keep going.

"What it boils down to is that beauty should never be toxic."

Mona sucks in a breath. "Wait. Say that again." I smile as my sister picks up the thread.

"Beauty should never be toxic. Not the way it's made. Not the way it's sold. Not the way it's advertised. That's what you lean into. That's why people my age will buy it. Because you two care. And so do we."

There's another heavy moment of silence.

"Tilly!" Mona slams her hands down on the table, making me and Ollie jump. "That's fucking brilliant."

My jaw plummets to the floor. "Did you just say *fucking*?"

Mona waves her hands in front of her face. "No. Yes. It doesn't matter. What matters is that's absolutely genius."

"This beautiful brain," Amina says, leaning toward me and taking my face between her hands before landing a big kiss to the crown of my head. "How I love it."

"You . . . you like the idea?"

"Like it?" Mona says, standing and pacing around the room. "It's perfect."

"We could do so much with that," Amina adds, following Mona's path. "That could be influential enough of a niche that we could generate greater e-sales and focus on that instead of getting into stores."

"Oh, I absolutely love this," Mona says with (mildly terrifying) ferocity. She whips out her computer and props it on the bed, kneeling while typing with so much gusto it's amazing the keys don't crack. "Amina, do we have a competitor analysis on eco products?"

"No, but we need it now," Amina says, similarly booting up her laptop.

The two start talking a mile a minute, leaving Ollie and me as the blinkers.

"Uh . . . anything you need us to do?" I ask.

Mona shoos me with her hand. "Sorry. Sorry, but I'm way lost in a thought. Take the rest of the afternoon off, you two."

"Seriously?" I say, perking up. I had no idea coming up with a good idea would mean I got to spend less time actually working.

"Yes. Yes. Have fun," she says.

Ollie and I grin at each other, then bolt for the door.

"Did you see that?" I say in the hall, bouncing up and down as we move through the hotel. "They liked my idea!"

"Of course they liked your idea," Ollie says, grabbing my

hand and spinning me to him. I land with a sturdy thump against his chest, arms wrapping around his waist. "It's phenomenal."

"I feel like I really added something of value," I say. My heart is a bubble that will soon float away.

Ollie pulls back, eyes serious as he looks down at me. "Tilly." He says my name softly. Reverently. "A hundred good ideas or absolutely none, you add value just by being you."

A surge of emotions twists me inside out. I shake my head, letting out a tiny scoff.

"I'm serious," Ollie says, blinking up to the ceiling, dragging a hand through his hair. "How do I explain this . . ."

I watch the steady thump of his pulse in his throat.

His hand drops to his side, fingers tapping away. "Value in reference to color is the lightness or darkness of a hue, right? The less lightness a hue has, the lower its value. So, for example, something like a deep purple plum has a lower value than, er, a white peach, follow?"

"Uh . . . sure."

"Well, Tilly, you're as luminous as they come. Your value doesn't change based on an idea you have or what you offer people. It just is. And it's wonderful."

If I thought I was having a lot of feelings before, it's nothing compared to every delicious wonderful emotion that cracks me open now.

I push up onto my tiptoes, placing a soft kiss to Oliver's lips. He kisses me back, pulling a smile from me.

"I take it that was a decent way of explaining it?" he asks against my mouth.

I laugh. "What gave you that idea?" I ask, kissing him again.

Chapter 32

Avoidance and Other Healthy Coping Mechanisms

TILLY

I made the mistake of blinking, and now it's August. Which is terrifying, because that means my life-changing trip is getting closer and closer to being over, the real world sitting like a hungry wolf at the door, ready to devour me the second my summer in Europe is up.

And I don't know what to do. About, like, anything.

I don't know how to search for a job or create a résumé or figure out where I'll live or even what I want to do with my life and every time I try to make a plan my overeager brain twists itself into knots and shoots toxic darts of anxiety and confusion up and down my spine.

How am I supposed to have a future figured out? How am I supposed to know what I want to do every single day for the rest of my life when I don't even have a firm grasp on who I am? What if the next step I take is an awful one? A total disaster? And I literally ruin the rest of my life because I didn't know anything?

I finish typing the draft of my newest Babble post, wondering if anyone will understand how overwhelmingly unprepared I am for my own reality.

It was hard to write—each word forced out of me—but at least I finally got something down. The stress of being clueless has left my brain drier than a desert lately, and I can't get my fingers and my brain and my keyboard to work together.

I've never had the problem of not having ideas before—my mind is usually so flooded with them that I don't know where to start. But lately, it's felt like squeezing my brain through a meat grinder anytime I sit at my laptop and try to think of things to post.

I glance across the café table at Oliver. He's biting his lip as he stares intently at his computer, a wave of hair falling across his forehead. It makes me something close to furious that one person is allowed to be so obscenely cute. But then I remember that he's also sort of . . . mine, and then my heart feels fit to burst. Wonderful, lovely, ridiculous boy.

The surge of bubbly feelings is popped by an unwanted reminder: not only does August signal the conclusion of the trip, but it also leaves a big giant question mark on what happens with Oliver when summer ends.

And that question mark is wrapped around my neck and weighs a metric ton, dragging me down.

But, if ADHD has made me an expert in anything, it's avoidance, and I am pretending not to see my problems like a champ. Sure, the problems nag and gnaw at the back of my mind, slowly devouring me until I'm nothing but a flesh bag of subconscious anxiety, but it's better than actively sending myself into a meltdown by imagining literally every single rancid potential outcome. Such as me being a directionless loser back at home living thousands of miles away from the guy I really like and never seeing him and maybe having to . . .

No. Nope. Not today.

Ollie doesn't seem to operate on the same avoidance philosophy that I do, and he's regularly trying to talk about the future like it isn't the scariest damn thing in the world. But any time he tries to bring up what happens when summer ends, I distract him by asking about the impact of the first random color I see or I kiss his ridiculously cute face until his cheeks are flushed and his eyes are hazed.

Both methods are extremely effective.

I give my Babble piece another once-over, then hit *publish*, closing my laptop. Glancing his way, I find Ollie staring at me with a soft expression.

"I like that smile," he says, eyes tracing my mouth. "It's your writing smile. I think it's your broadest."

I touch my lips, giggling like a fool. "I didn't even realize I was smiling."

"You always smile when you finish writing something. Even when you slam your laptop shut and groan that you hate what you wrote, you still end up smiling. I find it incredibly fascinating."

I flap my hands in some wild attempt at self-preservation before I start squealing in public. Ollie smiles back, then his look turns thoughtful.

"Have you thought about trying to write for publications?" he asks. "Pitching stories or article ideas or whatever it is writers do? Or applying for, uh, writerly . . . jobs . . . if you'd rather not do freelancing? Maybe you could earn some money with your writing."

I choke on my iced coffee, some of it shooting out of my nose as I splutter. "No way," I say, hacking up a lung into a napkin. "I'm not good enough for that. I'm . . ."

"You're . . . ?" Ollie says, eyebrows furrowed as another

wheezy coughing fit hits me. He reaches over and gives me a firm pat on the back.

I wave my hand, trying to figure out the words to describe the bizarre mix of inadequacy that constantly swamps me and the willingness to fling my words out into the ether or the internet regardless. Writing silly little descriptions and newsletter emails for Ruhe is a detached albeit fun exercise in playing with words. Writing on Babble is terrifying and vulnerable, but I'm in control of it. I can blast any feeling into a text box and chuck it at random online strangers without anything hinging on it. No boss critiquing it. No livelihood depending on it. I love writing, but that doesn't mean I'm worthy of calling myself a writer like professionals do.

I never heard back about that job with *Ivy* that Cubby and Darcy told me to apply for, and the silence has been crushing. The gaping feeling of inadequacy is only just now scarring over.

"I'm not good enough for someone to *publish* my stuff, let alone pay me for it," I say, dragging the pad of my thumb through the condensation on my glass. "The stuff I write is just silly nonsense and emo rants."

And that's fine. It's enough. When the world is over and I'm long gone, I'll always have created those words and shared them with whoever wanted to read them.

"That's patently false," Oliver says, his voice rough. I'm surprised by how serious he looks.

"What?"

"I'm sorry, but you're wrong," he says, scooting his chair closer to me.

He reaches out, grabbing one of my hands between both of his, and the gesture feels as natural as my heart beating.

"You make people feel seen," Oliver continues. "You're like a . . . a . . . prism."

"Excuse me?"

"Like a crystal prism. You absorb the world around you but somehow release this brilliant spectrum of colors through your words that people see themselves in. It's a gift."

"I . . . no. That's not . . ."

"I've seen the comments people leave you on your Babble posts. People connect with what you say."

"You've looked at my Babble?" Lately I've been showing Ollie drafts of my writing or sending him little excerpts I like, but I didn't think he was on the app.

Oliver reaches into his pocket and fishes out his phone, squinting at the screen as he swipes across it a few times before turning it to face me. "The only notifications I get from it are when you post."

Sure enough, he has an account. The standard gray avatar is in the upper left corner with *user276527* below it. I slip my hand out from his grip and scroll. I'm the only account he's following and . . .

He's liked every single one of my posts.

Literally, all of them.

But it doesn't end there.

He's also upvoted countless kind and supportive comments from other users, even writing *agreed* with a little heart in response to some.

"You see," he says, tapping the screen. "It's a simple truth. People like reading your words. And you like writing them. So why not pursue it professionally? Isn't that what you want to do?"

Here's the issue: it is what I want to do. So badly. But wanting to do it doesn't suddenly make me feel like less of a mortifying imposter at the idea of attempting it.

My eyes scour Oliver's serious face. His warm smile. The crinkles at the corners of his eyes.

He believes in me. He genuinely, truly, believes that I can

write things worth reading. And even more, he wants me to do it because it makes me happy.

It's the first time anyone's ever encouraged me to do something for the simple fact that it brings me joy. It's the first time that's ever been enough.

If Oliver can believe in me like this, why can't I believe in myself?

I try the idea on—this vision of me being scared and going for it anyway. Flinging myself into the unknowns and trusting I'll make it out alive. It feels loose and vast and terrifying and the sharpest bit thrilling as I twirl around in it.

I kind of like it.

"Okay," I whisper, leaning toward him. "Maybe I will."

He grins like I told him he won the lottery.

And all of a sudden, it's the most important thing in the world to find a job *right now*. That I send pieces to whoever is accepting. That I take this delicious fantasy and turn it into my immediate reality.

It's the aura phase of hyperfocus, of immediate gratification, and there's no fighting it . . . not for me, at least.

I turn back to my laptop, and it feels like I'm plugging my brain directly into the keyboard, googling résumé templates, job positions, open calls for submissions.

I lose myself so thoroughly in this deep dive—in this irresistible need to hold on to this feeling of . . . of *believing* in myself, to make this happen—that the next thing I know, Oliver is rubbing my back and saying my name.

I blink for the first time probably in two hours.

"I'm sorry to pull you out," Ollie says, "but we better start heading back for dinner."

I rub my eyes and blink some more. I have about fifty-eight tabs open, six different Word docs, and twelve confirmation emails of jobs and open calls I've submitted to.

Sometimes the resurfacing from hyperfocus is gentle, gradual. Other times it's jarring and disorienting, like you're waking up in a new world. This definitely feels like the latter.

"Alright?" Ollie asks, continuing to rub my back.

I grin at him. "Out of it," I say, stretching my arms overhead and arching my back into his touch.

Ollie nods in understanding, smiling back.

I glance at my laptop screen and groan.

"What's wrong?"

"Well," I say, total and utter humiliation boiling up in me, "There's like, eight typos on my résumé I just sent out to a billion jobs."

Oliver turns my laptop, and the gasp he lets out belongs on a soap opera, I shit you not. Which doesn't help things.

Except, well, it's Ollie, so I can't help laughing. And then I laugh harder. Ollie looks at me, horror-stricken. Then he starts to laugh, too. We're both laughing so hard our table starts to shake. Oliver drops his forehead to mine as we try to catch our breaths.

"Well . . . I wish I could say spelling shouldn't be a prerequisite for any of the jobs . . . but I do imagine it plays a bit of a role."

I snort again. "Whatever. At least I tried."

He kisses my forehead, then pulls away, packing up his things. "Honestly, Tilly, I imagine you'll still get responses. Editors exist for a reason, and people can overlook some typos for talent."

Something sharp and self-deprecating sits on the tip of my tongue, but I decide to swallow it down. I choose to bask in his confidence. His faith in me. I absorb it. Make it my own.

I pack up my own stuff and we head out the door, Ollie grabbing my hand and holding it as we walk.

A block away from the hotel I stop, tugging his arm so he's facing me.

"Thank you," I say.

"For what?"

"For believing in me."

Oliver shakes his head then smiles, leaning down to give me a soft kiss. "It'd be impossible not to."

Chapter 33

She's a Rainbow

OLIVER

It turns out, heaven does exist on Earth, and it's stationed in an interactive pop-up museum about color in the heart of Barcelona.

Tilly reaches over, putting her fingers under my chin and closing my jaw from where it's dragging on the ground. But I can't believe it. An entire museum—*five whole exhibits*—dedicated to the history of color, pigments, and their applications.

This is about to be the best day of my life.

Tilly had started our free Saturday by hovering over my sleeping form until I woke up with a minor heart attack from her wild-eyed stare. She then dragged me out of bed, threw a bundle of clothes my way, shoved a stale biscuit in my mouth, and pulled me out the door, saying she wanted us to be first in line for a big surprise.

I've never been so surprised in my life.

"Come on," she says, grabbing my arm and marching us to the entrance.

I snap a picture of the large poster at the start of the exhibit that details the immersive color and pigment experience, then send it to Marcus.

> sorry but I've officially replaced you as my best friend

Marcus's reply is almost instant.

> This is a lovely message to get after you've ghosted me most of the summer

> Who's the poor soul?

I grin at my screen. Marcus really is my best mate. I can disappear into my own world for weeks then text him out of the blue and we pick up right where we left off. He never makes me feel bad when I take days to respond to him or breaks from communication altogether.

"Come here," I say to Tilly, wrapping my arm around her shoulders.

Holding my phone out, she blinks in surprise for a second before breaking out into a giant smile right as I take a picture. She turns, smashing her face against my cheek with a kiss. I make sure to capture that moment, too.

I send them to Marcus.

> This is Tilly.

I follow it up with a second message.

> I'm fairly certain she's my girlfriend

A call from Marcus rings through and I hit *decline*, then receive about four thousand texts in a group message with him and Micah.

Micah
> OLIVER

Micah

OLIVER!!!!!!

Micah

YOU HAVE A GIRLFRIEND???

Marcus

you wanker

Marcus

how have you not told us sooner?

Micah

OLIVER OH MY GOD

Micah

I'm going to pass out this is incredible

Marcus

isn't she your boss's sister?

Micah

oh my gawd is she? The scandal. I love it

Micah

TELL. US. EVERYTHING.

Marcus

you look really happy

I grin at my phone, then shake my head.

happiness doesn't come close to doing it justice

I send them a few more pictures of me and Tilly together from the past few weeks then turn my phone off, pocketing it and turning to Tilly.

"What are you smiling about?" she asks, narrowing her eyes at me.

There isn't an adequate way to explain that I've never felt so wholly connected to another person. Like I can show her every piece of myself and she'll give me that wonderful smile. It's borderline ridiculous how much I want to brag about her, announce to the world that this peculiar and wonderful person *likes* me. Wants to be around me. It's not something I ever expected I'd have in life.

"I told my best friend, Marcus, and his partner, Micah, about you."

Tilly's eyes go wide like a cartoon character. "Oh. Okay. Wow. I am very okay with that and not desperate to know what you said and not internally freaking out at all and wondering what they'll think of me and everything is extremely chill and calm and totally fine."

I laugh, reaching out and pulling her to my side. She nuzzles closer.

"I told them the truth," I say, placing a kiss on the top of her head.

"Which is . . . ?"

"That I'm unbelievably glad to be here with you," I say, moving my arm from around her shoulders to twine my fingers with hers. Tilly stares at our clasped hands then looks up to my face.

I'm not usually good at reading facial expressions, but her smile speaks volumes.

"No time to waste," I say after a moment, tugging her toward the entrance. "We've got a world of Technicolor to explore."

We spend hours wandering through the colorful explosions

of the exhibit. Tilly listens closely as I go on and on about the various topics showcased, even asking me questions. I explain metamerism. Chroma. How saturation differs from value.

We go on a visual journey through the history of red—the endless and often futile pursuits of ancient artists and dyers trying to re-create its vibrancy, using deadly minerals just to capture the color's power, and how the pigment is, quite literally, steeped in blood. We both walk out a bit woozy from that one.

Tilly lets me linger for nearly an hour at a section dedicated to Picasso. One wall showcases his famous Blue Period. Cool and moody paintings of blues and blue-greens pulling you in on a chilly gust, daunting and haunting as you fall into them. They have a few of his original pieces on loan while a slideshow of the other works is projected onto a blank spot of wall.

It's contrasted with examples of his Rose Period on the opposite side of the room—vibrant pinks and earthy oranges warming you when you cross an invisible line in the space.

"Isn't it incredible?" I say to Tilly, moving back and forth across the room. "You can actually *feel* the temperature change. Right here," I say, rubbing my chest. "And even the subjects of the paintings. They aren't painted certain colors, they *are* the colors. Absolutely remarkable."

Tilly beams at me, following my aimless, happy wander. "So *cool*," she says, pointing at a particularly frigid blue painting and wiggling her eyebrows. "Buh-dum-cha."

I laugh, pulling her toward me and placing a kiss on the back of her hand. "Good one."

"What color am I?" Tilly asks, twining her fingers through mine as we stop to admire the rich reds and warm browns cast from the Rose Period projector.

I look at Tilly, my eyes scouring her raven hair. Those thundercloud eyes. The bright yellow of her dress and the touch of pink in her cheeks.

But she's more than those. She's the sweetness of cotton candy blue, the effervescence of gold, and the complexity of copper. She's deep like emerald and light like lilac.

"Tilly, you're the entire rainbow."

When we eventually leave the museum, I check my phone and have close to fifty new texts from Micah and Marcus and half a dozen missed FaceTime calls.

"I think someone might be trying to get ahold of you," Tilly says, leaning her head on my shoulder as we walk.

I chuckle, dragging my thumb across my forehead. "Putting it mildly."

"Call them back," she says, giving me a nudge.

I glance at her. "Would you . . . er . . . How would you feel about meeting them? Marcus and Micah? We could Face-Time."

Tilly's smile is, quite simply, radiant. "I'd love that."

We cut into a nearby park, finding a bench that offers a little shade from Spain's punishing summer heat, and I ring Marcus back.

"'Bout fucking time you called us," Marcus says by way of greeting.

"Marcusssss, don't be so rude," Micah says, batting him on the shoulder.

"Yeah, Marcus, don't be a wanker," I say, goading him.

Marcus rolls his eyes. Micah registers Tilly smiling next to me and proceeds to push Marcus out of the frame as they lean closer.

"Oh my God, you're Tilly."

"Guilty," she says back with a light giggle.

"I'd like to say we've heard so much about you, but seeing as Oliver has all but forgotten us during his jet-setting summer, you'll just have to fill us in on how extraordinarily lovely you are."

Tilly shoots me a goofy, terrified look.

"Micah isn't one to ease people into their energy," Marcus says, maneuvering to at least get part of his face in view.

"Wouldn't want it any other way," Tilly says, scrunching up her nose as she laughs.

"Enough small talk," Micah says. "Truly, tell us everything. How is the trip? What have you seen? How did *this*"—they gesture wildly between me and Tilly—"begin?"

Tilly and I glance at each other, then smile. We start with today, launching into a probably way too detailed play-by-play on all the museum's exhibits. We work backward, revisiting Granada and Stockholm and Copenhagen. Reminiscing on Amsterdam. Laughing about Rome. It isn't long before Tilly and I are both hyper and flushed with color, our voices loud as we remember so many wonderful moments that shaped us.

"You two are unbearably cute," Micah says. "If it weren't so endearing it would make me sick."

"What are your plans for after the summer?" Marcus asks Tilly.

He has no idea how big of a landmine he just stepped on. Tilly's smile wavers. She tries to recover it, but it falls flat until it crumples.

"Still have a few things I'm figuring out," she manages to say.

And I want to save her. I want to ease that worried crease between her eyebrows. But the problem is, I don't know how. Because I'm in the dark about what happens after this summer, too.

And it's killing me.

I want a plan. A firm, clear definition of what it looks like. I need routine and order and enough lead-up to recalibrate my mind to what comes next. But every time I try to have the conversation, Tilly distracts me. And I don't know what to do.

"Oh, I'm so sorry, but my sister is calling me," Tilly says suddenly, taking her phone out of her dress pocket and waving it wildly. "Gotta take this. It was so great to meet you."

She scuttles away before she can hear Marcus and Micah say their goodbyes.

"Did Marcus say something wrong?" Micah asks quietly.

I sigh, rubbing my knuckle over my eyebrow. "No. Everything's fine," I lie.

I can tell by the resulting silence that neither of them believe me.

"I better go," I say, watching Tilly pace back and forth under a tree, phone pressed to her ear.

"We love you," Micah croons as Marcus waves.

I end the call, slapping my phone against my palm as I worry.

Chapter 34

The Reckoning

Something kind of miraculous happened.

I'm officially a published writer.

Dead ass.

Now, don't get me wrong, it's not like I wrote some ground-breaking piece featured in the *New York Times,* but my name *is* attached to a guest post on Wander Media's website, which, honestly, feels just as good.

Wander is a budget travel site that has open submissions and, riding the high of Oliver's encouragement, I sent in a short, satirical (and partially autobiographical) argument for bringing every pair of underwear you own on vacation. About a week after sending it in—and obsessively checking my email every four minutes—I got a reply from the section editor that they loved it and encouraged me to send them other pitches I might have.

To top it off, they're even paying me twenty-five dollars for it, which is basically like winning the lottery when you blow through money on coffee and sweets like I've been on this trip.

After reading the email out loud to Ollie for the third time, I sprint around the hotel room, jumping and spinning.

After my fourth loop, I charge full speed at Oliver. He braces himself at the last minute, eyes wide and mouth dropped open in a little *O* of fear before I jump into his arms, clinging to him like an overly excited baby monkey. He stumbles a few steps before the backs of his knees hit the edge of the bed and he collapses with an *oof.*

Mona and Amina secured another deal in Barcelona, and are out for an oh-so-subtle "celebratory business dinner" that neither Ollie nor yours truly were invited to, so we don't have to worry about being discreet.

"Sorry," I say, nuzzling into his neck, not sorry at all. "I'm just really excited."

"I'm so proud of you," he says, voice muffled from the fact that I'm pretty much suffocating him at this point.

I rear up, beaming down at his flustered face until I can't resist any longer and pepper rapid kisses all over his forehead and cheeks, making him laugh. My phone starts blaring from across the room and, with a sigh, I slide off the bed and run toward it.

GUARD THY LOINS flashes on the screen. Oh good, a call from my mom.

"Hi, Mom," I say, pressing the phone to my ear and chewing on my cuticle.

"There she is," Mom says in a falsely cheery voice, artfully passive-aggressive in her reference to how many times I've let her calls go unanswered. I didn't mean to make a habit of avoiding our check-ins, but it feels so brutally painful every time we talk, I can never force my finger to accept the call. Mona's been covering for me a bit, sending Mom frequent texts about how much I'm contributing to the team or some nonsense.

"I was starting to worry about you," she says. "How are you? Have you been taking your medicine?"

I sigh, pressing my forehead against the wall. "Yes, Mom." And I'm not lying. I've actually become really good at taking it regularly. I've found that setting a morning alarm as a reminder makes all the difference.

"Good girl," Mom says, and I wilt at how much her voice perks up. "And you're being good for Mona?"

"Yeah. She even gave me a lollipop today after I ate all my vegetables."

Mom's laugh is forced.

"The trip is winding down soon, isn't it?" she says casually. "Can't believe how fast the summer went by. Have you thought any more about your plans for the fall?"

How subtle.

"Well, actually, I have," I say, scratching my nose and tapping my feet.

Mom blows out a breath. "Tilly, that's wonderful. Where do you think you'll apply? Will this mean starting in the spring semester?"

I gnaw on my bottom lip. "No, the college thing hasn't changed. Not for right now, at least. I'm . . . I think I've figured out what I want to do."

"Oh?" Mom says, her voice dripping with disappointment.

I square my shoulders and clear my throat. "I've decided I want to be a writer," I say, my voice a bit wobbly. This isn't necessarily a new realization, but it's the first time I'm speaking it into existence. Declarative statement and all. "I've actually already sold my first article and if I can get a regular income flow from maybe a barista job or something at first, I can focus on my craft and refine my ideas and I'll—"

"No." Mom's voice is flat and final.

"What?"

"That's not a good job, Tilly," she says, and I can almost hear her shaking her head. "That's what people living in la-la land say they want to be before they end up waiting tables for the rest of their lives."

"What's wrong with food service work?"

"That's not the point," Mom says with an exasperated sigh. "The point is, you need to figure out a real job. Actually, a degree first, then a job."

"But why?" I ask. "Why does that have to be my set path? We both know I don't do well in school, and even Dr. Alverez said that traditional educational environments and formats aren't conducive to the way I learn, so why would I force myself through college?"

"I'm not limiting you here, Tilly." Mom's tone is one of ominous warning not to push it. "I'm just trying to be realistic. I—"

"You want to talk about realistic, Mom?" I snap. "My brain is my reality. I'm not some choose-your-own-adventure novel for you to dictate every experience I have. I'm sorry I'm not what you want me to be, but this is the best I've got."

"Tilly, don't raise your voice. I'm not saying that. There's a certain way things are done and—"

"But you *are* saying that. You've always said it."

Even without words. It's the way she quickly snatches at my hand if I reach for something in a store. The way she squeezes my shoulder in warning if I start talking to someone too fast. Too loud. It's the warning look she gives me if I get too excited about a special interest. She's said it a million silent ways. She wishes I was "normal."

"I'm just trying to protect you!"

"You treat me like an inevitable fuckup!" The words come out harsh. Sharp. And my mom's silence screams across the line. I let out a shaky breath.

"I'm not treating you like a . . . a mess-up," she says. "It's the way of the world, Tilly. It's what Mona did. She even went on to get advanced degrees."

I start pacing a vicious little loop across the hotel room. I can feel Ollie's eyes on me, but I can't look at him. "I'm not Mona and Mona's not me, Mom. You can't keep comparing us. It does nothing but wedge us apart. I want my sister as my sister, not some untouchable creature of perfection I'm constantly chasing the shadow of.

"And Mona deserves to be free of that pressure. It isn't fair to her, either, to carry the weight of needing to be perfect. To be some ideal daughter and uber successful older sister. She's human. She's allowed to make mistakes. I am, too. I—"

"I'm not having this conversation. You're completely missing the point. You need to get serious about the real world."

I stop my pacing, deflating at the harshness in her voice that leaves no room for argument. No way I could ever convince her that what I want is worthy of pursuing.

She lets out a sigh. "I'll be there in a little over a week to visit Mona and bring you home. I expect you to have a plan by then. A real one. Is that understood?"

I swallow, my stomach in knots and blood rushing in my ears. All I manage is a hiccupping sound.

"I'm being hard on you because I love you," Mom says, voice cold. Then the line goes dead.

I crumple to the floor, crying into my knees.

Oliver lets me quietly sob by myself for two minutes before marching across the room and sitting on the floor next to me, pulling me to his chest. He doesn't ask for details. Doesn't need a play-by-play. He tucks my head under his chin and rubs soothing circles across my back.

And I feel . . . safe. Secure. Cherished.

Three scary and vulnerable words almost bubble to my lips, but I tuck them away for later.

I stop crying long enough for Oliver to coax me outside for a walk where he then proceeds to buy me food from every vendor I look twice at. This gorgeous angel has really cracked my love language.

It's nice, being with Ollie, but I still feel this empty ache through my limbs. All this sadness and fear and confusion about the future has weaved its way so deeply into my muscles, I'm pushed out of the present.

We eventually wander back to the hotel, and we hear Mona and Amina talking through our shared wall. Somewhere along the trip, their own need for privacy won out over the always-open-shared-door rule.

Like we do every night, we wait for sounds of sleep to drift in from their room before I crawl into Oliver's bed, cuddling against him in a cozy nest under the comforter.

We usually end up whispering till the sun comes up. Sometimes, it's hours of jokes and teasing, punctuated by kisses and touches. Other nights, Ollie will risk it all and keep the lights low, spending hours holding color swatches up to the moles on my cheek, brow furrowed and tongue between his teeth, flipping through the wheel aggressively until I dissolve into silent giggles at his frustration.

He always ends up pressing his lips to my freckles with a growl, turning my laughs into a delighted sigh.

Tonight, we're serious. Vulnerable. Mumbling confessions and fears of the future.

"I feel like I'm constantly failing," I whisper, tracing my fingers along his cheekbones. "I feel like I'm not good enough. Like I'll never be good enough."

"Good enough at what?" Ollie asks, eyebrows furrowing.

I rub the pads of my fingers across the lines between his eyes, smoothing out his worry. "Good enough at anything," I say. "Writing. Creating. Being a person. An adult, I guess. I feel pretty lost. All the time."

Ollie is silent for a moment, staring at me like my skin holds the answers to questions he's always wondered about.

"I feel lost, too," he says at last, turning his head to kiss my palm. "Want to be lost together?"

Chapter 35

French and Kisses

At the start of our last week of the business tour, Mona and Amina come flouncing into our room, perching primly on the edge of my bed.

"Wear something nice tonight," Mona says. "We're taking you two out to dinner. We have important things to tell you."

"Mo, no offense, but we all know you and Amina are dating," Tilly says as she shoves clothes into her suitcase by the handful.

Mona's jaw drops and, after a momentary silence, Amina starts cackling with laughter.

"She's got us there," Amina says through her giggles. "But if we have to admit it, you both do, too."

Tilly and I are anything but subtle, our gazes whipping to each other in fear. Amina cackles some more.

"We're leaving in an hour," Mona says, brushing invisible dust off her lap like she can brush away the awkwardness with it. "It will be . . . fun."

"Try not to sound so devastated by it, darling," Amina says, laughing again. Mona rolls her eyes then marches out of the room, Amina giggling behind her.

After a shower and shave, I pull on my nicest black trousers and a matching button-down, smoothing down my hair. Walking out of the room, I find Tilly crouched on the floor, still in her shorts and T-shirt, hair thrown into two messy buns at the top of her head. She's scribbling on her shoes with a . . . Sharpie?

"My flats were scuffed," she says by way of explanation, continuing to, uh, color the tips of her, rather worse for wear, black dress shoes.

A loud knock rattles the connecting door. "Ten-minute warning," Mona calls through. Tilly screeches, then tosses her shoes aside, grabbing a rumpled dress out of her suitcase and scuttling to the bathroom.

Somewhere along the trip, we all realized that giving Tilly periodic reminders about time saved a lot of the frustration of her being late.

And, five minutes later, she comes out of the bathroom. Looking like a dream.

No, a dream doesn't do Tilly Twomley justice. She's so much more than that.

Tilly gives me a goofy twirl, showing off the open back. The full skirt of her black dress swings around her hips and she laughs. "How do I look?" she asks.

The dress is simple. Structured. So different from the usual bright and flowy dresses she wears. If I'd seen it hanging in a closet, I would never have been able to picture Tilly choosing it.

Yet, it makes her glow. It's a frame for her energy, her charisma, everything about her that shines.

I walk across the room to her, brushing my hand across her cheek, then cupping her neck.

"Perfect," I say. Because it's the only word that even kind of describes it.

Tilly scrunches up her nose then reaches up to give me a kiss. I hold her close for a second one.

"Time to go, lovebirds," Amina says, knocking then opening the door, pretending to shield her eyes. "Get all your odds and ends situated."

Tilly and I share a glance and silently giggle, then meet Amina and Mona in the hall and follow them out of the hotel.

"So," Mona says, folding her hands on the table after we've all placed our orders. "Amina and I have been talking—"

"I'm sure that's the extent of it," Tilly says, giving me a gratuitous wink. I bite my lip hard to not laugh.

"I hate you," Mona says. Tilly beams.

"As I was saying, we've been discussing the future of Ruhe, and we'd like to incorporate you into those conversations."

Mona and Amina turn to me, and I tilt my head to the side as I listen.

"We've *loved* the work you've done this summer, Oliver," Mona says.

"Blown away," Amina adds, nodding in emphasis.

"We've seen tremendous growth on social media and our online sales. And some of the boutiques we're working with have expressed interest in using your photos for ads in their stores. We'd like to figure out a way to keep this momentum going after the trip ends."

I blink at them.

"What we're picturing," Amina says, "Is keeping you on as a Ruhe employee, even in a part-time or consultation role."

"We know you're starting school soon," Mona continues,

"and I'm sure you'll be very busy, but we'd like to still pay you to take photos for Ruhe, even if it's on a non-regular basis. You've built up a great image database for us so far, and we'll continue to use those, but it would be wonderful to keep you on as you're available."

I process this, then smile. "I'd love to," I say, meaning it. "It's hard to know exactly how much time I'll have when classes start, but even on weekends or whatever you need. It would actually help me to continue building a portfolio, too."

"Fabulous," Amina says, smiling then squeezing my shoulder.

"You're a dream to work with," Mona adds.

Tilly's looking between us, leg bouncing. She's uncomfortable.

"That leaves you," Mona says, turning to Tilly. Tilly starts chewing on her lip.

Mona looks at her sister for a long moment, then beams at her. It's the brightest smile I've ever seen Mona wear.

"I'm so proud of you, Tilly," Mona says, reaching across the table and holding Tilly's hand. "You've had so many clever ideas. Done such a great job in helping us build a fun, exciting website and newsletter that speaks to people your age. I hate myself for underestimating you as much as I did, but you've been a huge asset to this team."

Tilly blinks rapidly at Mona but doesn't say anything.

Mona clears her throat. "And, if you're interested, we'd like to make you an official Ruhe employee. Full disclosure, the salary will definitely suck as we try to build capital, and it won't be the most glamorous job, but we could figure out a way to coordinate with you on work visas or the like if you wanted to stay in London. Stay on with us."

Tilly's rapid blinking stops, and she stares with wide, frightened eyes at Mona.

Then she bursts into tears.

"*Really?*" she sobs. "You really mean that?"

"Of course, love," Amina says, her voice soft and comforting. "We'd be honored."

"And I could stay in London?"

Mona nods. "You can stay with me for a bit while we get things figured out."

"Or me," Amina says. "I have a two-bedroom flat if you get sick of the couch."

Tilly sucks in a shaky, gasping breath. Then jolts up from her seat and body slams Mona in the world's most enthusiastic hug.

"Yes!" Tilly says, her voice loud enough that other diners start to look at us. "Thank you so much."

Wait . . . okay . . . hold on. Things are moving fast. So fast.

Mona just offered Tilly a job. A real job. In London.

Holy shit.

London. Tilly.

Tilly has a job in London.

I live in London.

"Oh my God," I blurt out, blinking at Tilly, then at Mona and Amina. "Tilly, you'll be in London."

Tilly, lady of refinement that she is, grabs a napkin and blows her nose into it, then smiles.

"Sounds like you aren't getting rid of me yet," she says, walking around the table and wrapping her arms around me.

I squeeze her back.

"Have you told Mom and Dad?" Tilly asks Mona.

"Not yet. I thought it would be a fun surprise to tell her when she's here next week."

Tilly nods, rocking back and forth a bit. "And, uh, this isn't like . . . I don't know, a pity hire, is it?"

Mona's face creases. "Tilly, no. Of course not." She reaches across the table, taking her sister's hand. "I mean, on a selfish level, am I excited to keep you closer and spend more time with you? Of course. But you have so much to offer. Ruhe is lucky to have you."

Tilly scrubs at her cheeks furiously as a giant smile glows across her lips.

"We have one more surprise," Amina says, grinning at Mona.

Tilly opens her mouth, likely to make yet another innuendo about their relationship, but Mona points at her. "Don't," she says sternly. Tilly clamps her mouth shut.

"We're taking you to the beach," Amina says, clapping her hands together. "As a thank-you for the work you've both done. The next four days are for nothing but rest and relaxation."

"What beach?" Tilly asks, eyes going almost feral in instant excitement.

"A small town outside of Marseille," Mona says.

Tilly looks at me with an arched eyebrow.

"South of France," I tell her, and her grin is more lovely than any landscape we're likely to see in the idyllic area.

"*Hein hein hein. Baguette. Oui oui,*" Tilly says in an awful and exaggerated French accent as she pretends to swoon, falling back into her seat.

Mona rolls her eyes but can't hide the smile that pops out. "Our train leaves on Saturday," she says, taking a sip of her wine. "I'd recommend you brush up on your French in the meantime."

Chapter 36

Working Kinda Sucks

TILLY

To be totally completely ungratefully honest, my new position with Ruhe is not exactly my dream job. Mona had me hit the ground running the day after our dinner. My title is Executive Assistant, which sounds so pretentious I almost rolled my eyeballs out of my head when she told me.

It's a lot of detail-oriented administrative work. Scheduling, meeting minutes, writing emails, responding to emails, forwarding emails . . . so many emails (*cries in *I hope this finds you well!**).

But, it's a job—one that keeps me in London, no less—and that's really all that matters . . . right?

Plus, I still get to write the newsletter and some of the descriptions for colors—although it took a lot of coaxing to get Mona to agree to a rather innuendo-filled blurb for an eggplant purple—so I at least get to flex the writing muscle. Most of all, I'm feeling useful. I'm helping Mona and Amina reach *their* dream, even if this role isn't necessarily mine.

And I'm not about to look a gift job in the paycheck, especially one that gives me a chance to live close to Oliver. We hadn't ever discussed it, but I had this dark, looming fear that if I ended up having to go back to Cleveland, it would have meant an end to what we have. I mean, what eighteen-year-old guy would want to deal with a girlfriend living in a different country? It would be messy, and Ollie doesn't deal in messes.

But now, it's not even on our radar, and we're blissed out on our sturdy future.

"Got everything?" Ollie asks, zipping up his perfectly packed suitcase, knowing full well that 80 percent of my things are still strewn about the hotel room.

"Never felt more organized in my life," I lie, sticking my tongue out at him. He gives me a skeptical glance that makes me giggle.

I start walking around the room, trying to figure out where to start. I tend to take out everything in my suitcase when I get somewhere. If I can't see it, it's like it doesn't exist, and my brain feels better when I'm able to visualize what I have. It does me absolutely no favors when it comes to packing up, though.

I do laps around piles of clothes in one corner, shoes in another. Cheap jewelry littered here. Even cheaper makeup there.

It's not surprising that my aimless walking eventually turns into pacing—stimming in response to the cloud of overwhelm hovering above my head.

What is surprising is realizing that Ollie is also pacing, his fingers tapping at his sides and face lined in deep concentration. It stops me in my tracks, a little smile breaking across my mouth. We're two neurodivergent tornados spinning around this hotel room.

On his next pass by me, I grab his hand, pulling him close to my chest as I wrap him in a hard hug. He's tense—short waves of stress radiate off his shoulders—then every muscle in his body relaxes like a released rubber band. He hugs me back.

"You okay?" I ask against his chest.

I feel his nod on the top of my head. "I got a bit stuck in my thoughts," he says. "Overwhelmed."

"I noticed," I say, pulling back. I grab his hand and place a quick kiss to his palm. The smile that blooms across Ollie's mouth is prettier than a rose opening its petals to the summer sun. "But you know what they say."

He tilts his head in question.

"Couples that stim together stay together."

Ollie's silent for a moment, then laughs so hard he starts to wheeze. There is nothing, *nothing*, in this world I love more than making Oliver laugh.

"What's on your mind?" I ask when his laughter dies down, lacing my fingers through his.

Oliver blows out a breath as he drags his free hand through his hair. "A change in environment makes me a bit on edge as I lead up to it."

"Do you not like traveling, then?" I ask.

"No, I do," he says. "I really do. But I struggle with change, even when I'm excited about it. It takes me time to adjust to new places. Or even just the idea of them. And today while I was packing up, I think it started to hit me that school will be starting soon. And that will be even more new environments to navigate. And people and social interactions. I guess . . ." He blows out another breath. "I guess I'm a bit nervous."

My heart swells up like a balloon in my chest, and I crush Oliver to me again, wrapping my limbs around him like an aggressive (and oh so loving) python. "I will, quite literally, kill anyone that causes you any issues."

Oliver laughs, and tries to pull back to look at me, but I hold him even tighter. He easily gives in.

"You'd make a great bodyguard," he says. "All five foot four of you. But I'm not necessarily worried about people, I don't know, bullying me, or the like. I can't control how they act and God knows I can't anticipate it. It's more the unknown of change. The disruption of my routine. Need a bit to wrap my head around it all. Prepare for what's coming so I can accommodate it."

I eventually release him from my death-love-grip.

"I get that, I think," I say, picking at my nails. "My struggle comes with thinking about and organizing all that goes into a change. Like the steps I need to do to get there. If that makes any sense."

"It does," Oliver says. "Speaking of, do you want help organizing . . ." He gestures vaguely at the chaos of my stuff around us.

"My, my, Oliver. You certainly know how to make a girl swoon," I say, fanning myself.

He blushes bright red and he's so cute I could die.

I start off trying to help Ollie help me pack, but I end up disrupting his system and he shoos me away.

I do a few more things for Amina and Mona before our vacation, and it ends up using way more of my bandwidth than I expected. By the time I finish, my brain bank feels depleted and all I can do is curl up on the bed. I hate this feeling—like someone hooked me up to an IV and drained my energy. I've felt it a lot this week.

Oliver, on the other hand, looks as flushed and energized as an adrenaline junkie finishing up a skydive.

We spend the rest of the night watching a movie, holding each other tightly.

Being with Ollie makes me feel so safe. So free.

Which is why the little nagging feeling that's burrowed at the base of my throat, that reaches up and scratches at the back of my mind when I'm not moving, not doing anything, scares the shit out of me. I have the boy of my dreams and a job that lets me stay near him . . . so why don't I feel 100 percent happy?

Chapter 37

You and Me and Us

Mona and Amina rented a small, old cottage, not far from the beach. Its pale stones perpetually hold the sun's warmth, and white lace curtains sway with each breeze that curls through the open windows. The floors are a faded and aged wood, each stair creaking as you climb to the second floor.

It's perfect.

Our first day in the small coastal town is spent exploring. Tilly and I walk for miles along the beach, and she stops at every tide pool along the way to marvel at the oceanic architecture created within.

"I love it here," Tilly declares as we watch the sunset, cuddled close together in the sand.

"I love you." The words slip out so much easier than I ever expected. Tilly's body tenses for a moment, and then she turns her head to me, eyes wide and vulnerable, the dying sunlight reflected in her gray irises.

"Do you mean that?" she whispers.

I nod, words getting trapped in my throat, but I push through. "I've loved you for a while, I believe," I say, rubbing a hand across the back of my heated neck. "The name for the feeling finally came to me."

Tilly swallows, then licks her lips. "I love you, too," she says. "So much." She emphasizes the point with a kiss that sends sparks of energy bursting through my stomach.

We turn, watching the sun's last few minutes of the day, the sky a near violent red with slashes of violet and orange across the sky.

At the last moment, I lean back, capturing Tilly's silhouette framed by the vibrant sky, tendrils of her hair lifted and curling in the wind.

The sky wishes it could be as lovely as Tilly Twomley.

Back at the cottage a few hours later, Tilly is curled against me, sleeping peacefully, as I stare at the photo.

I don't edit it or tweak it or label every individual color I see. Somehow, they're all one.

I swipe open Instagram and upload the photo.

This color right here, I type, is love.

At first glance, it's bright. Shocking, almost. It instantly gets under your skin and into your veins. Your impulse is to blink away, turn to something safer. But that's not the point of a color like this, is it? No. You take a step closer. And, at a different angle, the color morphs. It's soft. Inviting. Draws you closer still. And you go back and forth, feeling jarred and comforted. Like you're safe in bed or on a free fall through the stratosphere. You feel comforted and thrilled and terrified. And that's why it becomes your favorite. Because life is too boring without the multitudes this color holds.

On our second day at the ocean, we continue our wandering until we find a hidden inlet between steep walls of rocks with warm sea and even warmer sand. We spread our blanket and fling off our shoes.

"I have a confession to make," Tilly says, turning to me abruptly.

"What's that?"

"I stole something from you."

My eyes bulge a bit, which makes Tilly laugh. "You robbed me?"

She digs through her tote bag. "A momentary theft," she says. "Because I . . . uh . . . always intended to give it back to you."

She thrusts out her hand, dropping a thin silver square into my palm. It takes me a second to recognize it's a condom from the . . . er . . . care package Cubby left me.

I look at the foil for a moment, my eyes growing even wider, then my gaze shoots to Tilly.

"You want to have sex with me?"

Tilly's face bursts into red splotches and she lets out a snort of laughter. "Yes," she says, looking at me. "I do. I've . . . uh . . . never done it before so—"

"I haven't, either," I rush out.

"So are you . . . what are your thoughts on the matter?" she asks, dragging her foot in the sand.

I tilt my head back, looking up at the cerulean sky, then swallow, brilliant yellow happiness swirling through my system. "I think there's no one in the world I'd rather share this moment with. I think . . . well, I think my heart's yours and my body is, too, whenever you're ready."

"I'm ready," Tilly whispers.

"Can . . . Can I touch you?" I ask.

"God yes thank you please," Tilly fumbles out, loud and fast.

There's a beat of silence as I pause my reaching hand.

Then we both burst into laughter.

"Someone's rather keen," I say, a laugh still in my voice as my hand rests at her side, fingers splayed across her ribs, drawing her closer to me.

"You have no idea," Tilly says back, nose scrunching up as she tilts her head and smiles at me.

That smile makes it feel like sunshine is rushing through my veins, while small flashes of lightning crack through my chest and fizzle down to my fingertips.

"Can I touch you, too?" she asks.

I nod so fast my head is a blur. "Yes."

And she does. Greedy hands reach for my hair. My jaw. My shoulders. My chest. I touch her back, mirroring her movements until my palm rests right above the steady thump of her heart like hers does to mine. She presses closer again, and I want her pulse to embed itself in my skin.

I bend down until the tip of my nose touches hers, rubbing them together twice, and smiling.

Tilly smiles back, then kisses me, pressing up to her tiptoes and throwing her arms around my neck.

My hands start to wander again, moving slowly and lightly down Tilly's sides, across her back. A featherlight touch against her hips.

And Tilly—master of keeping me on my toes that she is— lets out a mildly terrifying combination of a squeal and a honk and yells, "Stop!"

I jump back and Tilly sways forward, thrown off-balance.

"What's wrong?" I ask, staring at her with wide eyes.

She rakes her hands through her hair like she wants to pull it out. "Nothing! Nothing," she says, trying to press herself against me again.

I grip her shoulders, holding her at arm's length, while giving her a look that hopefully conveys that I won't be doing a single thing more until she talks to me.

She drags her teeth back and forth over her lower lip, staring at my throat.

"It's not you," she says at last, head drooping. "I don't exactly know how to explain it, but it's definitely not you."

"Okay," I say, using my fingers to gently lift her chin. "But would you be willing to try and find words for it? So I can learn?"

Tilly closes her eyes, then smiles softly, taking a step toward me and leaning her head on my chest.

"Soft touch can make my skin feel . . ." She does a full-body squirm. "It doesn't feel good," she says at last. "I love firm touch. Hard hugs. Stuff like that always feels great. But soft touches or tickles make my skin crawl and, again, it's not a you thing, it's a me thing, but the sensation is really overwhelming and then I get this weird jolt thing and—"

My hands move from her shoulders, back to her hips, gripping her butt with something that could only be described as determined gusto. Tilly sucks in a breath then giggles.

"Is that better?" I ask, looking at her with a completely serious expression while I continue to squeeze her bottom. Tilly laughs even harder, wrapping her arms around me.

"Perfect."

We touch each other, nervous giggles turning into a shared sigh. Smiles melting into kisses and parted lips.

We ask what feels good. Tell each other what doesn't. We're hungry mouths. Fumbling hands.

We're filled with more tenderness and trust than there are grains of sand on the beach we lie down on.

I make an effort to be as gentle as possible through my fumbling awkwardness.

And Tilly is, too. Every touch feels adoring. Special.

Then we both turn a bit frantic, chests heaving and teeth clashing as we move together. Closer.

Beautifully, terrifyingly, magnificently close.

"Are you okay?" I ask, my hand trembling a bit as I move my palm to cup the angle of her jaw, her eyes closed and brow furrowed.

I feel her relax after a deep breath, and when she looks up at me, something wild and wonderful builds between us.

Tilly's smile is nothing short of radiant as she reaches up and threads her fingers in my hair. Tracing them down my neck. Across my shoulders.

"I'm perfect," she says, leaning up to kiss me.

"I'd have to agree," I say with a tiny gasp.

We both giggle like the infatuated fools we are.

In the aftermath, we hold hands, lying on our blanket and staring up at the devastatingly blue sky. Reaching out, I tuck Tilly's head against my chest, kissing her hair. I breathe in the familiar scent of her skin mixed with the salty sea air. We stay like that for a while, preserving our infinite moment of perfection. Golden threads of happiness tethering us together.

Chapter 38

Besties

OLIVER

W e didn't come all this way to watch you two sleep," a voice—which sounds disturbingly like my sister's—cuts through my dream of warm beaches and soft kisses.

"Get up," another voice says, jolting me fully awake with a shove.

"Oh, Marcus, *don't*. They look so cute cuddled together."

Is that . . .

I sit up, scrubbing my eyes then blinking rapidly as Marcus, Micah, Cubby, and her band all blink into focus. Surrounding the exceptionally small bed Tilly and I are squeezed into.

It's another moment until I realize that I'm not wearing a shirt.

"What the hell are you doing here?" I say, scrambling to pull the duvet up over my chest like a scandalized mother.

"Surprise!" Micah cheers, throwing their arms out.

"You're here!" Tilly yells, extremely close to my ear, as she sits up, too.

"What . . . you knew about this?" I ask, turning to her.

"Tilly *planned* it," Darcy says, moving forward to give Tilly a hug. The two collapse back onto the mattress with a squeal and I'm effectively shoved out of the bed.

Trying to sit up in a more dignified position on the floor, I wedge myself against the wall. I'm a bit overwhelmed by this, er, surprise and the resulting commotion. Cubby notices, pressing her back against the wall and sliding down to sit on the floor with me while Micah, Marcus, and Harry fight for spots to look out the window at our gorgeous view.

"Tilly thought it would be a nice surprise for you to have all your friends around. Sort of an end of the summer celebration thing," Cubby says, leaning her head against my shoulder. "She asked Mona and Amina if it'd be okay then called me to tell me about it. I coordinated the rest."

A relieved sigh leaves my chest. Okay. Good. Facts and explanations help. And now I can focus on the fact that all of my favorite people in the world are in the exact same, beautiful place. I look at Cubby and grin.

"I can't believe you're all here," I say, glancing around the room. Then I frown. "Where's Connor?"

I feel Cubby's shoulders stiffen, then she shrugs. "I don't know. He isn't my problem anymore."

My frown deepens. "Did you break up again?"

Cubby shrugs again. "We're taking a break."

"What does that mean?"

"It means, mind your own business, Oliver."

"Does this mean he's no longer in Tongue-Tied?"

"Oh my God, Oliver, we aren't called Tongue-Tied anymore," Darcy says from the bed. "That was a totally different era for us."

"That was literally last month!"

"We're called Ivan on My Mind, now," Cubby says, looking at me like I'm incredibly dim for not keeping up with her band's daily name changes.

"Who's Ivan?" I ask, looking between Cubby, Darcy, and Harry, who's walked over from the window.

". . . What?"

"Who is Ivan?"

The three Ivan-ites look at each other in bewilderment like I asked them to translate all their songs to Portuguese on the spot.

"Don't overthink it," Cubby finally says, waving away my question.

"I *so* love all this chatting," Micah says, stepping into the center of the group. "But could we do it, like, on the beach? In the sun?"

Tilly scrambles off the bed and dives for her suitcase. "I like the way you think," she says, stopping only long enough to give Marcus and Micah hugs. "It's great to finally meet you in person, by the way," she says, giving them both a grin. "Now let's get to the water."

We spend the day at the beach, alternating between lounging on the sand and splashing around in the water. I spend most of my time in the sea, loving the way the aquamarine water feels as comforting as a hug as I float, holding Tilly's hand.

By the time dusk falls, all our energy is drained from the endless sunshine, replaced by a lovely, heavy calmness. All of us, that is, except for Tilly. She seems to have absorbed all that sunlight, and is now reflecting it back to us, keeping us giggling as she talks over dinner in town.

"God, I love her," Cubby whispers to me, after Tilly tells a particularly ridiculous story about running into her neighbor's immaculate shrubbery after first getting her license.

"I do, too," I whisper back, then reach out, twining my fingers with Tilly's and holding her hand under the table.

Part of me wishes I could capture this moment in a photograph, look at it over and over from every angle until all the details and colors and shapes are imprinted like a tattoo on my mind. But I know a photo wouldn't do it justice. It wouldn't capture this warm and bright glow in my chest. The gentle hum in my arms and legs. The comfortable stillness in my head.

It wouldn't do justice to Tilly's laugh or the way my sister smiles. The unspoken words in every look Marcus gives Micah.

This moment is more than any picture could capture.

And it's ours.

Chapter 39

Paris, You Fickle Wench

TILLY

I've come to associate the specific ding my phone makes when I get an email with disappointment and rejection. It's this wild roller coaster of emotions where, at the first trill of the synthy note, my hopes *soar* and my brain chases its tail around my skull saying *OMG this is it, this is it.* Then, a quarter of a second later, I remember that this ding, historically, is bad news. It's a form rejection on one of the jobs I applied to. A curt but kind decline on an article pitch. And then I'm so over-whelmed with dread, I have to lock myself in the bathroom and talk myself up for a good seven minutes before I can open the email.

But the subject of the one I just got, my phone clutched in my clammy palm as I crouch in the upstairs bathroom, has a new riot of emotions burning through me.

Ivy Application—Time to chat?

With a shaky (and tragically sweaty) thumb, I open the email.

Hello, Tilly,

This is Ellen Yu, with *Ivy Online*. I wanted to connect with you about some of your writing if you have a chance. Is now a good time? If not, when are you free this week?

I reread this message about forty times before I scream and chuck my phone into the sink. I'm glad everyone—minus Oliver, who's taking some alone time to recharge in the back garden—went into town so they don't come questioning why I'm shrieking like a banshee.

I get up and start pacing. Okay. This is a little terrifying. Is this Ellen person wanting to tell me—*on the phone*—that I'm not getting the job? That my writing sucks? Is this a uniquely cruel way to reject me? And, I'm sorry, but who wants to talk on the *phone* anymore? Can't she give me three to five business days plus shipping and handling to digitally respond to whatever it is she has to say?

Maybe she actually likes your writing, a gentle voice whispers in the back of my mind.

I stop my pacing.

Why is that just as terrifying as thinking this is a rejection?

Chewing on my cuticles, I turn and look at where my phone sits in the sink. Slowly, like I'm approaching an explosive, I inch toward it, then pick it up and start typing.

Hi Ms. Yu! Now's a great time to talk if you're still available, I type, adding in my number before hitting *send*.

I'm gnawing on my cuticles again when a call from an unknown number rings through a few minutes later.

Ohmygawdohmygawdohmygawdokaywowicandothis.

With a deep breath, I accept it.

"Hello?" I say, picking up my pacing again in the small space.

"Hi, Tilly? This is Ellen. So glad we could connect. How are you?"

A nervous laugh escapes my dry throat. "Great!" I say, way too loudly. "How are you?"

"Very well, thanks," she says in a rich French accent. "I heard that we have acquaintances in common, although through many degrees of separation," she says kindly.

I boom out another laugh. Oh my God I need to chill. "Yeah, if I'm following the chain correctly, you're my boy-friend's twin's bandmate's friend's cousin . . . twice removed."

My stomach flips a bit when Ellen laughs. "Something like that. But, the fact remains, I saw your application for the Editorial Assistant position and I wanted to talk with you about it."

I make a bizarre guttural sound that comes out something like "Oh *hmmggmmuu*?" which Ellen, thankfully, interprets as me encouraging her to continue.

"I'm not sure how familiar you are with us, but I'm one of the founders of *Ivy*, a relatively new online magazine. Our ar-ticles run the gamut from book reviews to reproductive health to trans rights advocacy to general humor and cat content. Our goal is to create an internet space for people to feel com-fortable and truly seen in the content we produce while also feeling empowered for existing just as they are."

"I love cats," I blurt out. Wow. Really adding to the con-versation here.

Ellen laughs again. "Good. Our team is composed almost entirely of cat ladies. You'd fit right in."

I laugh, too, and now it's a breathy, panicked sound.

"But the reason I'm calling," Ellen continues, "is I wanted to see if you're still looking for work, or if someone else has snatched you up already."

I clear my throat and try to tamp down the pukey nervous

feeling in my stomach. I don't know what to say. My mind goes incredibly blank.

I have a job. A good job. But for some reason, instead of telling Ellen that, I say, "I'm still on the job market, yes," which I really hope sounds mature and like I have any idea what I'm talking about. "I've been doing some, uh, freelancing as well. Primarily for travel magazines."

"Fabulous," Ellen says. "I started reading your Babble posts. It certainly seems like your summer adventures gave you plenty to pull on for that."

"Some could be better classified as misadventures," I say, hoping I sound witty and not like I'm sweating so badly I need to change my shirt. And my underwear. Thank God I have so many pairs.

Ellen laughs, and it sounds genuine. "I was particularly drawn to your essay on traveling with ADHD and some of the obstacles it's presented. How you've coped with it."

This makes my breath catch. "R-really?"

"Oh yes. Mental health and carving out our own safe spaces in the world is an incredibly important topic," Ellen says. "And one that's gaining more public discussion. Lots of catching up to destigmatize it, but I'm hopeful."

I nod, even though she can't see it, feeling both daunted and thrilled at what she's saying.

"To get to the point, I loved your application," Ellen continues. "The position would be reporting directly to me. At this point, the work would likely end up being more part-time than full-time, but I imagine as we continue to grow as a media source, work will pick up. Aspects of it are, admittedly, rather unglamorous administrative tasks that come with the role—content scheduling, ad copy, meeting and event organization—but the role would also involve regular writing for the website, and we try to be as flexible as possible on allowing our staff to cross over to different editorial sections if they're inclined."

I'm feeling a bit out of my depth here, and can't get any words to come out.

After an awkward beat of silence, Ellen continues. "What I'm getting at here is that I'd love to offer you the job. I have this vision of you writing a regular column about the reality of being a Gen Z woman navigating the edge of adulthood and being neurodiverse. Obviously, there are so many angles and approaches to such a broad and meaningful topic, but to start, at least, we could narrow the lens to specific beats that speak to you."

More awkward silence as I try to process this.

"Wait . . . really?" I manage to choke out. Wow. So professional.

"Of course," Ellen says, giving another tinkling laugh. "You have a freshness about you. An earnest vulnerability that I think will resonate with readers."

"I . . ." I really don't know what to say. "Thank you. So much," I finally land on.

"If I can be honest with you," she says after a moment, her voice a bit softer. "I also have ADHD, and the openness with which you discuss it really resonates with me. I spent so much of my early career masking to try and make headway, until I burned out and had to start from scratch. That burnout was, essentially, where *Ivy* was born, and I'm glad for it, but I wish I'd been able to be more open about my experiences. More true to myself."

"I know what you mean," I whisper, sharp memories of every failed social interaction, every exhaustive collapse from masking so hard I didn't even recognize myself, hitting me at once.

"I don't want that cycle to continue," Ellen says, voice

stronger. "I think we need to amplify those voices instead. That's what we aim to do with every writer on the team. It's our mission at *Ivy*. And we'd be so thrilled to have you be a part of that. What do you think?"

What do I *think*? My head is so full of excited, buzzing thoughts, I don't know that there are actual words to explain them. I mean, this is kind of incredible? Like . . . absolutely huge? I'm being offered a chance to write, the thing I want to do more than anything. Let my mind frolic and play in new thoughts, stretch it until I come up with something clever and fresh and meaningful. Make others—especially those like me—feel seen.

But I technically have a job. Would it hurt Mona if I took this position? Could I somehow manage both?

A voice in my head—one that's loud and practiced in doubt—immediately tells me no. I'm not organized enough to pull something like that off. Not clever enough to create content for two jobs. Not worthy of both opportunities.

I chew on my lip as I think about this. Just because this voice is louder than the one telling me I *can* do it, doesn't make it true. I don't have to do what it says.

"When can I start?" I manage to ask, making Ellen laugh once more.

"Oh, Tilly, I can't tell you how pleased I am to hear that! We actually have a team meeting next Tuesday, where we're discussing our end-of-year goals and visions as we prep for the final quarter, and it would be so wonderful to have you there."

"That would be incredible!" I say, a few searing, happy tears rolling down my cheeks. "I'll be there."

"Wonderful."

"Oh, wait," I say, realizing that I'm, uh, technically on

vacation and actually not quite sure where their offices are located. "What's the company's address? Probably something I should know."

"We'll send you an email with onboarding information," Ellen says. "But, as I'm sure you saw on the application, we're right in the heart of the greatest city on Earth. Paris."

Chapter 40

This One Hurts

TILLY

Paris. Paris. Paris.

The city, which once sounded so magical and wonderful, plays on loop in my head until it's nothing but two terrifying, beautiful syllables.

Did I . . . Did I just accept a job in Paris? Paris, *France*? Like . . . what business do I have working in Paris?

A city where I don't know anyone.

No Mona. No Amina.

No Ollie.

As if summoned by my heartbreaking thoughts of him, Oliver pads into the living room and smiles at me as I sit on the couch in stunned silence. When I see him, I stand up, too, retreating to a corner across the room.

"Hi," I say, my voice hoarse.

"What's wrong?" he says immediately, head tilting. He walks toward me, but stays a few feet away. I hate that space between us. Despise it.

I swallow. There's no point in holding this in. I'm confused and elated and terrified and, well, Oliver is the only person in the world that I want to talk about it with.

"I . . . I got a job," I say, glancing down at my phone.

"I know," he says, eyebrows furrowing. "I was there when Mona offered it to you."

"It's a different job," I say slowly, looking at him, then away. "It's . . . well, I didn't even mention it because I thought it was such a long shot but it's one I applied to that Darcy and Cubby told me about. Some friend of a friend's bandmate's cousin . . . anyway. It's working as an editorial assistant for an online magazine."

"Oh . . ." Oliver says, looking confused. "Are you going to take it?"

"I . . ." My throat feels raw. I kind of already have, haven't I? And it all feels so confusing and so fast and so much and . . . "The job is in Paris," I blurt out.

Oliver looks as bewildered as if I'd told him it's on Mars.

"But that's not . . . London," he says at last, dragging his thumb across his forehead. I don't know what I expected, but it might have been something slightly more enthusiastic than that.

"I know," I finally say. "What . . ." I'm scared to ask—terrified—but the question is inevitable. "What are you thinking?"

"That Paris is definitely not London," Oliver reiterates. I'd laugh if his fixation on that detail didn't absolutely shatter my heart.

I'm silent as I look at Oliver. He stares back, frowning like he's staring at a puzzle he can't solve. Like he can't see a solution to some massive problem dumped on his lap.

"I'm going to take it," I whisper. He doesn't react. He's frozen.

And for me, that's when it clicks.

He doesn't want a girlfriend who's living in another country. Who would? It's nothing but miles and time zones and airfare and missed calls and inevitable broken hearts. Why would he ever volunteer for that headache? That unavoidable mess?

A hot tear rolls down my cheek, but I scrub it away, blinking back any others.

"I get it," I say at last, forcing a smile that creates a crack through the center of my chest.

"Get what?" Oliver says, still giving me that stare.

"That Paris isn't London," I whisper. "I won't be in the same city as you. And I get what that means for us. What you're thinking."

"Please enlighten me," Oliver says, rubbing at his temples and looking genuinely desperate.

I clear my throat then square my shoulders. "Our summer will always, *always* be the happiest time of my life," I say.

Oliver nods.

"And, um, I'm really thankful to you for believing in me. Helping me to believe in myself."

"I'll always believe in you," he says, his voice rough.

My smile is nothing but sadness. "This summer was perfect. And we'll leave it just like that. Preserve that perfect little world and not set ourselves up for hurting in the real one."

Oliver's face falls slowly—so slowly—and I watch every line form.

"Are we . . . Are we breaking up?" he whispers. I watch his throat move as he swallows.

Two more tears slip out from the corners of my eyes. I brush them away. "I think so."

Oliver's silence is, once again, devastating.

Eventually, he nods. "Oh," he says, eyes fixed on my shoulder.

We stand there, neither willing to move, neither willing to step out of this last moment of us being together. Pop our happy bubble forever.

Oliver reaches toward me like he's going to brush his hand against my cheek—across my freckles. But I never get to feel the warmth of his skin. Not even this one last time. He leaves his touch hovering between us.

Then he turns.

And walks away.

Chapter 41

Shouldn't It Be Enough?

OLIVER

Numbness is an odd sensation. I know, technically, it means to be devoid of feeling, but—while I'm not exactly an expert on the subject—I think emotional numbness is different. It's heavy. It's hollow. It's a dull ache. A delicate pain.

It's something that fills you so thoroughly, it's not that you don't feel anything, it's just that you don't feel anything good.

I walk out of the cottage and down the beach, my limbs stiff and clumsy as I move. I don't know how long I walk, but, eventually, the sun sets, and I turn, stumbling across the sand in the dark until I'm at the back door of the cottage, contemplating how to sneak in so no one sees me. So no one talks to me. I don't have the capacity for words right now.

I'm lucky—I guess—that, when I quietly let myself in, no one seems to be home. I climb the stairs, aimlessly searching for somewhere to land. Somewhere I can actually think.

There's light coming out through the crack under the door of the room Tilly and I share. I don't dare go in there. Everyone else is already filling up the other two small rooms on the second floor, and the only place I'll find peace, find solitude, is the small bed in the converted attic.

I pull down the ladder from the ceiling and climb the stairs as quietly as possible, trying not to recoil at the musty, hot air up here. There's a bed and sheets and pillows. That's all I really need.

I'm okay, I tell myself, burrowing under the duvet and rubbing a fist against my shattered chest, waiting for the pain to go away. I have my family. I have my friends. I have school starting soon and colors and my camera.

That's more than enough.

But all I really want is Tilly.

"Oh my God, *there* you are."

I'm jolted awake, yet again, by Cubby.

I would love—truly *love*—for my sister to stop interrupting my sleep. Next family counseling meeting, I'm bringing it up with Dr. Shakil.

I turn, squinting one eye open to see Cubby, Marcus, and Micah circled around my bed. I groan.

"Go away, please," I say, dragging a pillow over my head.

Cubby snatches it from me, then hits me in the face with it. "You gave us all a heart attack, Ollie. You and Tilly both. You've been missing for hours!"

I glance at my watch.

"Cubby, it's three in the morning," I say, staring at her incredulously. "The most I was missing was a few hours at dinner. Also, why are you all even up?"

The three of them blink at me, eyes a bit glassy.

"We may have stayed out a bit too late at dinner," Micah says.

"Drank a bit too much wine," Marcus adds.

"All of that is irrelevant," Cubby snaps. "As soon as we realized we hadn't seen you in nearly nine hours, we were worried *sick*."

They all nod.

"I'm serious," I say, pulling the duvet up to my chin. "Go away. I don't want to talk."

"What's going on?" Micah asks. "Tilly's in a similar state of anguish. Darcy attempted to talk to her before she and Harry both pissed off to bed."

A cold and sharp laugh escapes me. "That doesn't seem quite right, seeing as she broke up with me," I say. "She doesn't want to be in a relationship."

Micah gasps.

"What?" Cubby says, darting over and sitting on the edge of my bed. "Did she actually say that? She literally said, 'I don't want to be in a relationship with you'?"

I chew on my lip for a moment. "Well . . . no. But she might as well have."

"What happened?" Marcus asks, hovering over me.

I explain the conversation as briefly as possible, but it still has me rubbing my chest where the ache is so deep, I don't know that it will ever feel right again.

"Did you tell her *you* don't want to break up?" Cubby asks, frowning at me.

I blink. "Uh. I mean . . . no. But she didn't ask."

"Oliver!" Cubby smacks me on the shoulder. "Oh you absolute twat," Cubby says, standing up to start pacing. "Both of you! I mean my *God*, use your words, people. All of this could have easily been solved with a very simple conversation."

"Because you and Connor are so great at talking things out?" I snap.

Cubby stops pacing and blinks. "I . . . He . . . we're *not* talking about my relationship here."

"Similar approach you and Connor take, no?"

Cubby marches across the room and smacks me on the shoulder again.

"Ow!"

"Oh, I want to *strangle* you, Ollie. Sitting here moping when you should be groveling!"

"Groveling? What could I possibly have to grovel about?"

Cubby opens her mouth—to say something scathing, no doubt—but Micah steps forward, placing a hand on Cubby's shoulder.

"Oliver, darling," Micah says (in an exceptionally kinder tone than my sister). "Have you and Tilly talked about the ways you communicate?"

I blink at them then look at Marcus. He shrugs.

"I'm not entirely sure what that means," I say. "We use . . . words? Is that what you're asking?"

Cubby groans.

I'm not great at reading facial expressions, but the pitying smile Micah gives me is pretty hard to miss.

"Okay. I think that's the best place to start." Micah clears their throat, and Marcus stares at them like they placed every star in the sky. Christ.

"Oliver, how do you like people to talk to you? Explain things to you?"

I blink some more. "With words?" I repeat. I feel like I'm really missing something about this pointless exercise.

Cubby groans again. "Okay, what Micah is trying to say is, you're autistic, right?"

"Yes." That, at least, I can answer definitively.

"Remember sessions we've had with Dr. Shakil? Where we all talked about the best way to express ourselves to prevent misunderstandings?"

"Yes."

Cubby blows out a deep breath. "Remember how you and I had to go back and forth about it for *ages*? Because we couldn't grasp that we communicated so differently?"

I nod again, a knot forming in my throat.

Cubby had explained, with tears in her eyes, how *frustrated* she'd get that I couldn't tell when she was cross with me. How she'd feel so hurt when I'd go about my business, seemingly oblivious to her silent sulking. It made me cry in frustration, too. How was I supposed to know something she didn't tell me? How did she know some foreign language of facial expressions and posture and hidden meanings that I couldn't crack?

We'd had to work through this topic for weeks and weeks, and it still comes up years later, but unraveling our differences has allowed us to be closer.

Cubby reaches out, giving me a quick hug.

"That's the type of conversation you need to have with Tilly. It's all well and good that you love each other and make each other happy, but that won't mean anything if you don't understand how the other talks."

I swallow, and look at the ground, fingers tapping. "What if I'm not able to learn how she needs me to communicate? What if she doesn't want to? What if what I need is too much work? What if she doesn't want this at all? What if—"

Marcus steps in front of me. "Listen to me," he says, squeezing my cheeks between his palms until my lips pucker like a fish. "I'm not going to sit here and let you jumble this up with what-ifs. Do you love Tilly?"

"Ywesh," I say through my smooshed mouth.

"And do you want to be with her?"

I try nodding this time, hoping to come across at least slightly more dignified. Vain attempt.

"Do you care that you'll be living in separate cities?"

"No," I say, pulling away from his grip. "I'll love her no matter where she lives."

"Good," Cubby says, standing and patting Marcus on the shoulder before planting her hands on her hips. "Now haul your arse to her doorstep and tell her as much."

Chapter 42

The Art of the Grovel

OLIVER

Standing in front of Tilly's door feels like standing on the edge of a cliff. It's terrifying and magnificent and makes my palms sweat and my heart thump hard enough I'm worried it's going to pop out of my chest.

I can do this. I can knock on her door.

Any second now.

Oh my God, *knock*, you wanker! Do it already!

My internal pep talk finally gets my hand moving, and I tap softly.

The squeak of the floorboards from the room might as well be gunshots for how loudly they reverberate in my chest.

A moment later, Tilly opens the door, head jerking back a bit when her eyes land on me. She stares for a moment then says, "Hi." She sniffles and brushes the backs of her hands across her cheeks.

"I think I'm pretty shit at talking," I blurt out, while also confirming my suspicions.

Tilly blinks rapidly then frowns. "What? I love your accent. Who told you that? They're wrong."

I blow out a breath and shove my hand through my hair. "Communicating, I mean. I think I'm kind of bad at it. And I want to get better. With you. If you want to. It's okay if you don't. But I wanted to, er, well, I guess, communicate this to you. That I want to be a better, uh, communicator. So . . . yeah."

Tilly is silent for a moment, arms wrapped around herself as she stares at me. "Word vomit is generally *my* thing," she says at last, giving me a small smile that doesn't reach her eyes.

I shake my head, feeling words get clogged in my throat again. I take a deep breath, trying to untangle them.

"I think we communicate differently," I say. "And I want to learn your language. I want us to figure out how to talk to each other in the best ways possible. Because if you're moving to Paris, I want to understand you, and for you to understand me. I don't want to lose you."

Tilly's lips part. "You don't want to lose me?" she echoes.

I clench my jaw in frustration. Why am I unable to make this clear? I'm getting all jumbled. I'm doing this wrong. I . . .

"Tilly," I say, taking a step toward her and placing my hands on her cheeks. Her eyes are wide. Vulnerable. I love her so much it seems impossible. "I didn't want to break up when we talked earlier. I don't want to break up now. I don't want to break up ever. I *love* you. I'm comfortable with you in a way I never even hoped to experience with another person. Being around you—seeing the way you shine—is like discovering a new color of the rainbow every single day."

Tilly is properly crying now, and she sucks in a breath. "Why didn't you say any of this before?"

I blink up at the ceiling and laugh bitterly. "Believe me, if it were that easy for me, I would have. I'm slow to process. When plans change, even small ones, my body and mind lock up. I'm flooded with so many sensations, I can't discern what they all mean. It's hard to put words to what I'm feeling, what I'm thinking—even right now. And it's scary to say that out loud because all my life people have told me I say the wrong thing."

My gaze flicks back to Tilly and I feel . . .

I feel safe.

I keep going. "My silence in that moment is the biggest regret of my life. Because I should have taken it to celebrate you. To appreciate you. To tell you no matter where you live, I'll love you. You are noise and charisma and joy and that's what I should have been for you."

"Ollie," Tilly says, reaching out for me, her hands landing gently on the nape of my neck. "I don't need you to be anything but you."

I start to say something more, but she places her hands on my lips, silencing me. "And this is something you've told me. You told me change is hard for you to adjust to. That you need a little time. I always thought of it in the sense of travel, and that was dumb."

"It's not dumb," I whisper. "We're just learning."

Tilly's smile is real now.

"I'm very sensitive," she blurts out. "Like, extremely sensitive. And I tend to react before I think. I can misread pretty much anything. A look. Silence. Something simple someone says. And I turn it into rejection. Like I'm a failure on a fundamental level. And I think some awful voice in the back of my head has lied to me all my life and told me I deserve that rejection—that hurt—because I'm a lot to deal with. And I try to shut that voice up, I really do, but sometimes it talks on a loudspeaker, and I start to believe it. Find moments for it to be true."

"You should speak with a therapist," I say, a small bubble of excitement growing in my chest that I can help her with this.

Tilly blinks, mouth dangling open, then bursts out laughing. She wraps her arms around me, hugging me close.

"Why are you laughing?" I ask.

She laughs harder, her whole body shaking. "Because, generally speaking, telling someone they need psychiatric treatment can come across a bit offensive."

"Why?" I ask again, pulling back to look down at her.

Tilly's eyebrows furrow, and she nibbles on her lip. "I . . . I actually don't know. It's not like people get offended when you say, 'Oh, you should get a checkup,' or whatever with your regular doctor. Regardless," she says, waving away the left turn in the conversation. "I think you're right. A therapist would probably be good for me."

I reach out and grab Tilly's hands, lacing our fingers together in that strong, secure way I know she likes.

"So, you're okay with the fact that I won't be in London?" she eventually says, raising our clasped hands to rub her lips across my knuckles.

I clear my throat, unhooking my thumb to lift her chin so she's looking at me. "You could tell me you're moving to Brazil. Or back to Cleveland. Or some moldy cave in a forest, and I'd love you all the same. You'll always be the place that feels most like home."

Tilly pushes up on her tiptoes, kissing me until I feel dizzy with it. And I kiss her back.

We eventually crawl into bed, talking and holding each other for hours, until we both start trading yawns.

"I don't want to fall asleep," Tilly whispers, eyelids heavy as she nestles closer to me. "I don't want this moment to end."

I wrap my arm around her and kiss the crown of her head.

"End?" I whisper. "Tilly, this is only the beginning."

Chapter 43

Hellos and Goodbyes

TILLY

My attention is split between painting Marcus's and Micah's nails. After seeing how damn photogenic (and adorably touchy-feely) the couple was at the beach, Mona recruited them as additional hand models. Micah is practically vibrating with excitement.

"Not to be dramatic," Micah says, voice dripping with exactly that, "but I'm fairly certain this color was made for me."

Micah lifts their free hand, tilting it in the sunlight streaming through the window. "Like . . . am I a Ruhe muse or what?"

"Calliope has nothing on you," Marcus says, leaning over and giving Micah a kiss on the cheek.

"Where are you shooting today?" I ask Ollie from where he's perched on Mona's couch. We've been back in London for almost a week, and he's walked me all over this gorgeous city, pointing out things only his sharp eye seems to notice.

"Queen Mary's Gardens is our first stop," Ollie says, looking up at me. "Then off to the library. Mona helped organize access to some old book collection or the like. Going for a bit of a back-to-school theme."

"Love it," I say, putting the finishing touch on Marcus's nails. "Don't you dare smudge," I add, giving him a stern look. He sticks his tongue out at me.

"Oh, Tilly, I wish you could come with us today," Micah says wistfully.

"Seconded," Ollie grunts from the couch. I laugh at him.

"Believe me, I would much prefer to wander around gardens and libraries than meet my executioner."

Ollie looks at me, tilting his head, before closing his laptop and sliding off the couch to the floor. I bear crawl to him.

"We have all the time in the world to explore," he says, wrapping his arm around my shoulders.

I grin, a golden swell of feelings swallowing me whole.

He's right, we do have as much time as we need.

I went to the onboarding meeting with *Ivy* a few days ago, and it was absolutely amazing. Everyone on the team seems smart and kind and filled with so much passion I thought my head would explode.

And, to top it off, the company actually seems to *care* about its employees . . . what a novelty. After going over some logistical points with Ellen, she was more than willing to let me work remotely, especially as it's part-time right now.

"Many of our employees transitioned to the hybrid model," Ellen told me. "I see no point in forcing people to come into the office space if it isn't working for them. Accommodation seems to only spur creativity and work output in my experience."

Needless to say, I'm totally obsessed with my badass new boss.

I'll still go to Paris a couple times a month for various meetings and other work that will be easier to do in-person, but I couldn't be happier to let my roots grow in London.

It feels like, for the first time, I'm exactly where I belong.

I'm willing to do a bit of commuting and hustling to keep this dream.

"It'll be good to see your mom, rip the Band-Aid off," Ollie continues, tapping his fingers against my leg.

I groan. "We do not speak of it!"

My mom arrives today, and I'm nervous as hell to see her. Part of me, of course, is excited. It's my mom. I do love her, no matter how much I don't get along with her. But it's easier to lean into the dread—this premonition of things going wrong— than to get my hopes up that things will go right.

A knock echoes through the room.

I freeze, staring with wide eyes at the door.

"Damn it," I whisper to Ollie. "You've conjured her."

"Stop it," Oliver says.

"Should I be afraid?" Micah stage-whispers.

"Yes!"

"No."

My voice tangles with Ollie's and we both frown at each other before bursting into giggles.

"Miss Two-Jobs is suddenly too good to get the door?" Mona asks, power walking out of her room and shooting me a goofy look. "Come on, Tilly."

With a deeply tortured sigh, I stand, my friends following my lead.

The door creaks open and Mona's voice rings through the apartment, punctuated with a short giggle. "Mom!"

"Oh, my baby!" my mom says, voice muffled.

I feel my pulse in my palms as the pair rounds the corner and enters the living room. Mom stops, looking at me, her smile only growing as she takes me in.

"Tilly," she says, crossing the room and pulling me into a warm, consuming hug. It feels . . . genuine. Comfortable.

"Hi, Mom," I say into her shoulder, hugging her back.

After a few moments, Micah clears their throat, pulling a laugh from me.

"Mom," I say, untangling myself. "These are my friends, Micah and Marcus." I gesture at the duo.

"Pleasure," Micah says, leading the charge and shaking my mom's hand. Marcus follows suit.

"Nice to meet you," Mom says.

"And, uh, this is Ollie. Oliver. Oliver Clark," I say, gesturing wildly at the person in question. "He's kind of, um, my boyfriend."

Mom's mouth drops open.

"Oh?" Her eyes bounce from Ollie to me to Mona and back in a wild loop.

I push my lips together, trying to tamp down the smile that wants to burst from me. It's hard not to absolutely screech in happiness every time I get to introduce Oliver as mine.

"I . . . Well. This is a wonderful surprise," Mom says, reaching out for Ollie's hand.

He shakes it, eyes fixed on her shoulder. "So thrilled to meet you. Tilly's told me so much about you."

Mom's laugh sounds a little forced. Maybe even . . . nervous? What could she have to be nervous about? I'm the one twisted in knots.

"Well, we'll leave you two to catch up," Micah says, grabbing Marcus's and Oliver's hands and leading them to the door. "Tilly, will we see you later?"

"Uhh." I glance at Mom and Mona. "I'll text you," I say, waving them off. "Have fun."

A hush falls through the room as they depart.

"Well, they seem lovely," Mom says, looking at me. She's smiling, but it's edged with something sad tugging at the corners of her eyes.

In a blur of movement, she reaches out for me again,

wrapping me in a second hug. "I really have missed you," she says into my hair. Eventually, she pulls back. "I'm so excited to be in London, oh my gosh."

Mona beams. "Happy to have you, Mom. Hungry? We could go get lunch. Or I could fix something here?"

"That would be great but, um . . ." Mom smooths a hand through her hair. "I was actually hoping to talk to Tilly for a bit? Alone, if you don't mind?" Mom's glance flicks between me and Mona.

"Whatever you need," Mona says, already backing out of the room.

I want to beg her to stay. Beg her not to leave me. To act as a buffer. A shield. Anything to delay the awfulness that could come tumbling out of this talk.

But she's gone, shutting her bedroom door behind her, Mom and me staring at each other in a tense silence.

"Want to sit?" Mom asks, moving to the couch and tapping the spot next to her.

My legs feel wooden, my lungs full of bubbles, my heart in my throat. But, somehow, I walk forward and sit next to her.

I take a deep breath. Then another. One more should do it. Then I'll say it. I'll tell her I've got a job—two, actually— neither of which she'll like. And I'll have to tell her that her opinion on it doesn't really matter. I can't let it matter anymore. It's what I want from life, and I hope, someday, she can be okay with that.

I open my mouth, choking on words as worry zips through my arms and congeals in my chest.

"Tilly, I've read your Babble posts."

Mom says the words so fast, so unexpectedly, my head jerks back and hits the wall behind me.

"W-what?"

Oh no. This is bad. Like, really bad. Because I'm rather,

um, honest about my frustrations with my parents on there. Is she going to scream at me? How could she not scream at me?

I brace for impact.

After a moment, she meets my eyes, sadness lining her face. "After our talk, I searched for the article you said you sold. Which was wonderful, too. But then I found your Babble posts. I've read them and they're beautiful. Heartbreaking, but beautiful."

Ummm what?

"I . . . you're so clever. I can't believe some of the stuff you come up with."

Once again, *what*? My eyes are wide as I stare at my mom, waiting for the other shoe to drop.

"But, they also made me realize just how . . . how much I've hurt you. And I'm so sorry for that, Tilly."

I try to suck in a breath, but it gets locked at the top of my throat.

Mom pushes on. "I'm sorry for what I said when we last talked, and for the pressure I've been putting on you." Mom's voice sounds more fragile than I've ever heard it before. "I haven't been able to stop thinking about our last conversation. I mean, I just had an exceptionally long flight to think of nothing *but* our fight. And I truly am sorry for how I spoke to you. I hope you can forgive me. You see, I worry about you, Tilly. You're so special. So precious. And I live in fear of the world hurting you. But in trying to do what I thought was right to protect you, I'm the one that caused pain. And I'm sorry."

"I . . . I'm not really sure what to say."

Mom reaches out, grabbing my hand. "You don't have to say anything. Or you can say everything. I've . . . well, I've realized I haven't been listening to much of what you've had to say. And I want to change that."

She's quiet, thumb tracing over the back of my hand as she gives me room to speak.

I still don't know what to say. Words zip around my brain, down my throat, through my limbs. I'm scared to say anything—to ruin this moment she's giving me. But I decide to be brave.

"I need the room to make mistakes, Mom," I say, my voice cracking. "I know I've made tons of them and I'll make so many more, but . . . I need to know that that's okay."

Mom nods, reaching out and tucking a strand of my hair behind my ear. "Keep going."

Tears start rolling down my cheeks as the words pour out of me. "I know that you want what's best for me, but I also want to know that you'll be there if I fail. I want to feel safe enough to make mistakes and know you'll still love me."

"I'll always love you, Tilly. That's not even a question."

"It feels like a question to me."

Mom's silent for a long time, and I'm worried she's mad. I can't lift my eyes to look at her, instead focusing on our held hands as emotions build in my chest. Eventually, I hear a tiny hiccup followed by a sniffle.

Oh no. Did I make my mom cry?

I glance up at her, and, sure enough, tears are rolling down her cheeks, too.

"I'm sorry, Mom. I didn't mean—"

"Tilly, no," Mom says quickly, her words soft but sturdy. She swipes away her tears. "Don't apologize for being honest with me. Ever. If how much I love you is ever a question, that's on me, and I need to know so I can fix it. I love you without conditions. Without expectations. And I'm sorry that I've failed you in showing that."

"Mom . . ." I say quietly, at a loss.

"And I'm not saying any of this to guilt you. I want you to know that I hear you, Tilly. I can't promise that from this point forward I won't mess up, but I want you to know that I'm going to try. I'm going to take what you've said and do better. Because I'll be damned if my precious, brilliant daughter questions my love for her exactly as she is one day more."

My mouth is clogged with emotions and a tangle of words I don't know how to say. "I love you," I finally manage.

"I love you so much," Mom says back. And I believe it.

She hugs me close to her, and I melt into it, crying at the soft comfort.

"I have something to tell you," I eventually say when I pull myself together enough to talk.

"It better be all about this boyfriend of yours," Mom says, stroking my hair. "I want all the details."

I giggle. I'm such a fool for Ollie I could talk about that silly boy for hours.

"Not about him," I say, pulling back to look at her. "I . . . uh . . . I got a job. Two, actually. And . . . well, I know they won't be jobs you consider ideal, but I hope you're proud of me. Or that I can make you proud, at least."

Mom lets out a sigh, shaking her head. "I'm already proud of you, Tilly. No matter what. I'm sorry I've made it so you think a job is what will cause that. I'm proud of you for just being you."

"*Mommmmm*. Please stop making me cry."

Mom presses her lips together, using her thumbs to wipe my cheeks.

I fill her in on everything. The job with Ruhe and my freelance articles and working for *Ivy*. All of it pours out of me, my heart on my sleeve and passion in my voice as I lay out every detail of my future that's equal parts exhilarating and terrifying and beautiful and daunting. When I run out of words, Mom offers me a few of her own.

"Tilly," she says, taking my face between her hands. "You're simply amazing. I can't wait to see what you do next."

We hug for a bit longer, then Mona eventually comes out of her room.

"I'm so sorry," she says, "but I really have to pee."

We all laugh, and Mona takes care of business before meeting us in the living room. "You two okay?" she asks.

Mom looks at me with a smile. "Not necessarily. But I think we're getting there."

I smile back.

"Still want to get lunch?" Mona asks.

Mom lets out a soft sigh and stands. "Absolutely. Wherever you want. My treat."

Mona grins and grabs her purse.

"Why don't you go meet up with your friends," Mom says to me. "Mona and I have a few things of our own to talk about."

I nod, giving her one last hug before scooping up my purse and leaving them to figure out their own stuff.

Out on the street, I stop in front of a gorgeous red phone booth, leaning against it as I call Oliver and ask to meet up with everyone.

It's a humid day as I make my way through the city, heat held tight by the old buildings and crowds, the gray sky pressing down on me. It's so beautiful I could cry.

Eventually, I find them in Hyde Park, sitting on a bench. Oliver offers me a kiss and doner kebab in greeting, and I sit next to him, pressing close just because I can.

While we eat, Micah talks about their groundbreaking poses and innovative ideas, Marcus nodding along with everything they say. Ollie grabs his camera, showing me picture after picture. Zooming in on this spot and that. Pointing out colors I didn't even know existed. Tapping his fingers and periodically squeezing my hand.

And that's when it quietly hits me. This is my future. My now. This moment, in a blink, will be my past. And it's better than I ever could have imagined.

I don't have everything figured out. I need to find my own apartment and come up with article pitches by the end of the week. I'm broke and nervous and still worry that I'll fail. But I'd rather give it my all and come up short than not try at all.

I'm sitting under a gorgeously gray sky in an electric city I can now call home with friends that I feel unabashedly myself with. I'm holding hands with the boy I love and, miraculously, he loves me back.

And there isn't a single thing I would change.

Acknowledgments

I wasn't diagnosed with autism and ADHD until my twenties, but looking back on my childhood, it's truly comical that we all went that long without knowing. Being a teenager is hard enough, but having undiagnosed neurodivergencies was a recipe for many tough (albeit hilarious in retrospect) moments and growing pains. Yet I wouldn't change anything about my path to diagnosis. Growing up knowing that you're different means you study those around you closely, trying to absorb social interactions and rules and intricacies so maybe one day you can fit in, too. I've given up on the pursuit of fitting in with what's defined as normal (I couldn't be happier with my sphere of oddball friends, many of whom are also ND), but all those years of studying people has given me empathy and a desire to see the world beyond my own point of view that makes writing books the most rewarding job in the world. And this book, this love letter to neurodivergent brains, wouldn't exist without the care and compassion of so many.

In a world where we still have limited and questionable media representations of autism and ADHD, I'm eternally grateful to my editor, Eileen Rothschild, for asking me if I wanted to write a novel about two neurodiverse teens falling in love. The opportunity to write about brains like mine is a privilege and an honor I'll never feel worthy of, but I'm grateful for it all the same.

Thank you to my agent extraordinaire, Courtney Miller-Callihan, for constantly talking me down during drafting spirals. I don't know how you do it, but damn do you do it well.

Thank you to Lisa Bonvissuto for being an all-around badass in publishing. Working with you is such a joy. The Cleveland references in the book are for you. Thank you to my lovely publishing team at Wednesday Books. Alexis Neuville and Alyssa Gammello, you two are a dream to work with, and I'm so thankful for all that you do to champion my books and get them into the hands of readers. Also, really appreciate the Harry Styles content you post. Thank you to Kerri Resnick for designing what I truly, unbiasedly believe to be the best cover ever created. You're a genius.

Thank you to Susan Lee for reading the *extremely* rough pages of my first draft and giving me the confidence to keep going. You're a force of nature, and I'm glad to know you.

Thank you to Emily Minarik for teaching me that auburn hair is actually red only after I had finished writing this book and was ready to die on the hill of saying Ollie was a brunet. Words are hard and you keep me humble. Thank you to Saniya Walawalkar for roasting me about not originally including a blanket in Tilly and Ollie's beach moment. Those two would have had a sensory meltdown without that crucial edit and we appreciate your public service.

Thank you to Megan Stillwell for being my best friend on the planet. You are sensationally petty and I love you for it. Thank you to Chloe Liese for being a fierce advocate for neurodiverse voices and always helping me find the humor in the ups and downs of autistic life. You are such a gift.

Mom, thank you for my love of reading and for always supporting my hyperfixations and big dreams. Dad, thank you for the mayhem and the humor. Some of my favorite memories in the world are of us laughing. Eric, thank you for believing in me. I'm so grateful to have you in my life.

And Ben. My sweet lil rascal. Thank you for being terrified of weird eighteen-year-old, pink-haired, way-too-keen me in freshman seminar, and letting me force friendship on you anyway. I've never had to mask with you, and that's pretty damn special.

Finally, thank you to my readers. These stories and characters mean the world to me, but it's nothing compared to the love you've shown them. I pinch myself daily that I get to write books, and your support means more to me than you could ever know. Stay messy, my dears.

Look out for

Late Bloomer

Coming soon from

HEADLINE
ETERNAL

HEADLINE
ETERNAL

FIND YOUR HEART'S DESIRE...

VISIT OUR WEBSITE: www.headlineeternal.com
FIND US ON FACEBOOK: facebook.com/eternalromance
CONNECT WITH US ON TWITTER: @eternal_books
FOLLOW US ON INSTAGRAM: @headlineeternal
EMAIL US: eternalromance@headline.co.uk